About Apollo Africa

The original Heinemann African Writers Series was launched in 1962 with the publication of Chinua Achebe's *Things Fall Apart*, Cyprian Ekwensi's *Burning Grass* and Kenneth Kaunda's *Zambia Shall Be Free*, with Achebe himself acting as an editorial advisor. Over the next 40 years, the series continued to publish the best writing from across the African continent.

One of the founding aims of the Heinemann series was to make books by African writers available to as wide a readership as possible. Apollo Africa – a collaboration between Black Star Books and Head of Zeus – is proud to continue this work, ensuring novels, essays, poetry and plays from the original series are once again made available to readers all over the world.

Orimili

Orimili

Amechi Akwanya

Black Star Books and Head of Zeus would like to thank the following organisations: The Miles Morland Foundation, The Ford Foundation, and Africa No Filter. This publication was made possible through their support.

First published in the Heinemann African Writers Series in 1991 by Heinemann Educational Books

This edition published in 2023 by Black Star Books and Head of Zeus, part of Bloomsbury Publishing Plc.

Copyright © Amechi Akwanya, 1991

The moral right of Amechi Akwanya to be identified as the author of this work has been asserted in accordance with the Copyright, Designs and Patents Act of 1988.

All rights reserved. No part of this publication may be reproduced, stored in a retrieval system, or transmitted in any form or by any means, electronic, mechanical, photocopying, recording, or otherwise, without the prior permission of both the copyright owner and the above publisher of this book.

This reprint is published by arrangement with Pearson Education Limited.

This is a work of fiction. All characters, organizations, and events portrayed in this novel are either products of the author's imagination or are used fictitiously.

9 7 5 3 1 2 4 6 8

A catalogue record for this book is available from the British Library.

ISBN (PB): 9781035900565
ISBN (E): 9781803288208

Typeset by Siliconchips Services Ltd UK

Printed and bound in Great Britain by
CPI Group (UK) Ltd, Croydon CR0 4YY

Head of Zeus Ltd
First Floor East
5–8 Hardwick Street
London EC1R 4RG

WWW.HEADOFZEUS.COM

For
BARBARA HAYLEY
ANGELA LUCAS
KEVIN BARRY
PETER DENMAN
at Maynooth,
and all the BROTHERS at Oatlands

1 | *The Afor Holiday*

Orimili spent most of that day at home. Lounging bare-bodied in his comfortable sling chair, a loin-cloth tied loosely around his waist, and on the floor beside him, a fan that he wielded every now and again to cool himself, he let his body relax completely, keeping his mind just within the fringes of consciousness, a station which was ideal for drifting in and out of sleep.

Ekwenze Orimili Nwofia's bungalow was of a type which was already going out of vogue in the lower middle-income sections of Okono, the large town down-river, where the farmers of Okocha sold their farm produce and bought modern household goods. But there were few such houses in Okocha; Orimili's being the very first one built by a townsman. So it was a wonder to the people; and in that wonder was a good deal of envy, and perhaps resentment; for the man was not assimilated as a full citizen despite the fact that both his father and grandfather had been born and bred in the town. In Okocha no one was ever known to have grown out of the secondary status of a naturalised citizen into the privileges of ordinary citizenship. The people must have taken it as part of the privileges of full citizenship to be accounted a social success. Hence Orimili's success seemed to touch upon their sense of propriety, more so as his people appeared to have been following assiduously the wisdom of the snail for the two or three generations they had been living in the town, and had remained a quiet and unremarkable lot. Okocha's ancients had been struck by the slowness of the snail to the point of making a proverb about it, saying that it was owing to its native cunning and judiciousness. With those qualities to guide it, it could make its way over thorns and brambles without coming to any harm. In the eyes of some of the leading people in Okocha, Orimili had set aside this wisdom by which his forebears had been conducting their lives. That was shown in the type of house he had built for himself. That they didn't forgive him that want of good sense, was something the man felt to be in the very air around him; and he often had a sense of their secret hostility in his intercourse with them.

The house itself was a four-room affair, with two rooms on either side and a veranda in front of the parlour. A central door and two windows opened into the veranda from the parlour. With similar apertures at the back, that sitting room appeared like a passage from the front yard through to the kitchen behind the house; and it was often used for that purpose. The two doors in front and behind had the further effect of dividing the house into two equal parts, one half occupied by Orimili, his wife, and little children; the other half reserved for his first son by a deceased wife. The young man's things were all in one room, but his father was looking forward to his marriage, and thought that the young woman, whenever she arrived, would keep her own room, as did his wife. The beauty of the edifice was mainly in its brickwork. The cement blocks were bossed, the two pillars in front of the veranda hexagonal in shape, and topped with moulded capitals and beams. The two rooms on either side of the veranda, one of which was the proud owner's bedroom, had a projection in front, producing a frontage and eaves of many angles and sides.

Orimili was lounging in his favourite corner at the door of the room tacitly reserved for his son's wife. From that spot, he had a clear view of the courtyard in front of the house and the pathway beyond, but he himself was partially hidden from the view of the passers-by thanks to the great kola-nut tree in the middle of the courtyard. The day was the great Afor, the townspeople's weekly day of rest which occurred at eight-day intervals, with the minor Afor as a halfway point between one great one and the next. Orimili's children had gone to school, however, for the school ran on a different pattern; while his wife had spent most of the morning in the village freshwater stream, with the rest of the women of Ebonasa, Orimili's village. The women's great public work on the holiday was to tidy up the freshwater stream. They also held a meeting in the afternoon in Ama Ebonasa – the village square – taking a break in between to give their families their midday meal.

Edwenze Orimili had the house to himself all day, dozing, coming awake, wondering what his children would be doing that moment in the school, dozing again – an extremely short one this time, but long enough for him to have a vague and complicated dream in which his son Osita was fighting with someone on board Orimili's boat, while he himself was trying to overtake a passenger who had departed without paying her fare. It was a woman, he was sure of that; and moreover, even though he was running inland from the waterfront, he was following the progress of the fight on board minutely! Orimili considered the matter briefly, and hoped that it was only a dream. All the same, he offered a prayer for Osita that the spirit of Okocha might protect him, and give him success (victory, actually) in his studies in Europe.

Not long after his younger children came home from school, and had been chattering for some time in the kitchen, Orimili told himself that the period of quiet and peace he had enjoyed all day was definitely over; and it was time for him to make a move. He put his hands upon the arms of the chair and levered himself to his feet, giving out a great sigh at the same time, as though he had tired himself just resting. Yawning, and arching himself for a stretch, he felt his wrapper coming undone. Cutting out the yawn halfway, he reached down quickly to stop it slithering to the ground. Fully awake now, he made the wrapper fast round his waist, let it hang down to his calves, and pulled it up in places at the waist for a disorderly effect at the lower fringes, to avoid the smooth and even flow favoured by women. The latter went with graceful movements, whereas the former emphasised freedom of movement and suggested warlike readiness. But one would misjudge the man if one sought to determine his mental attitude from the way he tied on his wrapper. His propensities had very little indeed to do with violence – at any rate, of a warlike sort. He would avoid such violence almost at any cost.

The present occasion, however, was entirely peaceful, and he was about to go out for an evening of ease and enjoyment. He went into his bedroom, found the cotton jumper matching the wrapper, and threw it over his head. Shaking himself a little to ease its folds, he plunged his arms one after the other into its wide sleeves, and brushed it down the front towards the knees. Orimili shouted towards the kitchen that he was going out, picked up his things and went off to Amanza to have a drink with his friends and so bring the holiday to a fitting end. Amanza was the town's main square, where the public gatherings were held and public events celebrated. What was being celebrated on this day was only the Afor holiday, this part of the holiday ritual being very popular with the menfolk. For the palm-wine tappers brought their wine-yield of the day to the square for the people to entertain themselves and their friends with. The wine was poured out into calabash gourds of various sizes, which the men paid for and took away with them, sitting down together with their friends to talk and amuse themselves. Orimili never missed these Afor evenings; none of the townsmen did, for one would scarcely know what was going on in the town if one kept away.

Ekwense Orimili was a busy man. He was especially preoccupied during this season of the year, the early dry season, when the townspeople went to sell their produce at the market at Okono. Orimili ran a ferry service to that great market town down-river, conveying the people and their goods on the lesser Afor days, and transporting freight on other days for Guy & Son's Trading Company, which had a trading post on Okocha's side of the great river down which one sailed to Okono. The company's freight consisted of cash crops, usually palm produce, for export. Orimili shipped this cargo to the company's warehouse at Okono, and fetched up-river their consumer imports. During the rainy season he found that he was kept in business largely by the trading company, though even then there wasn't much work for him to do. But he would rather not think of that season of dearth. This was the dry season, and there was work to look forward to.

As the evening of the Afor holiday was approaching, Orimili was rehearsing his plans for the coming week. First thing the next day, he must call at the company office and see if they had taken in sufficient stores of produce for delivery at Okono. It would be a nice way to start the week, to make an early trip to Okono. Putting the goods on board the barge – supposing that the stores had accumulated – would keep him occupied all afternoon the next day, to get everything ready for the trip very early the following day. He was quite used to starting his mornings before cockcrow: hadn't he been doing it all his life, really? It made sense, especially on market days with all the delay and trouble one went through, ferrying market women; else one would never be able to return to Okocha before midnight. As it was, he usually returned not long after dark.

It made Ekwenze Orimili happy to think that his income came mainly from his work for Guy & Son. It would have been very bad indeed if there were no Guy & Son, and he did business only on market days. He would have kept a farm, of course; but he was inclined to think that he wouldn't have done well in it. In any event, he would have been nowhere near as well off as he was. He had the advantage of being able to draw cash at short notice from his savings

– which was not the case with most farmers, especially during the planting season. So he considered that it would have been intolerable to him, were his circumstances worse than they were. What couldn't he do with a little more even now? There were some who said he was rich – how he wished they were right; you know, really right! Many of them were resentful, of course; but who cared? They were entirely mistaken, if they thought that he would oblige them by being poor like a craftsman, and in that way proving to them that he didn't make his profit at their expense. No, he wouldn't be like Okoye the blacksmith, who made hoes and knives and diggers-and sold them too, and yet could not afford new roofing mats to mend his leaky house! It was good not to have to prove anything to anybody, but to be his own man. Okoye could go on proving that he didn't make money out of his skill; Orimili didn't care about that.

What Orimili could not frown away, as he had done the slight uneasiness he felt over the fare he charged for the ferry service, was his sense of moving up-stream all the time, as if the river turned with him or changed the direction of its floods whenever he turned his boat, causing him to be moving against the direction of the current all the time. Of course the problem had little to do with the river, but rather with the rhythm of life in Okocha as a result of which the people seemed to be coming when he himself was going. Take the present season, for instance. Everybody was at leisure during the dry season, but the only leisure time Orimili could share with them was the weekly holiday. He saw little of the townsmen after that since he was busiest during that season of the year. At the end of the season, of course, the rains would come, with the townspeople going to work precisely at the time when things were slack for Orimili. Well, thanks to Guy & Son, he was much busier now in the rainy season than was the case when his father still ran the ferry, and Guy & Son was only setting up shop at Okocha. With an average of two, plus the odd three, delivery runs a week to Okono during the planting season itself, well, that was work. Before Guy & Son, one used to feel idle, guilty even, as one set out early in the morning for the waterfront, passing people going in the opposite direction towards the farmlands. Why, it made one feel like a fisherman – which nobody was during the planting season, and which only a handful carried on after the subsiding of the floods, marking the end of the rains. But now, on account of the certainty that there was work to do at the waterfront, one went out in the morning with a sense of urgency, and didn't feel self-conscious when one passed the townspeople going the other way.

However, Okuata, Orimili's wife, kept a farm, just as did every villager who was not old or bedridden. The man never said a word to her, good or bad, as to her preoccupation; and this was rather characteristic of the relationship between the two. Orimili seemed not to know what he might say to her. For her part, Okuata knew what she wished him to say to her. For instance, she wished he would say encouraging things to her; she wished him to promise to come and help her in the farm when he wasn't travelling to Okono. But she never asked him to do any of these things. One reason why they said so little to each other was probably because they were so far apart in age, Orimili being so much older.

Besides, Okuata was sure he hated farmwork, and often told herself that it would have been a good thing for her to give up farming. Then Orimili would have had to pay for every single one of their household needs. She would bet that after the experience he would see what she meant; and she wouldn't at all be surprised if it turned out afterwards that he was the one making the offer to come once a week to the farm! However, she had her children to worry about. Suppose Orimili went away one day to Okono, leaving them no money? How would she cope with the hungry children?

Meanwhile, Orimili struggled with his sense of detachment from everyone else: he who had every conceivable reason to be in the thick of the crowd of townsmen. Okuata knew nothing of this struggle. Not that the knowledge would have stopped her grumbling. More likely, she would have said, 'Serves him right!' and, anyway, why didn't he do something about it if he felt so bad?

In fact, Orimili regularly did something about it. Since he was wont to connect the unpleasant feeling to his manner of employment and the profits that derived from it, he often reasoned with himself that there had to be someone to do the odd job. He had reassured himself so often in this manner and had become quite certain not only that someone had to do the odd job, but also that it was in the order of things that the man for the odd job was none other than himself. He kept at that job even to the point that some of the townspeople did on occasion suspect him of insensitively serving outside interests against the very people he claimed to be part of. For the moment, however, he was greatly cheered, as he strolled to Amanza, by the prospect of two delivery runs for Guy & Son, with the market day one in between – by far the noisiest and most wearying and, moreover, the least profitable.

Orimili arrived at Amanza, wine-horn under his arm, and with a light folding wooden chair. He exchanged greetings with his acquaintances as he made his way deftly towards the sacred tree, where the wine-sellers were; at the same time, he was discreetly looking round the crowded square to locate any of his particular friends with whom to share a drink. He saw Ogbuefi Oranudu sitting on a goatskin mat spread on the ground. With him were two men, one being Ogbuefi Edozie Nwanze of Amanna, whom he recognised at a glance because of his red cap. This was an emblem of rank as a member of the *ozo* society – the ruling class of wealthy people in Okocha of which the title of peerage was 'Ogbuefi'. Nwanze wore his cap at all times as if it were quite ordinary. The other person with Oranudu was a younger man, the company clerk: what was his name? Strange. Someone he saw quite often, and yet never seemed to remember his name! How did people remember all the names of all the people they knew? He racked his brains, knowing that the young man's name was there somewhere. Be that as it may, he would go and join the group for a chat, before moving on. It should have been best, of course, to have everybody's name at the ready, when one was going to sit and talk with them. At the foot of the sacred tree, where all the palm-wine-sellers had congregated in order to take advantage of its shade from the afternoon heat, he bought for himself a calabashful of the milk-white wine, and picked his way towards Oranudu in front of whom one gourd was already lying on its side, showing that it was empty.

'Ugonnaya *ogalanya*!' Orimili saluted. That was the name Oranudu had taken when he had been inducted into the *ozo* society. That rite which made one a life member of the durbar was usually marked by the taking of a nickname.

The old man acknowledged the greeting, and at the same time invited '*Ogbuefi* Orimili' to join them. Orimili was delighted, and his good humour rose still higher when he heard Ogbuefi Edozie Nwanze welcome him with the title of 'Ogbuefi'. It was as though the two titled men were trying to give him a hint that they were in favour of his becoming a member of the fellowship of title-holders. They must have heard, thought Orimili, that he had applied for membership. The man flattered himself that Oranudu and Nwanze were probably not using the title merely as a courteous greeting. Orimili had held the idea long enough that the title was a most worthy and compelling goal to aspire to, had so often imagined himself decked out in the robes and emblems of *ozo*, and felt how becoming they were that he had begun unconsciously to associate the title with himself. But he did not carry the flattery to the point of supposing that he could see himself through to the possession of the object of his quest. It was true that he was thought to be one of the wealthiest men in Okocha, which was a point in his favour. But it was also well known that neither Orimili's father nor his grandfather had taken the title. There was a certain handicap in that, though not insuperable, as long as he carried the majority of the aldermen with him. That was why he needed such an ally as Ogbuefi Oranudu, who was well respected in Okocha. If he had the man behind him, and Nwanze too, surely that would bring him a long way. To think of it, shouldn't he be using his evenings at Amanza to try to cultivate such people as Oranudu and Nwanze, and as many of the title-holders as he could? Get them all behind him, instead of letting the matter be decided purely on the merit of the case, especially as he himself would not take part in the debate? The merits of the case: what were they? What did the sodality ask, really? Orimili put an immediate check on his thoughts by reminding himself proverb that a farmer would have done well to have tilled the ground properly and sown his yams. It wouldn't do him any good to sow worry into the bargain. He had made his application; that was all. If there were questions to be asked, what was his friend Ogbuefi Obiefuna Emenogha there for, other than to answer them? Or try to answer them, he quickly amended.

Orimili placed his wine-gourd before the group, as though he were making them a present of it, as if he were already getting to work, cultivating the worthies. He handed his drinking-horn to the young man from Guy & Son, in answer to whose greeting a while earlier he had good-humouredly said, 'Oh... er... Record-taker! Are you here too?'

He had handed his drinking-horn to the young man so that he could unfold his chair, but he was obliging enough to fill it and hand it back to Orimili when he sat down. The latter beamed:

'Thank you, Record-taker. You are a thoughtful young fellow, for you seem to have guessed that I haven't had a sip all day. Little wonder that they are very pleased with you at Guy's, and won't part with you! Had you a good day at the office today?'

'Oh, busy as usual; only don't let them hear at the office that I am not to be parted with. What if they think it is I giving out the stuff, and try to prove me wrong?'

'No harm will come to you,' answered Orimili, taking a sip of the palm wine. Then he stopped to consider its quality. 'May it never be said that Orimili brought anyone misfortune.' He raised his head, and had a long draught of the wine, stopping only when the wine-horn was empty. Then he nodded briskly, and commented: 'Good and strong!', handing the horn back to the young man to fill up again for him. Now, sitting forward, his second hornful in his fist, he faced the old man and enquired politely about his health.

'I'm fine, today,' answered the old man. 'Fine now, I should say: that's as much as an old man may say with certainty. Who knows what will chance in another moment?'

'There will be no such thing,' Orimili quickly told him, 'only good fortune! Also you are looking well, I am glad to see that.'

For an answer, Oranudu breathed deeply, and went on to enquire about Orimili's family. Orimili answered that all was well when he left the house, and he couldn't say whether anything had happened since. To the old man's specific enquiry about Osita, Orimili answered that he had recently received a letter from his son. At the same time he turned towards the young man from Guy's, as he recalled that the letter had not yet been read and that this fellow, who was obligingly filling his wine-horn that evening, had actually failed him. Wasn't he the fellow he had asked some days before to come and read him the letter? The severity in his look lasted only an instant. Orimili smothered it because it wouldn't do for him to be angry. What if the fellow said, 'Fine, read the thing yourself!' Also, maybe he had come when Orimili was out. Orimili asked, quite mildly:

'Can you come tomorrow, er... Onyeme?' (Of course, that was the fellow's name; Onyeme Umunna. How did he forget?) 'Rather, the day after tomorrow...' He stopped, embarrassed. Was he then so preoccupied that he couldn't spare a moment for his son Osita? An entire day, even, to know how his boy was doing? Suppose Onyeme offered to come and read the letter for him tomorrow evening, would he give up what he had planned to do tomorrow so as to hear what Osita had to say?

That was the kind of question which set Orimili arguing mentally because his mind re-echoed the common opinion, as if with a clamour. It said now that, of course, he should give up everything just to know how Osita was. What common opinion did not know, naturally, was that the business of the day after tomorrow was connected to the one he must do tomorrow, and that paying Osita's tuition was connected to both. No, he wasn't being mean not to spare the next day to his son. What he was doing was more like what was said in the adage that in preserving oneself from danger or illness, one was only preserving oneself for death. What was meaning of his work? Was it something he was doing entirely for the young man? If he saved the next day for work, whose benefit was it, if not Osita's? The problem, he told himself in a matter-of-fact way, was that he could neither read nor write; were he able to, he would have dealt with the letter long ago, and forgotten about it. Yes, that was the problem – his having to depend on someone for something he needed. When he was working for himself, and everything depended on him, he was fine: he rarely failed to attain what he had set his mind upon. But it was something else when other people were involved. Then it was either that whatever else he had to do had to suffer, while he followed up what the fellow was supposed to be doing for him, or he never got anywhere. Was it because he wasn't sailing down-river with all the rest of the people? Where would he be, otherwise? Would Onyeme Umunna have been more obliging, had he been following wherever the people were, and doing whatever they were doing? Would he have been able to sustain Osita? And would there have been any letters then?

Likely not.

It'd be a lot more practical to try to make the acquaintance of the school teachers, so that one's letter would not have to wait until it pleased this impudent young man here to oblige one. They would be much more dependable than Onyeme, except that they always tried to make a convert of one: a choice between two kinds of impertinence. It was a wonder that the teachers were not content to do the job for which they were paid. Were they given prizes for bringing people to church?

Orimili used to know a teacher, the one Osita had in his last year in the primary school. A good fellow, he was, and didn't hold much store by that prize; nor did he give one to think that he had set his mind on making one his first catch in the town. He understood after the first few tries that Orimili took very seriously his kinship with the river god, and was equally staunch in doing his duties to the last of the earth-bound divines. But he had continued to visit every so often to talk about Osita – it was always Osita. It was this same man, Teacher Okoye, everybody called him, who had persuaded Orimili to send Osita to the teacher training college at Okono. But the boy had not continued there. For some reason, which was never fully explained to Orimili, he had transferred to the government grammar school, which neighboured the former school. And when he had finished at the grammar school, he had told Orimili of an admission he had to study law overseas. The man had regarded his son for some time with incomprehension. 'What about taking a job?' Orimili had finally asked, for the colonial administration had work for everyone who was qualified. Osita had said that he would get a job of course, after his studies overseas, and that it would be a very high-paying one. Orimili found out further that the job in question was three or four years away. After turning this over in his mind, he had decided that the boy was only being adventurous. Why wait for four years in order to take a lucrative job? Didn't the proverb say that the gleaner who went to work at first cock-crow had a good chance of filling his basket before midday? But Orimili's son would wait until after midday, before going to work! After some time, he had said to himself: All right, let him have his adventure – in Europe; especially for that. Not until Osita was ready to sail did his father realise that the adventure in question was to be paid for by himself.

Osita was in a way an only son, which was why at the end of the day he always had his way with his father. He was the only successful live-birth of Orimili's first wife, Ekesi, who had followed her one success with a series of miscarriages; and had died, as a matter of fact, in the last of these. So Osita became his father's greatest friend and, what was more, the souvenir of good Ekesi, which had been mercifully left to him. It was to be treasured above everything.

Ekwenze Orimili had come a long way from considering how to get Osita's letter read. In fact, he had forgotten about the letter, having let his imagination wander. He was only just then regaining awareness of his companions. That moment, Nwanze was talking about someone's illness, Orimili listened closely to see if he could pick up threads to piece together. When this failed, he enquired of Nwanze: 'Do you mean the man himself?'

'Of course,' answered Nwanze; and noticing that a query still lingered on Orimili's face, he added, 'don't you know Edoko Uwadiegwu?'

'Of course, I know Ogbuefi Uwadiegwu. Wasn't I talking to him here in Amanza last Afor?'

'You must have been,' old Oranudu interposed. 'I saw him too. But, mind you, that was a week ago: eight days. Wasn't he talking to his wife and children one moment, only to fall unconscious a twinkle of an eye later?' He finished off with a shake of the head, sad.

'He fell unconscious,' echoed Orimili. 'Dreadful! It must have been the heat; hasn't it been terribly hot during the past few weeks?' No doubt, it was the hottest and most humid part of the dry season. With the rainy season about a month or so away, the sky seemed anxious lest its work over the past season be too quickly undone by the rains. So there was a panic release of heat, and people poured with sweat at all times, day and night, especially at night. There were times when Orimili woke up in the middle of the night to find that he was lying in what seemed like a pool of fairly steaming water.

'That was what everybody thought, when the incident first occurred,' Nwanze explained. 'They said it was the heat. Later, however, the herbalist arrived, and confirmed what all the neighbours feared, but dared not broach.' His voice fell to a whisper. 'It was a stroke of the elemental spirits.'

Orimili snapped his fingers in horror: 'The silent-disease!'

Incongruously, there was an outbreak of raucous laughter quite near them. Shocked, they turned at the same time and saw Ogbuefi Obinagu Nwalioba and Okandi Echebido still full of mirth, and coming towards them. Ogbuefi Nwalioba had a loud and croaky tone of laughter, making it seem as if he drew the sound from his entire frame, which was tall, lanky and slightly stooping. He and Okandi sensed immediately that something was wrong, and their laughter ceased. Their eyes opened wide as their embarrassment was quickly overtaken and swept aside by their curiosity and foreboding. Orimili was impressed at the way in which Nwalioba's high hilarity had been suppressed. For it gave him a weird sense of what must have happened to Edoko, when, bludgeoned in broad daylight by the elemental spirits, darkness descended abruptly, gripping his very bones and sinews. There was also another reason altogether why it was shocking to see Nwalioba so merry. Orimili was vaguely aware of it, but hadn't the time to reflect in order to pinpoint it. It was some moments later before he remembered why: that Nwalioba had a grievous weight upon his mind.

While Nwanze gave Nwalioba and his friend a gist of what had happened, Onyeme was having a hard time maintaining his good manners, and not departing in the middle of an account of an illness. He endured the account to the end. His rising to leave, when it was over, seemed to lift the spirits of the company a little. In any event, Orimili took advantage of the young man's departure to fix Nwalioba, who was one of his particular friends.

'Come, you must have some news to share with us. Have you people settled?' He was referring to a land dispute between Nwalioba and another titled man, Ogbuefi Ikedi, who was his neighbour.

'Settled?' repeated Nwalioba. 'Of course not. I'd say there is very little chance we shall.' They all turned to him. He took them all in at a glance, looked away, and remained inscrutable. The only concession he made after a while was to shake his head a little, with: 'It's a tiresome business.'

'It must be,' commented Orimili doubtfully. In a moment, he pursued: 'Didn't you tell me the last time we were talking that you were going to meet with the arbitrators? You mean they did absolutely no good?'

'No... no they didn't.' And Nwalioba hung fire. Orimili felt, in fact, that he saw him draw back, as if something had stirred inside him, and he had to restrain it to prevent it from issuing in bitter words. The man kept his gaze in space for a while, ground his teeth to steel himself, and then let it come: 'What good did you think they would do?

What good could an arbitrator do, if he was afraid of the truth? Well, the people who came to us looked everywhere but at the evidence pointed out to them. I tell you, there is very little chance of our settling anything! Not unless the landmarks are taken for what they are worth! You know, they dared to mention sacrifice and compromise to me.' He gave a dry laugh, and continued: 'Well, it is all very well to compromise, as long as the property in question does not belong to one. But I shall not compromise because it belongs to me. You understand, Orimili; it is mine!'

'Still,' remarked Edozie Nwanze after a pause, 'you and Ogbuefi Ikedi are neighbours, I'd say relatives even. So,' he hedged, 'it ought to be settled amicably. You know, a give-and-take – I mean, on all sides – it is hard to do without it once a quarrel has begun, and must needs be settled. I see nothing that can be done with the present one except to settle it; you see?'

'Therefore, a give-and-take,' cried Nwalioba. 'On whose land, though? That's the point you miss! What you are saying is: I *give*, in return for *nothing*. You mustn't have seen the place we are talking about; I am sure of that.' He was altogether full of the sense of the justice of his cause. Nevertheless, he turned to old Oranudu with an appeal: 'You know the place, don't you? The thing is so clear!'

Oranudu knew the place from Nwalioba's description, but he didn't know which families owned land there. 'Well,' answered Nwalioba, a little put down, 'I assure you that there isn't the least difficulty in finding the old boundary line. I pointed it all out to the arbitrators when they came. But were they interested? No. All they wanted was that I should agree to have portions of my land handed over to Ikedi so that there will be peace! Would you call it *peace*, when your enemy is in possession of your property? Well, I don't. Not as long as I am there to make him give it up!'

'I think you are wrong to blame the arbitrator,' remarked Oranudu. 'Is it his fault that someone no longer knows the extent of the inheritance from one's father? For one of you is encroaching on his neighbour's property' – glaring at Ogbuefi Nwalioba, as if daring him to gainsay him – 'else there would be no dispute. If you do not know the boundary, you who work the land from year to year, why should the outsider be believed, if he says that it is *here* or *there*? How can he know?'

They all considered it in silence. As to Orimili, he knew Ogbuefi Obinagu Nwalioba pretty well; had known him since they were little boys. To him, there was no question at all that Ogbuefi Ikedi was the one encroaching. He was the one who deserved to be glared at by Oranudu. That was it: the old men did a great deal of glaring, but rarely in the right direction – that was what he thought was wrong with Okocha. He didn't say this, however, to old Oranudu. He rather addressed the aggrieved man:

'Ogbuefi Nwalioba, it is said that the ear that gets boxed is one that happens to be at a convenient distance. It is also said that if a rope is cut and retied, it will be shorter than before. You will admit that this present quarrel cannot now be wiped out together with the mistrust and suspicion it has engendered. That is being realistic. I believe that this is the reason for the view taken by the arbitrators. Think about it; I'm sure you'll see there is something in what they have said.'

'Yes, yes; I have considered that,' Nwalioba hastened to assure him. 'But one begins walking, starting from step one. That's where I want us to begin – with step one: the facts of the case must be established and recognised by all concerned. This is what the arbitrators have refused to do. How can we go on to the next step?'

'You have every right to speak as you do,' said Nwanze, reasonably, adjusting his cap at the same time. 'We all know how hard a decision it is to give up one's ancestral property, even for a good cause, to say nothing of its being snatched, so to speak, from one. I am not saying that what you have told us is all that there is to say about the case, one has to hear from Ogbuefi Ikedi as well to know which is which. I am saying rather that you have very strong feelings on the matter, and that is why you won't hear of making the least concession. Fair enough! Does not the proverb say that the one who is certain that his father told him so-and-so will come to no harm, should he swear even by the most pitiless of all the gods?'

Nwanze broke off, struck by the wider implication of what he had said. Finally: 'And, there you are! How do we know that Ikedi's father hasn't told him something different from what your own father told you? You weren't born with the land, neither was Ikedi. So how do you know that his claim is not as genuine as your own?'

'No, it isn't,' said Nwalioba firmly. 'Because his father never over-stepped the boundary.'

'All the same,' observed Orimili, 'mediators have been

called in. Don't you see that you are putting yourself publicly in the wrong to reject what they say?'

Nwanze adroitly took over the argument from Orimili: 'Shouldn't one have objected to having mediators from the first? But then,' he had now turned to Nwalioba, 'One would have been accused of not co-operating. One can hardly be in the right now unless one continues to co-operate; don't you think?'

Nwalioba was silent a moment. He saw now that what he hated particularly was being pushed into a corner by such a crook as Ikedi. It even struck him that his friends were helping Ikedi to achieve his purpose, and he spoke with some heat. 'Why is it that I am the one being told by everyone: 'Yield', 'Give up what belongs to you'? Yet no one has taken the trouble to point out to me where I have gone wrong. Why is nobody saying to Ikedi the kind of things you people are saying to me?'

'Listen to me,' Oranudu quickly interposed. 'You are a happy man that everyone is saying exactly the same thing to you, with no one at your elbow, urging you not to…'

'No, no! Let's have this clear,' cried Nwalioba, stormily. Leaning his spare frame forward, and sitting at the edge of his light wooden chair, it was as if he would topple over. With eyes still flashing fire, he fairly spat out his words: 'I need no one to tell me to stand up to Ikedi. I shall stand up to that greedy man. He must be checked now, or he will do worse later.'

'Precisely the way it should be,' commented Oranudu ironically. 'Be careful, though; and I mean both of you. For, as you know, there have been deaths resulting from land disputes. There have been whole families wiped out, fighting over a piece of land which then went to someone else! You are a sensible man, son of Nwalioba.'

Orimili was a sensitive man. He took things a great deal to heart, especially things that didn't concern him personally. He took them to heart because they touched off a chord in his own mind and caused some vague fear to stir up and give him hell for a spell, before subsiding again to resume its vague form at the back of his mind. Ogbuefi Oranudu, master of ambiguity, had just come out with a blunt warning; and his listeners were doubly impressed; on the one hand, by the very fact that he had spoken so bluntly, and on the other, by the import of the warning. For some moments no one said anything, so Orimili took the opportunity to reconstruct Nwalioba's case with Ikedi, connecting it to his own experience in order, so to speak, to draw as much terror from it as possible. Only in this way could he see it clearly.

He hadn't seen the disputed land yet, though he had promised Nwalioba that he would come and see it. However, he had been told about an ancient shrub, called *echiechii*, which demarcated Nwalioba's land from Ikedi's. Another shrub called *ogilisi* was more commonly used for marking boundaries. The former was very slow in developing, and survived very harsh conditions and ill usage. For instance, if its trunk was destroyed by fire, it was sure to sprout up again from its roots. Orimili was frankly struck that an *echiechii* had been used. It suggested that the site had been contested at least once in the past. Anyway, he knew nothing about that. The fact was that the shrub was standing where it now was; or rather, that the spot where it used to flourish was still known. For Nwalioba had reported that Ikedi had been burning heaps of twigs on that spot for several years in succession. But no one had suspected his motive. It wasn't until he began clearing Nwalioba's field the year before that the latter understood what was going on and raised the alarm. Both men were then forbidden to farm their portions until the matter was settled. It didn't seem to Orimili that they would be able to make use of the fields that year either; not unless Nwalioba decided to accept the new boundary proposed by the arbitrators; and this lay roughly midway between the *echiechii* and a spot well inside Nwalioba's land, claimed by Ikedi to be the real boundary.

Now, suppose he was in Nwalioba's position, what would he do? Take his own counsel? Would that not mean that he must retreat every time an acquisitive neighbour stirred? Perfectly terrifying! For he hadn't reserves where he could retreat into. In comparison with Nwalioba, he was just like the dry wood to the green. Orimili had excellent reasons for this bleak view of his situation. Therefore, he had to oppose any move against his own property from the very first instant, and with everything in his command. Well, even that would be already late, in that the mere fact of the encroachment would be like stripping him naked. Clearly, he should not wait until things came to that stage. What he ought to do was to go and wall his compound, and so discourage his neighbours from ever dreaming the dream! Ha! ha! Was not the building of a wall a way of letting everybody know that he was afraid? Would not the man with designs on his property say to himself upon seeing a wall going up: 'Come, get hold of something for yourself, before he seals off everything.' No – Orimili sadly reflected – a wall was not the thing. It would be too dangerous.

Of course, he had heard of no one being forced to give up portions of his own compound. However, this did not mean that a thing of the sort could not happen; nor did it follow that if it didn't happen to other townsmen, it could not happen to Orimili. The compound, where his house stood, comprised all the land he owned – which made his interest in the case still more understandable, and made him appreciate all the more how right Nwalioba was, to say that he would not concede even half a span of his land to a greedy man, for anything. That was the spirit, really. Such an attitude would be far more helpful in the long run than striving through compromise to avoid conflict. Old Oranudu was only trying to blackmail his friend with that stuff about being 'a sensible man, son of Nwalioba'. What a sensible man should do was exactly what Nwalioba said he was going to do: stand up to the greedy man!

Needless to say, Orimili recoiled from airing these views, knowing what consternation they would cause among his companions. Nor was that all. One had to assume that, as a titled man, Ogbuefi Ikedi would not lie; and that was a good enough reason for the arbitrators to take it that both Nwalioba and Ikedi were speaking the truth. Orimili saw it all now. Wherever they said was the boundary between their two properties, then that was the boundary. For both were titled men, and could not lie. Therefore, if their claims failed to coincide, it must be owing to a genuine confusion. All that one had to do was to find the halfway point between Nwalioba's boundary and Ikedi's and make it the common boundary for the two worthies!

So, Nwalioba could not in fact reject what the mediators had said? Ikedi had won the case; Orimili saw it very clearly. There was no limit to the privileges of the titled man, unless the man himself put on the restraint.

Okandi Echebido was saying that there were things which one had to put up with; injustice, for example. For if a fellow were to insist on pulling out every last piece of hair sticking out from a *khaddar* in order to make it perfectly smooth, there would be nothing left of the cloth by the time the fellow had finished with it.

Obviously more reason was being piled on what had already been said to persuade Nwalioba to compromise. As Orimili saw it now, what they were all doing was commiserating with him over the loss of a tract of his land. It was as clear as that.

Ekwenze Orimili showed every sign of haste in finishing off the dregs in his drinking-horn, and looked about him to see if he had dropped anything. Okandi stopped speaking, which was the effect that Orimili desired. 'Don't mind me, Okandi,' said Orimili, politely. 'Go on with what you are saying. I'm sorry that I can't stay to hear the rest of it because the evening light is beginning to fail, and I am to meet someone. It's important too; I nearly forgot.' In point of fact, he only wanted to see his friend, Obiefuna Emenogha. His evening at Amanza would be quite incomplete without this ritual meeting. He didn't get off immediately, however. For Oranudu had something to say to him. As a result, Okandi Echebido's speech was never completed.

Oranudu had heard that Orimili had asked to be conferred with the title of an alderman.

All that the man said to that was: 'Oh yes,' not knowing what else to say; whether it was more appropriate to ask in return what the old man thought of his chances, or to say that he was sorry not to have discussed it beforehand with Oranudu. Anyway, did everyone who desired the title do the rounds, discussing the project and gaining endorsements, before applying? To be sure, Orimili would very much have liked to be endorsed by Oranudu, and by as many titled men as possible. The best thing, however, was that they should do it without his asking them; do it purely on the basis of what each of them should be able to say about him as a person.

Oranudu did not mention what he thought of Orimili's chances. He only mentioned that the society of title-holders was to meet within the month, and that he expected to attend – unless something happened – to listen to the debate.

Orimili cast a quick glance in the direction of the sodality house, which lay just on the rim of Amanza at the far side, knowing that it was in that house his fate was to be decided. However, he faced the old man and spoke with the assurance of a priest giving a blessing: 'No harm will touch you. I count on you to be at the meeting and help carry the day for me.' Putting his wine-horn under his arm, he finished off in a pleading tone: 'Don't draw back now, do you hear?' He didn't wait for Oranudu's assent, but folded his chair, picked up the calabash jug he had brought with him – now empty of course – and went his way wishing the company good health. No sooner had he turned away than Ogbuefi Nwalioba remarked that Orimili was a rare man. It warmed the man's heart greatly to overhear the remark.

When he had left Orimili and his friends, Onyeme Umunna, the clerk at Guy & Son, meandered his way through the people, who sat or stood together in clusters. He was in search of Ogbuefi Ananwemadu, the man whom the colonial district administration had appointed head of Okocha, with the title of 'Chief'. Only a small number of the local people ever referred to the man by that title. Onyeme Umunna was one of these few, though he confused matters quite a bit by using the title as a convenient mode of address when he spoke about any of the *ozo*. As to these leaders themselves, who had taken it from Onyeme that *chief* was the English for *ogbuefi*, they took care, as if by common consent, not to use the word in reference to Ananwemadu. They would not let it be supposed that they took any particular notice of the man, laughing at the notion that he was their leader. The administration seemed to know nothing of the people's hostility to their chosen man, and continued to take notice of him. Onyeme Umunna's search for him this evening was entirely at their behest. Picking his way through the crowd of townsmen enjoying themselves, he felt as if he had been moving from one world to another: now he was passing by a group arguing noisily and hotly; now it was another in which the men stood in a conspiratorial attitude, heads thrust forwards and close together, keeping their voices low and completely oblivious of the group of revellers huddling together nearby, with some sitting among the empty calabash jugs in the middle of the group, and facing away from some of the company.

It was becoming difficult to distinguish the individuals from a distance because of the failing light. Anyway, he could call at Ananwemadu's house on his way home and leave a message for him. He searched on, nevertheless. He made his way through the crowd, which had become quite thick around the sacred tree, to enquire of the wine-sellers if Ananwemadu had been seen in the square that evening. Someone told him that the man he sought had bought a jug of wine only a moment before and had disappeared into the crowd. At length he heard the boom of Ananwemadu's voice among a fairly large number of people sitting together. He went over to the man and whispered in his ear. He rose immediately to go aside with him, but before they made a move someone spoke up in a tone of shock:

'Strange! Do you not know, Record-taker, that that man has the white man's warrant, making him a chief? How come you are calling him away without due ceremony?'

There was a roar of laughter. Onyeme and Ananwemadu joined in. At the same time, Ananwemadu was making ready his retort to Ogbuefi Nweke Nwofia (no kin to Ekwenze Orimili), who had just made the remark. He waited for the laughter to die down so that he would wonder aloud about a certain wealthy farmer, who failed to pay his tax and was made to scud through the market, hotly pursued by a brace of court messengers. However, Ogbuefi Ikedi, Nweke Nwofia's crony and Nwalioba's enemy, was the first to throw in a gibe as the laughter was dying down, and thus prevented Ananwemadu from getting at Nwofia. Speaking as if in answer to Nwofia, Ikedi had said:

'I shouldn't worry about that, if I were you. Can you think of anything more in point than to have the white man's record-taker get hold of' – strongly implying a formal arrest of – 'the white man's tax collector?' The company laughed louder and longer. Ananwemadu gave up, and went aside with Onyeme.

'Chief,' began Onyeme, 'can you call at the office tomorrow about midday? The manager would like to speak to you.'

'Tomorrow? What about?'

'No idea, only that it is urgent.'

Moments later, they rejoined the group. The company clerk found himself the target of many a lewd joke; and he was nettled by a fellow who enquired of him what he thought of the widows of Okocha. Why should he think anything of them, he had retorted angrily, and had been drowned out with derisive laughter. With every new jest, his head was growing hot, despite the cool evening breeze. Whatever he himself found to say sounded grotesquely defensive. How he wished he could get himself out of the firing line by throwing a clever gibe at some fellow in the group, causing him to draw fire to himself. He knew, however, that had he found anything clever, it would have been difficult to put it into words; for his companions were all men much older than himself. Younger householders tended to congregate at the fringes of the square. But Onyeme was not even married. Joining his elders at Okocha was a sort of privilege arising from the fact that he wasn't a native of Okocha, being of Ezinda, a neighbouring town. When he dealt with the townsmen individually, he often detected a certain deferential attitude which he thought must have something to do with his position in the company. On the whole, he was disposed to be patient with them, for he was looking upon one of their daughters as a possible bride. A joke or two at his expense couldn't possibly do him harm.

The warrant chief, for his own part, had been as mirthful as the rest. He even managed to get in a few jokes of his own. But on his way home after the company had broken up, he began to wonder what the manager of Guy & Son wanted to see him for. He hoped that it hadn't to do with the tax returns. At the thought of the tax returns, bitterness rose in his heart. Hadn't he made it clear to the district officer himself that he must not count on a native of Okocha to carry on tax drives for the administration, and that the office must find a way of making their court messengers more effective if they were still not satisfied with the returns? Ananwemadu did not see the way in which he could so much as suggest to the people that they should pay their taxes. He didn't want to believe that he was unpopular in the community – wasn't he drinking and joking with them as of old? Still, he could feel that some of the people resented him, especially among the menfolk, and he thought that some of the gibes he had received that evening were intended to wound him. However, he didn't want things to get to a stage when someone could tell him to his face that the district officer had been fooled by his great stature and fair appearance, and had appointed him a warrant chief without knowing that he had no brains! That was one of the more notorious and mortifying comments being passed around in Okocha. He knew, of course, that it was all jealousy. But he couldn't deny that they had found something that would appeal to their coarse imagination to cloak that jealousy in. No, he couldn't take on his detractors on an issue like that. He would bide his time, and in the meantime keep up the air of understanding and friendship.

Ananwemadu was suddenly angry with himself for accepting the district officer's appointment. He had thought that it would give him some advantage among his peers. Instead he had been the one trying to win their favour and respect: treating them to numberless jugs of palm wine, for instance, week after week at Amanza, and drinking little of it himself. How many jugs did he buy today? Three? Four? He tried to recall each instance. He counted off three on his fingers… There was a fourth one, he thought, squinting into the darkness to focus more minutely into his memory. Four full jugs, there must have been.

At any rate, he got a commission for the job, which was something, though far short of what seemed right for the inconveniences, which were quite numerous. Think of having to join in laughing at oneself and pretending to be unperturbed! If only one could know all the scandals which people secreted away; have all ready, one or two for every Okocha man. He would be very glad any day to be in Amanza!

Ananwemadu also considered whether it wouldn't be best to tell the manager of Guy & Son, when he saw him tomorrow, that he was done with the warrant chieftaincy, and that he desired him to mention the fact to the district officer. Be rid of it, and be able to make plain, honest jokes with his peers! Of course, one of them would quickly take his place. Who would it be? Suppose everyone said they didn't want the job? The district officer would send someone from his office to look after his tax. How he would enjoy hindering that officer a little just as some men of Okocha were doing to him, paying their own taxes but showing two or three others how to avoid paying and also stay out of harm's way! After one or two years, that officer would be sent away, and another appointed, who would fare no better. Then would be the time to smile.

Ananwemadu actually smiled in anticipation of this clever stroke, though it quickly fizzled out at the thought of Nweke Nwofia. Of course, Nweke Nwofia would go like a shot for the job, if it were on offer; and he would be sure too to turn it round to cause his voice to resound all the more loudly. Give him a chance, and he would do something for himself with this job. It would be unwise to let him. It wouldn't be beyond him to give out that he had been sacked. And that would ruin him utterly.

Ananwemadu was in an impossible dilemma. And he recalled the ancient story of the bat, who had been unable to decide whether to be a bird or an earth-bound mammal. Hurrying to and fro between the air and the land, enquiring about this or that in order to know all the advantages that each of the two domains had, the bat did not notice that the time allowed for the decision was quickly flitting by. Then, click: catching him at the halfway point between the two worlds. So the bat was caught in the in-between state for ever: part mammal, part bird. Ananwemadu felt that he had been cruelly forced into the middle position between the administration and his people. Had he been allowed a period of time to decide, just as the bat had been given? So, that was the main difference: that whereas the bat had been courting trouble by not deciding as quickly as the other animals had done, he himself had been given only an instant to decide. And what had he been asked to decide upon? Whether or not he would *serve* his people? See what he got instead!

This moment, however, Ananwemadu was playing the bat at another level. Between the decision to stay or resign he now stood, unable to say he was in or out, and damn the consequences.

The warrant chief slept little that night, feeling like an animal in a trap. He wondered whether there was another soul that night in Okocha who was staying awake into the small hours of the morning. Obviously not: what worries could they have? The odd land dispute? A sick wife? How to avoid paying the tax? What?

Ananwemadu's meeting with the manager the following day didn't touch on any of the things that had troubled him, but that didn't mean that he was now a happy man. By no means. He was self-conscious and suspicious, imagining that the townsmen knew every detail of what passed in his mind, and that a great many of their gestures towards him were aimed at showing him that they knew what was going on.

We shall need some wine, thought Ekwenze Orimili, to keep us occupied while we talk. So I'd better…

'Ogbuefi Orimili! How lucky to see you now!'

It was Uderika Nwanne's voice. How he longed to become a real Ogbuefi!

'That sounds like Nwanne,' answered Orimili. 'Is it you really?'

They met and exchanged greetings, enquiring about each other's family. Uderika then went straight to the point:

'My son says he needs money: will you be able to send him some from me on your next trip to Okono?' That was how it was with Uderika Nwanne. If he needed something, he knew where to go for it; and how to succeed in it.

Uderika's son, Kanene, was a student in the teacher training college where Osita had studied for some time. He was in his final year now, a great relief to Uderika. But then the final year brought its worries, chief of which, as far as Uderika was concerned, being that the young teacher might get posted to a strange place, just like Chiebo Oranudu, old Oranudu's grandson, who had been sent to Ikenga, a village far inland from Okono. Chiebo had not been seen in Okocha since he had begun teaching in Ikenga.

Orimili told Uderika that it would be no trouble at all to take the money to his son. He would be only too glad to go as he fully understood the poor fellows and knew all about their needs – which were usually expressed as sums of money.

Orimili's son was the model student, of course, and Orimili was so proud of him that he usually spoke as if to say that since Osita had gone farther in modern ways than any other of the young generation of Okocha, he had seen and experienced whatever the new age had to offer; and all the aspirations of the young consisted entirely in trying to be what Osita already was. Was it any surprise that they were all doing poorly, by contrast? Orimili had learned, thanks to Osita, everything it was possible to know about children: what going to boarding school meant to them, how they had to try to get on with strangers and endure long periods of separation from their parents. As a matter of fact, he knew a great deal more, for there wasn't another parent in Okocha, save Orimili, whose child remained in school from one end of the year to the other, and for several years in succession. Osita never came home on holidays from Europe, which meant to Orimili that he was never on holidays. Because he was unique in having followed closely the career of Okocha's model child, Orimili could lay down the law for the less experienced parents for bringing up their children. So he spoke of young people naturally as 'they', meaning, of course, the one and only Osita.

Uderika now said to Orimili: 'I have often wondered why Kanene is always writing home for money. He doesn't live on a diet of money, I'm sure; so what does he do with all the money I send him?'

One of the reasons why Kanene seemed always to be in want was that Uderika rarely gave him up to a half of what he asked. Orimili's reply, however, was to nod vigorously several times, saying: 'Oh, I quite understand your wondering like that. You know, it used to be said that sons are a sound foundation for wealth and power. That may still be true, but, as you are beginning to see, bringing up one child alone is enough these days to break any man's back! We are in a new age; that's what it is. Young people now seem to take for ever to grow up and fend for themselves. You are even coming off lightly since your son has only a few months to go, and then he will begin to look after himself. In my own case, it is like wrestling; and one has swooped and swept up one's opponent, ready to fling him to the ground, and so end the match. But, no; the referee says that I mustn't drop my burden: I must stand upright with my opponent on my shoulder, and do a dance too! See?' Orimili appealed. 'But what is the use complaining? It is the age of the young, the parents are condemned to slave for them.'

'Do you mean that there will be no end to this thing?' Uderika fairly cried; adding: 'I mean, that all one's children will go through college, and not be left to fend for themselves after learning how to write their names, or even passing their standard six?'

'You must be joking. You think your little children will willingly pass up going to college when their turn comes? Why should their elder brother have the advantage all alone? Do you know what my little boys tell their playmates? That Osita will come home and take them all back with him overseas, where they will become lawyers! Don't underrate those little things, my friend. They all want to go as far as their bigger brother has gone, and perhaps go farther!' Orimili stopped, wondering at what he had just said. When he first overheard his children boasting to their playmates, he had chuckled to himself: so the brats wanted to be like Osita? Interesting. Did they think he was going to let them trick him as Osita had done (*smart* was of course the word for Osita, which was different from 'trick', really). Strange! He must have welcomed this childish boast unconsciously. The children had a point, he now affirmed. And how was he going to cope?

'That's something I never thought of,' answered Uderika.

'Oh... er... You mean the children wanting to get on? Of course they will. However, bring the money to me any time: tomorrow, if you like. I shall travel the day after tomorrow, all things being equal. By the way, you didn't chance into Ogbuefi Emenogha this evening?'

'No, I'm afraid not. I shall bring you the money tomorrow, if you are sure it is not putting you to trouble. Thanks very much.'

Orimili told him that he was welcome any time. Then he took his leave briskly to resume his search for his friend Ogbuefi Obiefuna Emenogha.

Orimili bought another calabashful of palm wine and made his way outwards, listening as he went, quickly scanning the faces that made up the groups he passed, trying to maintain a purposeful aspect, which he hoped would discourage anyone who saw him from hailing him. But he was making little headway, not only because of the poor light but also because of the things he was carrying: his light chair, his drinking-horn and the wine jug. This made him wonder whether he wasn't putting himself to useless trouble. What if he squandered the remaining light dragging his things around the square, and not finding the man he sought? Maybe he should see Emenogha at another time, and in the meantime settle down with one group of people and have his drink. But he put this off with: Plenty of time for that. Give him another chance to show himself!

He tried to make a mental map of Amanza, cleared of all the townsmen except Emenogha. But this map refused to take shape; there was much too much noise to allow it. He stopped, craned his neck and tried to see above the numerous heads in the square, wishing he were taller. Pity he hadn't started the search sooner; and he was sorry too to have run into that blamed Uderika Nwanne. Moving on a little, he enquired of someone whether Emenogha had been seen in the square that evening. The answer came unexpectedly from Emenogha himself as he happened to be nearby. Smiling broadly, Orimili joined him and commented, tongue in cheek: 'Didn't know you could be so easily lost and swallowed up, even though Amanza is rather sparse today!' He busied himself shaking hands all round, while listening for Emenogha's riposte, which wasn't long in coming:

'Of course, I am distinguished, though not luminous. How did you expect to make me out in the darkness unless you are a cat?'

Orimili burst out laughing. 'I don't look like a cat, at any rate.'

'No, you don't,' said Emenogha with mock thoughtfulness. 'A vulture then?'

Orimili touched his hairless head instinctively, and the men roared with laughter. To be sure, if the height of the shoulders had been taken into consideration by Emenogha rather than the baldness of the head, the designation would have reflected more nearly upon the speaker himself. Orimili didn't stop to pick that up, of course; but moved to defend himself: 'What vulture would boast of these muscles? Just look at my arms and legs! As to you, you can hardly stand on your two feet without toppling over since yours are only canes!' The men greeted this remark with another burst of laughter.

Emenogha scratched his stubble and grinned. 'You are quite right about your sturdy limbs,' he said at last. 'But the proverb says that the breadfruit is most abundant where the people have no idea what to do with it. Give me a set of limbs like that, and I shall subdue any forest, and crop it with yams too! I should die of shame, if I were idle like you.'

'Idle? No, you couldn't mean me! By the way,' Orimili became confidential, 'have you heard about Edoko?'

Instantly, Emenogha's face became serious, and he exclaimed, wasn't it dreadful! Yes, everybody had heard. For some time they talked about how life was so beset with surprises and dangers. Then Orimili and Emenogha detached themselves from the group.

Orimili and Emenogha were the best of friends, but they bantered notoriously. The one often sought the other's company as if for the mere pleasure of inflicting this violence, and getting flayed in return. At any rate, they had little else to talk about when they were together. They had grown up with several other boys as playmates, and the two had stuck together despite the difference in their pursuits and preoccupations. When they were boys, Emenogha was *Obiefuna*, and Orimili was *Ekwenze*. The former grew up into what they called *his* father's son-which is not to say that other people were deemed to be any less their own fathers' sons. For the people of Okocha, it was a great virtue not to appear to be a distinct personality from one's sire. This was what entitled one to answer without irony the old man's name. Some who didn't know old Emenogha in person – he was already over ten years dead – were assured that to have seen Obiefuna was to have seen the old man. *Obiefuna* was dropped; thanks first of all to his father's age-mates who had shown early on that they preferred to know him by the name of the grandfather, whom he attended at the *ozo* ceremonies, bringing his stool or trumpet. They never did pick up his own proper name, but called him Son of Emenogha. *Obiefuna*, fine name though it was, ended up eclipsed by a finer one still, which sounded like a nickname deliberately chosen for oneself because of its ethical import; for it meant, 'Do nothing vulgar!' Orimili might have said that in his dealings with that gentleman he usually acted as if he took that precept very much to heart. Unlike his friend, he had given himself his own name, Orimili; at once an act of homage to *a* father – the god of the river where his barge was – and of rebellion from his own father. He was after all the male survivor of his line, and yet rather careless with the family name, and not particular about the one they had given him, preferring one of his choosing.

When the two friends had moved aside where they could be by themselves, Orimili enquired about his 'son's wife'.

Emenogha showed his irritation: 'How should I know, since you didn't bother to mention to me that your son was getting married, nor showed me his intended?'

'Didn't you know? Adoba, daughter of Emenogha, that's who!'

'Look, Orimili, you can't go on joking like this. Adoba is no longer a baby. It is quite ridiculous to apply such a title to a woman of her age, especially when you know perfectly well that there is nothing in it.'

Orimili was shocked. 'What do you mean, I know perfectly well that there is nothing in it? How can you say such a thing?'

'I see,' Emenogha grunted ironically. 'In that case, I am glad for my daughter!'

Orimili thought this over, before declaring that he didn't understand his friend's attitude at all. Did he mean to refuse him the girl now? Had they not agreed since she was a baby that she was going to marry Osita? Now that they had just come of age?

'I am not refusing you anything,' Emenogha answered evenly. 'You can't say that you stretched forth your hand for anything, and I said no.'

Orimili eyed him and found that he was looking away as if to show that he wouldn't even take notice, much less attempt to stop him, should he stretch forth his hand.

'Fine; we are where we were then,' remarked Orimili, cautiously.

Emenogha found this mildly amusing. 'And where would you say that we were?'

Orimili saw then that he could make excellent use of his friend's metaphor: 'I had put out my hand. I had laid a claim.' Emenogha only gave a short laugh, which gave Orimili a sense of how wrong he was. In the matter of marriage, there was nothing for a claim that was not witnessed by other people, except to laugh at it. This gave Orimili yet another sense.

'I am sure we shall do everything right. Wait until Osita returns. It is next year, you know; I think!'

'You *think* it is next year?'

'I'm certain of it. If all goes well…'

'All will go well!' Emenogha quickly rounded off, striking his fist on the ground to give force to his prayer. 'Of course there is no great hurry, for a year is not such a long time. They say that a thing worn down to one unit only is fairly done with. Still, a good many things can happen in one short year. For instance, we can't rule out someone coming and knocking any time – a good thing, mind you. Anybody with a marriageable daughter would wish that. You wouldn't mind if a thing like that occurred?'

Emenogha was obviously hinting at something, thought Ekwenze Orimili. Who was the villain trying to spoil Adoba out of his son's hand? However, he saw immediately that it would serve no good purpose to know who. Once he knew, the struggle, which he would win handily, would be hard to disguise for what it was; and one would have a grudge chalked up for one. It hadn't come to that, obviously. The thing was to make a quick and decisive move, and warn off any aspiring suitor. Emenogha was such a fine man to give him the hint; and it would be nice for him to reciprocate with an equally striking gesture.

'You know what?' said Orimili in an exalting tone. 'I mean to pay you an early visit!' Now more thoughtfully, 'It is only fair that a man charged to guard another's treasure should be given suitable weapons for the task. How would tomorrow evening suit you?'

'Tomorrow?' repeated Emenogha, suppressing a genial smile. 'What do you want to do tomorrow?' He was evidently thrilled. Try as he might, he couldn't keep it out of his voice.

Orimili put it in a nutshell for him: 'To knock and announce what I intend for my son.'

'So soon?'

'So soon!'

'Why so?'

'For a start,' philosophised Orimili, 'any time is *soon*, from some point of view. That's why our people say that a man of action will strike out, if he is obliged to do so, without bothering to find out whether the conditions are suitable or not. It is the outcome of such a stroke that I call an achievement. That is what a man relishes. I don't see what there is to relish, when the action was planned, measured and all the consequences calculated beforehand!'

'No,' observed Emenogha, 'a man is no good if he is not active and daring. Still, the haste seems excessive. Tomorrow evening will suit me personally. I shan't be going to the farm, after all…'

'Oh, fine. I don't see my way clear beyond tomorrow, and can't afford an eight-day or four-day notice. It would have been much easier, of course, if Osita had been here. But he prefers to remain in school until he is grey, leaving me to manage his affairs for him!'

'Well, he can't very well be here and there at the same time,' commented Emenogha in defence of the young man.

'What's the use of a father, if not precisely to look after his son?'

'No matter,' answered Orimili. 'Tomorrow, then. I'm glad it suits you. See if we can make a start... er... whether Adoba has a good opinion of my son.'

Orimili was sensitive, but happily that did not hamper him in making decisions. It helped him, rather. His deep yearning for a full sense of belonging caused him to reach beyond himself all the time. It was a curious strategy of survival, as if his entire life consisted in striving to catch up with an image of himself that was always somewhere else. His strivings were apparently on the point of reaching a certain term, with his brave man's sword held aloft and a handful of significant blows being struck. It couldn't be said that if he didn't stop to consider whether the conditions were right in every case, he was equally indifferent to the consequences. Take for instance his application for membership in Okocha's durbar. He knew for a certainty that he would be distinctly worse off, if he failed to achieve his goal. It must be said for him that he didn't let that fear deter him; nor did he calculate in what ways and to what extent he might suffer. Orimili was content to leave these calculations to fate, thankful to be spared the boredom of doing the sums and projections, but knowing that if fate was against him, and there was nothing to relish, well... That precisely was what he had consigned to the unknown. That dark side was always part of what he reached out for, always what became a little more clearly defined every time he reached out. So it was in the *ozo* affair. And so one fine day, he had asked his friend Obiefuna

Emenogha to apply on his behalf to the society. The latter had lost no time in getting the message across. Now what remained was the debate, which was expected to take place within the month.

Emenogha was used to Orimili's sudden decisions. The present one was even more agreeable to him than many another. Nevertheless, he politely enquired if his friend wasn't taking their conversation that night amiss. He would rather that Orimili took his time, for nothing could be farther from his purpose than to seem to push him.

'No, I don't call it pushing, if all you have done is to remind me to place a marker at my berth,' Orimili remarked genially, calling his boatmanship to his aid.

'It would have sufficed to know that you are still interested, but a marker, as you call it, is still better. For a couple of people have been looking lately in our direction; among them, the young man at Guy & Son, and...'

'What are you talking about?' said Orimili, shocked.

'I don't mean it in that way. But I'm sure you understand how difficult it can be, trying to invent excuses to turn away the callers. Adoba, of course, has some notion of our plans, but she needs something more concrete in order not to feel frustrated by my turning away her suitors.'

'You are not telling me that you let a fellow like Onyeme open his mouth in your place and say that he had an interest! You really shock me, Emenogha. So if this were a free-for-all, you would stand and see my son locked in combat with... with... and not be outraged?'

'Hush, Orimili. People will overhear us. Mind you,

Onyeme has no idea of our understanding. So you can't blame him for thinking that the coast is clear. Only do as you say; there will be no further embarrassments once it is known that the couple are engaged.'

'Maybe you should have given me this hint sooner. There was I saying that I was going to devote this year to the saving up of money and building up because of the great deal of spending I must do next year.'

'You were right, of course, to be looking ahead, what with Osita coming home, and the title-taking…'

'That last depends on you, remember. But I must be ready with the money, if you do push it through.'

'Don't you think – let's face it – that it will be wiser after all to proceed as you had planned? Adoba is not running away, you know. Let's finish with the title thing; then come for her.'

Orimili wouldn't hear of this, however. He had fitted Adoba into his plans and she sat beautifully in them, as if she had merely taken up the lot reserved for her. He would begin visiting and negotiating. The marriage itself would come only at the end – after the title, and after Osita had come. He was the one to get married, wasn't he? Certainly not Orimili! Didn't he see how grand a picture it was all going to be?

Emenogha confessed it was quite breathtaking. Orimili gazed afresh on it, full of wonder, in which was insinuated a shaft of misgiving that it was altogether too good. Yet it was hard to imagine what might impair a picture so bright and nice and, moreover, so just. An accident, perhaps? To prevent his boy from coming? He quickly thrust the thought from him, put up the picture, unimpaired, and stood back until it filled the field before him, and nothing could be seen beyond it or at the corners – quite as if the picture could not be removed without uncovering an abyss.

Another aspect of the plan on which he often cast a fretful glance was the hoped-for investiture with the *ozo*. He had in fact begun to seek reassurances from his friends that he hadn't blundered to have applied. This need was involved in his search for Emenogha this evening. The latter told him that it was yet early to see how the vote would go. He had been canvassing the peers, and so had Udeagu Obimma, Echesi and Udozo, their mutual friends. Altogether, he was optimistic, despite his having been unsuccessful with Nweke Nwofia. All that Nweke could do, of course, was to give him a fight; and if so, so be it. What he would like to know beforehand was what side Ogbuefi Oranudu would support. This he had been unable to establish from the interview he had had with the old man. That was the personage whom, in Orimili's experience, was given to glaring accusingly at the innocent, neglecting entirely the source of evil. But he hadn't as yet accused Orimili of anything; one might even say that he was partial towards him and his Osita.

Oranudu had other tricks, besides the one of which Orimili had a recent experience. He had elected apparently to sound enigmatic to Emenogha, like an oracle. Orimili took this up:

'Doesn't he speak sometimes as if to someone not in the audience; as if he isn't aware of the people in front of him?'

'Yes,' Emenogha put in. 'One mustn't be misled that he looks strong and gets about on his own. He is ancient, and his contemporaries are all gone. You know the saying that one like that is already with his age-mates in the land of the dead?'

'Then,' cried Orimili, ducking into the third person, 'let him tell those friends of his what Orimili has set his heart upon, and how he values their support!'

'If one could be sure that he himself is with us,' said Emenogha evenly, 'then there could be little doubt about his friends, living and dead. So far, he doesn't seem to be opposed. I shall keep trying to get him to declare for us. There are also others to canvass… Ananwemadu? Should I speak to him?'

'Is he not more likely to spoil the thing rather than help?'

'I think so too. Anyway, I'd better not bring him in just yet. And… well, I hate to feel that I am pushing you into hastening up the other thing, when we should all be putting our shoulders to…'

'Oh, well; the shoulders needed are yours and mine, not such young, innocent ones as Adoba's and Osita's. Your shoulders in particular. Just keep them there, and leave the rest to me.'

Obiefuna Emenogha thought Orimili's resoluteness and purposefulness altogether rare. There were few men who could boast such qualities in Okocha; among them, a mere handful would not have spoiled things by making themselves odious in some particular way. To be sure, it wasn't purposefulness as such that he admired. He couldn't stand it in a female, for instance. In her, it was pure bad taste, and deserved to be rooted out and ruthlessly suppressed. He was rather taken with the way his friend exercised the quality. His own view of what was the matter with Okocha – it was uncommon to see a townsmen say what he found taking about it – was that the task of realizing themselves involved for far too many people the bringing down of their neighbour!

Orimili had a way of his own. Had he not known him since they were both little boys, he would have supposed that the man had been influenced more by the things he saw where he travelled than by the behaviour of the villagers of Okocha, where he had been born and bred. When he had agreed that his son should go abroad for studies, the townsmen had been shaking their heads at him, saying that he must be mad to throw away the staff on which he was leaning. Emenogha himself had not been charmed because Orimili's younger children were still very small. He had stopped short of telling his friend that he was anxious for him, being of a small race in which it was unknown that there was more than one male in any generation. Orimili hadn't bothered about any of those things; and now, everybody was wishing they were Orimili.

For all his admiration of single-mindedness and bold strokes, Emenogha was temperamentally cautious and conservative. Everything was taken in measure. Hence, even though the people of Okocha had said as if with one voice that there was no point sending girls to school, Emenogha had sent his daughter to school, and she had completed her primary education. Then the lady teacher had asked the girl, what about becoming a teacher like herself? All that she needed to do was to go to a teacher training college for two years, to begin with; the rest would be done at leisure, as it were. Adoba had said that she would be glad to go, if her father would let her. So the lady teacher had volunteered to go and speak to Ogbuefi Emenogha, if it would help.

A few days afterwards, she had paid the man a visit. After her speech, he had asked her if her husband was also a teacher, or was she doing all the teaching, and he all the learning? When she explained that she wasn't yet married, Emenogha had understood, saying that, on the contrary, his daughter was going to 'enter into someone's house', and that he doubted that the man would be the sort who would want his wife to teach him! So Adoba had resumed keeping her mother company at home and on the farm. Nearly three years later, Emenogha and Orimili were completing their plans for their children's union. Adoba herself was nearly as good as she was before she first went to primary school, except that she was big and mature and blooming. Little remained of whatever she had learned in school. What was more strange still was that it didn't occur to Orimili, nor to Emenogha, that the young man for whom they were reserving this young lady may have had a different idea altogether about whom he wanted for a wife.

Ogbuefi Emenogha was a kind-hearted man, though his family would not have said so. He was spare and dark, his shoulders two hillocks, which gave his neck a slightly sunken appearance. He had a longish face too and a prominent nose, with two large creases across his forehead – three, when he frowned. Upon the whole, he looked quite unyielding; nevertheless, he had all the graces of good social behaviour native in Okocha. Scarcely had he finished his conversation with Orimili this evening than he began to form his plans for extending material help to him. Orimili was thought to be very wealthy, and quite able to pay for anything he undertook. Still, one accepted help from one's friends and relatives if one was taking, say, a title. It would be ill-mannered to do as if one didn't need them. Emenogha was determined to help lighten the burden for him in whatever way he could. And he calculated that it would help to place the marriage arrangements on a firm footing, and make the engagement public too. In that way, he would be able to give assistance in the manner of discharging an obligation devolving on an in-law.

The two men remained in the square long after it had become deserted and quite dark. They seemed to have an infinite amount to talk about. For they met much less often than either of them wished, mainly because Orimili travelled a lot. They talked about a great number of things, including a great war that was said to be going on in Europe. The mention of this war made Orimili wince, but Emenogha could not notice this in the darkness, and he went on to wonder what the white people were quarrelling about.

Orimili said it was impossible to tell and, recalling Osita's letter, mentioned it to Emenogha, saying, 'Perhaps he will talk about the war in it. Then I shall tell you. But I'm still waiting for Onyeme…' He felt very hostile to that young man. 'Do you know that fellow deserves to be thrashed. He has kept me waiting these two weeks! Obviously, he has been busy with other things,' he chuckled ironically.

Ogbuefi Emenogha felt a certain lightness within himself. It was as though a weight had previously oppressed his spirit without his being aware of it, thinking that that was the order of things. Now the weight was gone, and it made him feel as if the ground itself had become insubstantial and sustained his weight by a miracle. But then, he hadn't a distinct feeling of being substantial himself; rather he had a sense of an airiness, the well-spring of which was deep in his bowels; just as if his belly was a pit, which, opening out at the bottom, had had an in-rush of air. Such a quick in-rush of air into his belly from beneath would have been sufficiently uplifting, for, unlike Ekwenze Orimili, who was broad, with thick flanks, his wrestler's calves firmly resisting the force of the rising air, Emenogha was a head taller and lankier. But what heightened his experience all the more was that the rising air suffused his entire being.

Ogbuefi Emenogha was in a communicative mood too. The first person he would have thought of when he felt the need, though having nothing particular to say, was Ekwenze Orimili. With him there wasn't a difficulty lighting upon something that would keep them talking for half a day. But it was his conversation with that same person that had put him in the present mood. So he had to find someone else to talk to. He had news anyway, and invitations for his neighbours. Why, they were the very people to go and talk with. The news would be communicated to his family backhandedly and in an unsmiling manner, this being one of the ways in which he had unintentionally disguised from them his essential good nature.

His first stop was at Ikenna Nwozo's house. The latter had just finished his supper when he arrived. Glad though he was to see Emenogha, his greeting was nevertheless couched in the form of a reproach:

'I wouldn't have believed it, had someone told me that you were one of those criticising me behind my back. But now I have seen the proof of it myself in your coming late for supper. Your idea is to be able to say afterwards that I have been mean to you, isn't it?'

'Oh,' cried Ogbuefi Emenogha, downcast. 'To have missed supper despite my haste!' Then narrowing his eyes in suspicion: 'Do you mean, anyway, that I am to have nothing to eat tonight just because of my being late? No, you are mistaken. Tell your people to bring me my supper; that's all.'

'Of course, of course!' Then he shouted into the yard, 'Hey, wife!'– which wasn't how he usually called his wife. In any event, the call brought not the wife but Emenogha, pleading that he was fine, really, and didn't need another supper, having had one already. He then shouted into the yard that Ikenna's wife should save the supper for him. He would come unfailingly and have it the next day. Only then did the woman amble across to the reception room to urge the guest to have the meal right away, and that tomorrow would take care of itself.

Those preliminaries over, Emenogha explained that he was going to have a visitor tomorrow evening, and that he would be delighted if Ikenna would be with him to make the visitor welcome.

'It is a joyful occasion?' Ikenna thought it proper to ask.

'It is – well, a happy occasion… and… As a matter of fact, it is Ogbuefi Orimili, and he wishes to enquire about Adoba on behalf of his son.'

'Now, isn't that wonderful! It is the son studying overseas, is it?'

'The same.'

'So Orimili will take away our beautiful Adoba for his son?' He answered himself: 'Well, I suppose we can't marry her into our neighbourhood as people do not marry their own daughters. Ah! Orimili: doing everything possible for that one son of his. You too; you have done the best for your daughter.'

Emenogha designed to be diffident: 'It is hard to please young people today. No one knows what they want. One only does the best that one knows. If one is lucky, they will appreciate and be thankful; but if one is unlucky, they will mess up everything, calling the presumptuous fellow their worst enemy! But then, people won't stop going to war for fear of dying, any more than the wine-tappers will be frightened off palm trees at the news that one of their friends has fallen off a tree to his death! So must we continue to do the best we can for our children, whether or not they understand what we are doing.'

'You are quite right about the young people. But you and Orimili are doing for yours what they will unfailingly appreciate. Moreover, they cannot cause their parents any further anxiety, once they are married off. Mark you, the advantage is entirely on Orimili's side, and we are the ones cheated; for our Adoba has never given anyone a worry, and never will.' Ikenna Nwozo added with mock bitterness: 'Orimili will not only gain in bringing such a perfect woman into his household, but also in using her to secure his son! That is the order of things, however. So we won't complain. We rather say, how happy we are that Orimili's son is marrying into our neighbourhood. Indeed we are happy and proud… Yes, I shall be there tomorrow evening, and thanks for inviting me.'

Obiefuna Emenogha next called on Udeague Obimma, arriving at his door when he was getting into bed. He nevertheless sat up to chat with Emenogha, assuring him, when the latter protested, that he was welcome at any time of the day or night. After all he was the ancient one of the neighbourhood, their father; and a witch coming in among them to attack a member would do so only at grave peril to himself, unless he had first done battle with him, and got the better of him. So why should the children themselves not come to him with whatever was on their mind, any time they felt the need to come?

Emenogha thanked him and explained that Orimili was going to visit him the next day, and that Obimma would be needed to guide them in the talks.

Flattered that his claim to be the father of the neighbourhood was implicity recognized, he congratulated Emenogha for having brought up Obimma's own child very diligently. It was in recognition of this that Adoba was being proposed to in the first place; for he knew a great many parents, whose daughters were all as beautiful as Adoba – or nearly as beautiful – and yet were living with their parents well past the age which their own child was at present. As to the young man himself who was coming to knock – or whose father was knocking for him, which was the same thing – the old man had nothing to say, since he was one, the like of whom there was none in Okocha. Yes, he would be at the meeting tomorrow and see that all due observances were followed.

When he went to bed that night, Obiefuna Emenogha felt perfectly satisfied, but had no inclination to sleep. He lay down, thinking, and feeling no stress whatever for all that. On the contrary, it was not until well into the new day that he began to feel the stress of his vigil and of his thoughts, which had become more and more heavy. This new, deeper, and obviously more permanent relationship he was entering into with Orimili seemed to require to be explored so as to bring out its full import.

Adoba was going to marry Osita Nwofia. Fine. He himself was going to put all his energy to work so that Orimili should be made an alderman. (Right?) He deserved it, being one of the most successful men in the town. There were men, of course, whose barns stretched from one corner of their compound to another; Nweke Nwofia, for instance. Still that wouldn't have done him much good, if he had a budget half the size of Orimili's. Think what it must cost to pay for his son overseas. It seemed to him that it would have required not one but several barns harnessed together. That was what Orimili sustained singlehandedly, without being any the worse for it. Instead, he and his family had continued to look even more prosperous by the day. Now, this was the man asking to join the *ozo* society. Had he not earned it three times over? What could the society ask, which Orimili couldn't give?

His mind secreted the answer, and let it rise slowly in his consciousness until it became clear and bright: Was he in fact a son of Okocha? That was going to be the sticking point. Orimili's background was obscure. His friendship with the man, his respect for the man had all conduced to making him trivialize that... well, blemish; for that was what it was going to be called when the debate opened. Even now Emenogha did not feel bitter towards Orimili for putting him in the awkward position of championing a cause that seemed so shaky. That was all there was to it. But not everybody was going to see it that way. That was why Nweke Nwofia had been difficult; why old Oranudu had been obscure. Clearly, the sodality was going to be divided; with some pretending to defend the tradition from Orimili who would break in and change it. As if there was any aspect of the tradition in which the man wasn't well versed! What business had anyone investigating another's origin, anyway? His first task must be to get Nweke Nwofia and all who would support him to come clean, and call their objection by name. Then he would put that question to them; what business of theirs was it? This was a cause well worth fighting – for its own sake, and not merely because the man at the centre of it was one's bosom friend. But because the man was one's bosom friend, one must win, otherwise how could they look each other in the face afterwards?

By the way, what was obscure about Ekwenze's origin? Was it not rather so clear?

That remarkable turn in the reflection might have led Emenogha to perceive that the objection boiled down to Orimili *having* a history – having it in its being known;

whereas Oranudu, or, for that matter, Obiefuna Emenogha himself, had no history, beyond the fact that they were the son of so-and-so, who was the son of so-and-so, until… nothing. Their history could not be traced; it did not matter. To be anybody in Okocha, one need have no history; one might as well be obscure!

Emenogha did not follow up this interesting turn in the thought of origins because he was beginning to tire out, oppressed by the weight of the thought. So he followed the track which led to practical considerations, which consumed less of the resources of the mind; but were no less interesting for being lighter. Emenogha never knew what those resources were, but he knew that they were easily depleted if one was thinking deep thoughts. However, he found that he rather liked this vigil; he was just in the mood for it. He had better not spoil it with heavy thoughts.

Obiefuna Emenogha's people had been in the sodality for generations. His grandfather had been a very successful man, and had had his son Emenogha inducted in his early youth. Thus Orimili's friend had stepped into the grandfather's title after the latter's death, and Emenogha's title had yet to be redeemed. The eleven-year-old Osaemeka would be invested with this title as soon as he came of age. This was a decision that had been made unconsciously. His father was far more conscious of the desire he nursed for that boy to travel and study abroad just as Osita Orimili had done. He didn't see an irony in his coveting for his boy what Orimili had already given his, though himself reduced to begging, cap in hand, for a privilege which the little boy had almost as a birthright. He only knew that Osaemeka's chances of achieving what he desired for him would be much improved if the marriage took place. He would have not only an older brother to guide him, but his sister would be helping as well. If Adoba and her husband would do this for his boy, what more could he ask? It was more to him than a hundred titles.

Osaemeka was of course only a primary school pupil. He was Emenogha's second child, but younger than Adoba by almost eight years, having arrived just as his father was beginning to give up hope of his coming, and was growing panicky about a successor. It was his arrival that saved his mother, Ojiaku, the inconvenience of having to live with a rival. Osaemeka became for him a sign that more of the same sort could be hoped for from Ojiaku; and was now easier in his mind since Osaemeka had two younger brothers and another sister.

Outside his family, his worries centred chiefly on the goings-on in the *ozo* club. First there had been the rivalry between Ananwemadu and Nweke Nwofia. These were men of whom he thought precious little. Yet like a fool, he had helped Nweke to defeat the other. Frankly, he hadn't known at the time that it was a simple case of rivalry. After Ananwemadu's appointment as warrant chief, he had begun to behave as if the white men had put him in charge of the aldermen as well. So they had opposed him as one man, and brought him to heel. Ogbuefi Nweke Nwofia, it must be said for him, had been loudest in his opposition to Ananwemadu. Maybe that was what he thought had entitled him to steal the victory, and begin in his turn to impose upon the peers. Why then were they fighting shy of Nweke, having only recently put down the ambitious man who was aiming to clamber over their shoulders and heads to the top? Was it because of his success, being the master of what was probably the largest barn in Okocha, and of a compound full of sons and wives? He had thought that they would say that enough was enough when, the other day, Nweke had the temerity to say *shut up* to a fellow alderman! Sadly, only a couple of voices affirmed that he had gone too far; among them, Nwalioba, who had demanded that he should apologize for the insult. But didn't Ikedi get up to say that Nweke had been right? Strangely enough, Oranudu seemed not to notice the outrage. He must have been too far gone with his riddles and altogether lost in conversation with his departed comrades. That was a tacit approval all the same, and Nweke had taken full advantage of it.

In a way, Emenogha was curious to see what Nweke Nwofia was trying to do. But he also foreboded it, and would rather nip it in the bud. However, he had the honesty to tell himself that whereas the idea of nipping Nweke's project in the bud sounded grand, there was little chance of success; Nweke being what he was, a ruthless schemer and manipulator. One could see that he already had a firm hold on such fools and noise-makers as Ikedi and Ugonabo. Ugonabo? Hardly a fool and noise-maker; nevertheless, Nweke's staunch ally. So much more the pity. As to Oranudu; the thought sounded indecent, even sacrilegious; but Emenogha was desperate enough to think it: wasn't he dazzled by Nweke to the point of forgetting himself? So Nweke Nwofia had a free hand to build up as formidable a force as he wished-and he was busy doing it. The other side, Emenogha's, was rather disorganised, there being no capital figure – one had to face it – who could mobilize all the others to put Nweke in his place. It was almost too late to do anything about it; but one could still make a start if Orimili could be brought in. There would be the initial drawback of being a freshman; but his very presence was bound to be felt adversely by Nweke, in that he was by far a more successful man.

The trouble was how to dribble Orimili past Nweke's inevitable opposition into the sodality. That gave him pause. He was sorry that it was so important that Orimili should gain the title, for, in his experience, the more important a goal was, the more elusive.

That evening, the herbalist paid a visit to his patient, Edoko Uwadiegwu. Nduka and his younger brother Nzeadi were expecting him. He peered into their faces and saw in a glance their dread and despair. Still he enquired in an even tone how the sick man did. Nduka answered that their father had shown no sign of improvement, and that his breathing was extremely laboured. The herbalist shrugged and shook his head sympathetically, telling the despairing man that their father was hovering between life and death, and that one could hardly expect less, when one had the misfortune of falling into the hands of the elemental spirits. The great difficulty in treating their victim was, of course, that they did not go away after the initial blow, but crowded together around him, sometimes trying to strangle him or stop him from breathing. They were very wicked, the elemental spirits.

The herbalist entered the sickroom, and reappeared some moments later. The brothers looked up to see the least sign of hope in the herbalist's face, but the latter had assumed a mystifying aspect. He only shrugged, went to a corner of the sitting room and arranged his things for divination, casting lots to see whether or not the patient still had a chance. Apparently, he had. So he cast other lots to decide which of the several preparations he had brought would be the most suitable. He returned the rejected preparations into his bag, and retrieved a bunch of herbs from it, which he handed over to Nzeadi, instructing him to burn a little quantity of it every so often in Edoko's bedside fire. Nzeadi glanced at the herbs and recognized them as ones they already had been using. Their smell was awful when thrown on the fire, and must do positive harm to the invalid. He said nothing, however.

The three men then filed into the room. No one spoke. The herbalist changed the amulet he had placed around Edoko's neck the day before, scraped off the clay-coloured cast over the man's chest, massaged the chest, and then pasted on a new preparation. He cast a small quantity of herbs into the fire, added a dash of a rapidly burning substance, which made the issuing smoke especially pungent. Edoko and Nzeadi put their heads out of the door, in spite of themselves. They couldn't wait to get out of the sickroom.

2 | *Adoba*

Ekwenze Orimili emerged from the warehouse of Guy & Son, where he had been seeing the company's stock of produce. Onyeme followed him out, completely unaware that part of Orimili's business that morning had been to see if he could detect a self-consciousness in the young man that would help him confirm whether he had meant to upstage his son and carry off his intended. Failing to notice this, he had considered warning him off, but checked himself in time with the reminder that the visit he was going to pay Emenogha this evening was all that was needed to cause the would-be rivals to fall back. So he had gradually warmed up towards Onyeme, and soon had quite forgotten that he had meant to give this young man a choice between holding his job at Guy & Son and staying clear of a certain young woman.

He was pleased also with what he saw in the warehouse. There was enough cargo for a trip next day to Okono. Furthermore, Onyeme had informed him that new supplies were expected at Okono, and that the supervisor at Okono might entrust him with the papers to confirm to the manager at Okocha that they had indeed arrived: precisely the kind of news Ekwenze Orimili wanted to hear. What would make things still more interesting for him would be to be entrusted with seeing the cargo safely to Okocha. They would see that he would never fail them.

Now he must send word to his men to come over and put the stock on board, and get the barge ready for the journey next day to Okono. Too bad he could not be there to supervise the work to the end. His men were never as good in his absence as they were when he was supervising. So departure tomorrow morning was likely to be late, as he must take a careful look before leaving to see that everything was where it should be. There was nothing he could do about that today. The call had to be made at Emenogha's; for having slept on the matter, he had frankly begun to wonder why he had waited so long to start. Had he done it say, a year ago, his hands should not now be as full as they were.

Orimili's hands were full because he was saving up for his title. Until the last harvest season, the idea of taking the title had been an object of fantasy for him. Now it had become a project and moved up from fantasy to the fore of his consciousness. What decided him was the conviction of one of his men for the profanation of a masquerade. Orimili had witnessed the incident and had been on the point of intervening to rescue the young man from five or six masquerades who converged upon him after he took hold of the cane with which one of them had been threatening him. In the scuffle one of the masquerades had accidentally knocked off the face-covering of its companion. Immediately there was a cry of outrage, and the boatman was charged with the abomination. The *ozo* society later took over the case, and a heavy fine on the unfortunate man. Orimili had had to help pay off the fine, but this was not the source of his complaint. What he found hard to take was that a careless young man had carried the day. Only the fellow in the mask, his companions and Orimili's man had been questioned, and the latter had, of course, been crowded out. Two titled men had interviewed Orimili privately, and he had explained to them how the accident had happened. To his surprise, however, the club finally decided that it was not an accident, but sacrilege. Did it mean then that Ekwenze Orimili could not be trusted to report accurately what he himself had witnessed? Why wasn't he called to give his evidence before the assembly? For he was sure that if this had happened, the assembly would not be able afterwards to give the verdict against an innocent man. Rather, they had brushed him aside, treated him like an uninitiate: like a woman! For this reason, Ekwenze Orimili had decided to ask the titled men, in a formal kind of way, what they thought of him. That was the meaning of his application to be initiated into the *ozo* society. But no sooner had he reached the decision than it dawned on him that there was no better way to gain a clarification as to what he was taken for: whether he was a citizen or a stranger.

The man's sense of destiny was growing, and this was probably owing to a nagging fear that he had overreached himself in making a bid for the title. What would he do if the bid failed? It wasn't like a snail coming out of its shell, and withdrawing again because he has found the place uncongenial. No, this was a blow which one struck, and war began; a blow which produced war in being struck, and not alone because it inflicted an injury which could not be put up with. The bid had to succeed, or…

What was Ekwenze Orimili to do, if it failed? The question played at the most distant corner of Orimili's mind. He was only remotely aware of it; never in a way in which it could challenge him to address and confront it, yet he was sufficiently aware of it to perform certain actions as if in response. He now had that fascinating sketch before him, which caused his whole life to rise before him like an inverted top. In what precisely the tip of that top consisted, whether in Osita's return or in his taking of the title, Orimili didn't know. Sometimes he acted as if it was the one; at other times, as if it was the other. Well, then, next year would be the watershed of his entire career: no need to be rigid about which incident should round it off. However it was, the marriage he was arranging for Osita had been drawn in as an essential part of the grand picture. A lot could come of that match. Not only would he secure for his son the finest wife he could think of, but it could also help win him important new allies: Emenogha's relatives and their friends. Moreover, the members of the club could not fail to be impressed with a man who set no store by the wisdom in the proverb that a dog couldn't answer two calls at once without breaking his jaw on the ground. He was going to answer several calls at the same time, and try to keep his jaw intact!

The sense of urgency was also beginning to build up, because the fates watched out for a fellow seeming to stand erect under pressure, maliciously piling on new burdens until the fellow collapsed and was crushed by the accumulating weight. He didn't see as a trick of the fates the sudden twist that had made him begin urgently to arrange for the engagement – how could it be that sort of trick since it had such obvious advantages? The only source of anxiety was the stretch of one year ahead: plenty of time for the fates to do havoc!

Orimili went over to his barge, feeling with satisfaction – tinged with a measure of apprehension – that the pace of things was quickening, and that if his luck held, the worst would be behind him within the year. He was thrilled to walk upon his boat. He surveyed it, went into the cabin then turned round immediately with the recollection that he had noticed in the cargo-hold what appeared to be decaying wood. He went over to inspect it; perhaps he hadn't looked closely enough at it, and had jumped to a hasty conclusion. He found, however, that the plank was really decaying, for it had soaked up water. He placed his foot on the spot; increased the pressure. The wood held. It would probably be good for another month or so. Still, why should he take any chances? When the farmers saw the river swell late in the wet season, did they say that it was not likely to overflow its banks for another month or so? Didn't they start immediately to harvest the crops which would most be affected in a flood? He went into the cabin, found a piece of chalk and drew a circle around the weak spot. Orimili did not care to speculate whether the decay of the bottom of his barge was the work of the vigilant fates. It was something that occurred every so often, for the simple reason that the hold was made of wood, and that it was lying in water all the time. What if the decay had affected a large part of the vessel? He shook off the thought as impertinent. What was necessary was to make sure that his men did not pile on stuff over the weak spot. He wasn't thinking of an overhaul at this time. Yes, in another month or two, with the farming season on, he would be able to have an overhaul without excessive loss of income. To have one now would involve him in chartering a vessel, and paying out much of his takings in charter charges. He knew about these charter charges, having once had his barge put up for repairs lasting nearly two weeks.

Ogbuefi Emenogha remarked to his wife and daughter that he expected an important guest that evening; so they should do well to be within call.

'Nothing untoward, I hope,' asked the wife for a hint as to how to prepare herself.

'Ogbuefi Orimili is coming to knock at our place.' He observed his wife and daughter exchange glances, and was satisfied to think that they were grateful to have been told so much.

'Do you wish us to give him supper?' put in the wife, in an effort to prolong the conversation.

'It is difficult to tell how things will turn out. There will be a few others besides Orimili. Some of our neighbours will be here to welcome him. You may as well have a meal ready in case it is needed.'

'Oh, good. We shall have something for them. Osita is expected back soon, is he?' knowing that she risked being scolded for impertinence.

Emenogha promptly frowned back at her: 'Not as far as I know. Why do you ask?'

'Oh, nothing! Just to see... Well... I mean, his father wanting to arrange this thing at short notice?'

Yes? Go ahead, and say what you mean. That was what Emenogha mentally shot back at her, enjoying her discomfiture. All the same he turned over the question, wondering whether he should explain, what good it might do to do this; and concluding: none. It would only encourage her to ask more questions. At any rate, this was a happy occasion. It shouldn't be amiss to be mild with her: 'You can be sure that Osita will come home some time, even if it isn't within a day or two.'

The manager poured Ogbuefi Ananwemadu a cup of tea from a flask at his side-table. He let the man begin to sip at it in his great, sharp hisses that he found tickling. Then he began to speak, pausing every so often so that Onyeme could translate. Ananwemadu was relieved that it was something altogether different from what he had feared, and had got a bad night worrying over.

It turned out that the district officer had ordered the manager – as the latter put it – to construct a complex which was to be used by two or three officers of the colonial detachment. The manager hastened to add that the officers would not be stationed permanently at Okocha. Their mission was only to select and prepare the volunteers who might wish to sign up for duty outside the colony.

Ananwemadu asked, 'From where are these volunteers expected?'

'Inland from here, I imagine.'

'And you say that they are going to be posted outside the colony. Will they remain outside, wherever it is, and not return to their people afterwards?'

'Oh no! Of course they will return. I'd say that they should be back here within a year.'

Ananwemadu said he thought that that should be the idea, since he figured that the volunteers were being called up for the war which he had heard was raging in Europe.

The manager turned over some papers on his table, as if he were looking for a particular document, which perhaps contained all the clarifications the warrant chief wanted. Meanwhile, he was saying, 'In point of fact, I have no specific information as to the nature of their mission, but it is possible that it is connected in some remote way to the war. Whatever the case, I wouldn't worry about their safety.' Giving up the search for the document, and fixing the chief with a gaze, he wound up: 'You would like to know, however, that the district officer has allocated land for the construction of the quarters; and he has directed that this should be mentioned to you.'

Ogbuefi Ananwemadu wanted to know which parcel of land the district officer meant.

The manager specified, adding, 'I think it is a nice spot, and should be most suitable for the facility – don't you think so? – as it is bordered by farmlands, and woods and the river.'

The warrant chief did not seem to have heard the

manager's good opinion about the site, but pursued his own thoughts. At length, he explained that the handing over of any part of Okocha's common property for any purpose whatever was beyond the power of a single individual, even that of the warrant chief.

'I quite understand that,' the manager hastened to assure him. 'However, that needn't worry you at all, as the district officer is not asking you to make the allocation.' He ceased.

'Does he wish me to present the request to the community?' queried the warrant chief, bewildered.

'No,' the manager was ready with the answer. 'It does not seem to me that he even requires you to do that. I am quite certain that he is chiefly concerned to let the warrant chief know that the project is being undertaken, which is gracious of him, I should think.'

Ogbuefi Ananwemadu was flattered, but that didn't lay to rest his unease. There was an aspect of this communication that quite surprised and baffled him. Previously, when the administration desired anything of him, instructions were given minutely. To his mind, that was how to go about things; for if he was to be a go-between, then the better he knew the terrain on either side the more efficient he would be in fulfilling his mission. This time, however, no instructions were being given. What then was he going to say to the townsmen when he met them? Or maybe nothing was desired of the people on the present occasion. What, in that case, was the meaning of his being sent for?

There was something positive in what the manager was saying, and he mustn't lose sight of that. The information about the facility would be useful. Obviously, the district officer wished him to be one or two jumps ahead of the rest of the people – several jumps, he meant, ahead of Nweke Nwofia! What pleasure it would give him some day to put it bluntly that way to the man himself! This reflection put a different complexion on the question. The manager had confessed that he was acting only as a messenger. So one might understand his garbling the message – didn't the proverb say that the fate of a message that passed from one hand to another was distortion and falsehood? Ananwemadu knew the district officer pretty well. He would have gone straight to the heart of the matter; for he did not play with words. That was why one always knew where one stood with him. The warrant chief decided to prolong the conversation a little further, for a chance of garnering something from a message that had obviously miscarried.

'You must tell the district officer that he has done well to let me know about the project. There isn't a difficulty I might help to smooth out for him, though?'

The manager considered a while. 'I doubt that there is one; he didn't tell me of any. I'd say the district officer has thought of everything; he always does. You should just leave it to him; and if he wishes later to make further contact with you on that, be sure that he will know how to get hold of you.'

They were, both of them, where they were at the start. It was particularly frustrating for Ananwemadu, who believed that he was meant to play a role in the affair. After all, the land belonged to some family. That was where he was likely to be needed – getting discussion going with the family and the elders – unless the land was going to be seized outright!

Well, this would be something entirely novel; something his titled friends should know immediately. Scarcely had this thought struck him than he was checked by quite another. If the sodality were to know what he suspected, they must learn it from someone else. Definitely, no one would thank him for the intelligence. He would be sooner denounced for collusion with the district officer; and they would clinch the case with the proverb that the rat could have known nothing of the fish hidden in the kitchen rack, without the mouse giving him the tip-off. The story would be that he had given away someone's land; thus he would have earned for himself a lifelong enemy. No, he wasn't going to mention to anybody what he knew. He himself didn't know anything. He would discover what the administration was up to when every other person did; and like them, he would be shocked – more so even.

But... why had they taken the trouble to inform him? This was knowledge which he could not use – a shame, that. So, if he could not use it, and was meant not to use it, what was the purpose of it? To torture him? Angry, and full of self-pity, Ananwemadu applied to himself the metaphor of the tree by the roadside, which was condemned to the unreflecting machete-strokes of the passers-by. Was he then no better than a tree stuck where it was for better or worse? He saw now how foolish he had been to think that he was safe from ill-usage from the district officer, and had only to contend with the aldermen of Okocha, who were mostly jealous. The white men had their own game, which they played with him, and didn't care whether they hurt him. They were probably laughing at him when they said they thought well of him! He was in the middle, all right; but not like the mythic bat. Certainly not. The roadside tree was the thing (it helped to know exactly how to state what was happening to one). The notion was that the bat suffered from being neither here nor there; but it was in fact both here and there, having the best of the two worlds, really. Quite different from the roadside tree, which was handy; always there, serving as the butt of irony to the one, and of malice to the other.

For all this, however, Ananwemadu stoutly refused to give way to pessimism. There was every chance that the administration were as well-meaning as they had ever been towards him. He had the cunning to keep a tiny window open in his mind for them, knowing that he would keep it so almost to the very last. Without that window, he would have had to abandon the comforting metaphor of the tree by the roadside – comforting because it was a sort of experience about which the fathers knew something, and which they, as it were, had foresuffered; hence they had enshrined it in the wisdom they handed on from generation to generation. Another advantage of that metaphor was that it took the place of the wall which a man conscious of attack from both his flanks might have deciphered behind himself. In the face of such a wall, a man could do only one of two things: permit himself to be taken prisoner by whichever of his enemies was nearest, or dig in and fight to the last. Ananwemadu kept his window open. So there was no occasion to take up arms against anyone. In any event, he had already fought one action against his fellows, the aldermen. Having had the wisdom to retire early from that encounter, he had survived to menace them with a formidable fact: he was *their* chief, in spite of themselves. Obviously, it wouldn't have helped him in any way to abandon his optimism completely, for he could hardly remain the warrant chief of Okocha if he did.

Orimili took with him a litre-bottle of dry gin, thinking how he and Emenogha deserved to give themselves a treat for arranging the engagement of their son and daughter. Since they enjoyed each other's company so much that they were never in want of a subject of conversation, Orimili's idea had been to keep their hearts warm with a dram now and again, while they talked. This was a day, if he knew one, when he should be content to let go and have no cares. He didn't mind if he should finish off being tipsy. He ended up, however, quite drunk; for Emenogha had made the meeting into a small feast of which Orimili himself had been the honoured guest.

He got his first jolt that evening, when on arrival he found that the setting was quite formal. Five people were sitting and chatting with the host, evidently waiting for him. He shook hands, and sat down to exchange pleasantries and enquiries with the company about each other's family. At the earliest opportunity, he directed a questioning gaze at Emenogha, who returned him a reassuring one. They talked about one thing, then another; now mentioning the awful heat of the afternoon, and then how nice and cool the evening was; why, one was already forgetting that a moment ago the footpaths were throwing up fire. One of the farmers said he was sure that the rain wasn't a long way off. He was really longing for it in order to go back to the farm as the long holiday of the dry season was becoming tiresome.

'Yes,' agreed another, 'the rains should arrive in a week or two; and that will be a welcome change.'

Orimili eyed the speakers, wondering whether they were having a dig at him, and dissenting wordlessly. It was hard to have been on the river in a rain storm, as he had been on countless occasions, and still say without qualification that the rainy season was a welcome change. Even as he thought this, he was brought up short by a follow-up from the first farmer, that if the heat should continue much longer with its present fury, the yams would begin to decay or shrivel up in the barns. His friend then recalled an experience of a few years previously, when the first rains were followed by a heat spell. The farmers had been deceived by these initial rains, and had sown much of their seed yams, only to have the precious crops destroyed in the renewed heat. The company dwelt at length on this, saying that some farmers were yet to recover from the catastrophe. One of the company confessed that he himself had been getting by ever since through share-cropping. Nor did they fail to mention Edoko's illness, concerning which the latest information was that he seemed to be worse.

The conversation continued to drift from one subject to another. Emenogha made no attempt to check it. He actually encouraged it, but Orimili could see that he was slightly worried. Presently, he called out for his son, Osaemeka. He whispered something in his ear, but before he ran off to do as he was bid, Udeagu Obimma was seen in the gateway. Old and drooping a little, Udeagu entered the sitting room, leaning his tall walking stick against the wall near the doorpost.

He greeted everyone and sat down, turning towards Ekwenze, and was going to say something to him when Emenogha announced the kola. The old man faced around, and accepted the kola bowl from Osaemeka, who had reappeared to make the presentation. Udeagu picked up the nut, waved it in the direction of the sky, sat forwards with his elbows on his knees, and spoke in an incantatory manner:

> Our noble host bids us welcome
> With this nut, a tight enfoldment,
> Bearing the seed of life, the promise
> Of fellowship, and token of oneness.
> Those, his good wishes to us,
> Shall redound ten-fold upon his house;
> No evil shall come near it.
> Together we shall continue
> In health, joy and peace.
> To the gods we offer worship:
> The power of the sky;
> Wide is your gaze, and close:
> You know our thoughts;
> May they conduce to good fellowship.
> Our fathers too, who shield
> In all their ways the sons
> Of this our land, this gift

We call on you to share.
And do remain and breathe in all we say and do.

He ceased. Then handing it over to the host, he said that it was all blessed now, and asked him to break and share it out.

While they were eating the kola, Udeagu turned again to Ekwenze Orimili to enquire about 'his daughter', meaning Orimili's wife. The old man had a revelation to make; he saw it in his attitude. Orimili was immediately alert and hopeful. Okocha was a dense network of kinship, but a lot of it managed to miss Orimili in its criss-crossings. There wasn't a man in the whole town who had as few relatives as he. He thought in fact that he knew every one of his relatives, and the total number could be counted on his fingers. Here now was old Obimma suggesting that he was an unknown relative. Orimili was thrilled. He told Udeagu that his wife was well, and then after a pause, enquired, 'You called her daughter as if you knew her well; do you?'

Udeagu Obimma brightened up instantly. 'Aha! Now I have it,' in a tone of mock disappointment. 'You know, I always wondered why you never spoke to me as one would to a near relation. I don't blame you, though. It is one of the evils of the age. Blood ties count for little now; in my youth, I can tell you, it was far different. But, do you mean, seriously, you have no idea that your wife is a great-grandchild of my family?'

'That's extraordinary,' cried Orimili. 'I couldn't have guessed that there was a connection.'

'Of course, there is; a very deep one too.' The connection

turned out to be that the mother of Orimili's mother-in-law was the youngest sister of Obimma's grandfather, and he asked Orimili whether he didn't know that the remains of the mother of his mother-in-law were buried in the property of Obimma's family.

'Oh,' cried Orimili, 'I am ashamed of myself not to know these things. You must have thought awful things about me for apparently failing to acknowledge you. Come to think of it, though, you hardly escape blame for failing to let me know earlier.'

'There never was a good opportunity, was there? And it didn't seem right to come and visit you, only to tell you.'

'Think no more of it, in-law. I believe you, since you have made use of the present opportunity to tell me.'

The old man went on to speak about Okuata's mother, a very hard-working woman, who had single-handedly raised a family of five children after the death of her husband. Ekwenze knew the story, of course. He knew also that his wife was made of the same mould as her mother. As it was, she was the one bringing up Ekwenze's young children – which was fine, thought Ekwenze Orimili. Gave him time, till he should be ready for them. Take Osita now – well, he started pretty early with him since the boy had lost his mother early. Okuata helped a little when she became part of the household, but Osita was growing into a man, and needed much less female care. So it was going to be one day with Ejike and the little ones. They would be passed over to him, and cease to be Okuata's concern.

Another trait Orimili knew that Okuata shared with her mother was her shyness. Orimili held this quality apart in his mind because this was what had drawn him to her in the first place. She still hadn't got over it, in spite of her marriage and years of living together with Orimili – and Orimili had begun to find it irritating. Now he tended to esteem her more because of her habits of self-dependence and resourcefulness, little suspecting how deeply they were connected to the shyness.

On the whole, he liked her, greatly; though not half as much as Ekesi. Okuata herself had seen how things were, and often marvelled that a dead woman could exercise such a hold on the imagination of a man after he had remarried. Yet the man had freed himself from this familiar to speak to a woman of flesh and blood – to speak to *her*. She had tried unsuccessfully to exorcise that shadow. Now she only feared and resented it.

The others were all listening to Ogbuefi Udeagu, who, pleased with the way in which Ekwenze had shown great joy in being acquainted with the history he had told, went on to talk about a similar incident, not long ago, when Ogbuefi Ananwemadu was confronted with the history of his own family, which also derived from the stock of Udeagu Obimma.

'How can that be?' cried Okandi Echebido in amazement. 'Unless you are talking about someone else, and not the Onyekwe Ananwemadu whom I know, the warrant chief, whose mother and my own mother are from the same kindred!'

'There you are,' returned Udeagu in triumph. 'Of course, it is the same one, as I know no other. It shows you that men are really held together by a single, tangled thread.'

Ikenna Nwozo chuckled, drawing attention to himself. He told the company that he was delighted with the discussion, and how appropriate it was that those facts were coming to light at the preliminaries of another alliance in which the thread would add yet another joint, and get all the more tangled. All the same, the discussion could lead to an untoward consequence. For instance, what if, in the course of the tracing of the movement of the thread the bride-to-be was found to be a near relative of the groom-to-be?

'I have seen it happen,' was Okandi Echebido's immediate reaction to Nwozo's caution. 'It turned out, however, that their kinship was distant enough; otherwise the thing we were blowing up would have burst in our faces. Both parties were scared and worried just the same; and before we could resume blowing, a rite of severing of blood ties had to be performed. That was the first I ever heard of such rites.'

The host's face had been clouding up as Nwozo's speech progressed. It wasn't that he feared that it might lead to the uncovering of cousinship between him and Orimili. There wasn't the remotest chance of that. Nwozo had overshot and spoiled the atmosphere which the conversation had been tempering as if purposely for the business in hand. It was simply indelicate of him to mention directly the object of the gathering. Emenogha felt like biting off Nwozo's head, but was angrier still because the setting was not appropriate for carrying out even figuratively what he felt.

Hastily, he greeted the company, calling each person by his nickname. Then he turned to Orimili, sorry for him that his speech was irretrievably behind time, and bereft of drama. He fixed him a moment, and spoke out: it was in the nature of story-telling to exaggerate. For instance, one might say that one had seen a rock python, though the truth was that one had seen a mere snake. Orimili had once told him something, but he hadn't known how to take it. Would he care to repeat it In the hearing of his relatives and neighbours here?

The company fell silent instantly. Orimili stood up, picked up his bottle of gin, and placed it beside the kola-nut vessel. He had quickly decided to make a presentation of it as soon as he perceived that the company had been called together to witness the betrothal of Adoba. How much more down-to-earth Emenogha was. He must mention to him afterwards that he appreciated the way he arranged the meeting. He had been calculating that it would be a small meeting in which Adoba would give her consent. But that wouldn't have changed things by much from what they were at the start. Now, however, there would be people to broadcast what was taking place.

He saluted, and began:

'It is said that there is a limit where growth just stops, but this does not apply to the growth in knowledge. There is always something new to learn. For example, this evening, I have come to a new knowledge of Ogbuefi Udeagu Obimma. Just think how glad my wife will be to hear, when I return home, that the father whom she thought she had lost was there all the time. Thanks again, Ogbuefi Obimma, father-in-law, for giving me the satisfaction of knowing where I am affiliated.

'As you all know, I am a great caller and visitor here; and

it is a wonder that people still take the trouble of saying *welcome* when they see me here. They even run around, looking for kola to set before me; can you imagine that?' There was laughter, and Orimili resumed, 'What I have come to do this evening is to show how greatly I am delighted with what I have been seeing here during these visits.

'Ogbuefi Obiefuna Emenogha, *nnadebeluaku*!'

'*Ehe!*' answered Emenogha, and returned to the speaker his due: 'Ogbuefi Orimili, the great flood that cannot be salted.'

'I address myself to you in a special way. If, while calling on my juju to destroy the thief who has made away with my property, the thief himself appears, do you think that I shall fall silent until he has passed by? Of course not. I shall point out the man to the juju, and ask him to go after him. That's why I have called your attention specially. I want you to hand over your daughter to me, that she may become my daughter, and my son's wife. That was what I asked of you earlier. At that time, you gave me no answer. Now your relatives and neighbours are all here. I see no reason why you should hold back and not answer.'

He paused a little as if he actually expected Emenogha to answer; but he went on presently: 'For reasons which you all know, my son is not here himself to tell you for himself why he thinks your daughter the most suitable match of all the young women in Okocha. But that makes little difference as I would still be obliged to speak for him, if he were in attendance. Do not our people say that as long as he lives, the father's eyes must serve the son as well?

'This suit means a great deal to me, not only because

marriage opens a bridge between families, like opening a way to the freshwater spring, with the endless coming and going one observes there. What is equally important to me is that rarely does a man's best friend become the father of his son's best friend; whereas, through marriage, bonds of friendship are apt to become as strong as blood ones. So, I am not really asking to take away your daughter, but rather, to have a share in her, and through her to enter into mutual sharing with you.' He ceased, and sat down to acknowledge the murmurs of approval. 'Welcome!' and 'Well-spoken,' they said to him, referring to his manner rather than to the substance of what he had said.

Emenogha went outside, and soon returned with Osaemeka. They set before the company two large casks of palm wine. Without further ceremony, the company fell to drinking. They were still at it, and talking in a desultory manner as evening approached. It was as if they had forgotten what Orimili had told them; nor did the man himself appear any more mindful. As it was becoming dusky inside, Emenogha offered to send and have the lamp lit; but Ikenna Nwozo said no need. They knew each other so well, down to the last modulation of the voice, that there would be no useful purpose in their looking at each other when they spoke. All the same, they might avail of the dwindling evening light outside. He went straight on, as soon as he had the party outside, to address them in formal tones:

'Ogbuefi Udeagu, *akukalia*!' he saluted.

'Eh! Nwozo *ngabi*!'

'Ogbuefi Emenogha, *nnadebeluaku*!'

'Nwozo *ogalanya*!'

'Ogbuefi Orimili Nwofia, welcome. The message you have brought to us is a happy one, for it is something we all know a great deal about, and wish to see happen to our children.'

Turning to his people, he pursued, 'Orimili has spoken to us about a matter dear to his heart. When he spoke of it earlier to Ogbuefi Emenogha, he gave him no answer because he was asking for something which no individual has authority to dispose singly. So Orimili has taken the case where it belongs; and he deserves an answer. Ogbuefi Emenogha will speak in our name; let that be his privilege for being our host. In case he needs help in working out an answer, I can vouch that Orimili is a worthy man. I can vouch for Osita too, even though he is not here with us. If you have seen Orimili, you have seen Osita as well; and I don't mean their resemblance in appearance only. Everybody can see that for themselves. What I mean is those qualities which distinguish one person from another: truthfulness and steadfastness, carrying oneself well, speaking one's mind, and doing it well – didn't you hear him speak a while ago? – feeling, and so on; in all those things, Osita is much the same person as his father. That's all I know about Orimili and his son. If any of you knows something different, which should help Ogbuefi Emenogha in deciding how to answer, let him say it now, while there is time.'

No one offered to contradict Ikenna. So the next move was up to Emenogha. Determined not to let slip any detail that contributed to the atmosphere of a communal decision and concerned lest it be supposed he had been laying up to Orimili for friendship's sake, Emenogha beckoned his neighbours to confer with him outside, leaving Orimili to his own thoughts and the wine. This did not perturb him in the least, his attitude being that as the event had become entirely public and formal, all he had to do was to go along. There was still a long series of meetings to be had, the setting and expenses of each of which would be more elaborate than the one that preceded it. He had been shamefully casual today, and must make up for it on the next visit. This was the bridge, and the traffic had begun, well before the marriage itself! Was not the marriage part of the traffic, really? – and the last, he might have added, since he himself did little with the marriage bridge, once it had been set up, but left it to his wife to see what she could do with it.

The re-entry of the others brought this reflection to a welcome end. They all took another round of drinks, before Emenogha addressed them:

'Ogbuefi Ekwenze Nwofia, Orimili *atu nnu!*'

'Eh! *Nnadebeluaku!*'

'My kinsmen have asked me to make their wishes known to you. They tell me that they do not reject your proposal, and that they have a high regard for worthy connections made through marriage. However,' making a dramatic pause, 'parents are little more than guardians. No matter how anxious or single-minded we are in trying to arrange an alliance, the work will be wasted unless our young people themselves are willing. So let us ask Adoba whether the suit pleases her or not.'

They all murmured their assent; whereupon Emenogha

summoned Osaemeka, asking him to call in his mother and sister. The two women soon arrived; and their appearance brought to Orimili yet again the sense of not having prepared in a fitting manner for the meeting. Emenogha had not been remiss in any particular. To be frank, Orimili had told his wife that he was going to see Emenogha that evening, but had given her not the least hint as to the purpose of the visit. She would have been astonished to see what he was up to that evening. There was nothing, however, to be sorry about in giving one's wife a surprise now and again. Moreover, a man had better be sure of his ground before bringing his people into it – Orimili held this principle, and it had been a factor in his planning for the evening. Still, he would have been horrified had he thought deeply about this caution, and unearthed the fear lurking underneath it; which was that he might be found not good enough after all. However, he congratulated Emenogha mentally for being so meticulous in his arrangements. The mother and daughter were not only prompt in coming to see the men, but it was also evident that they desired to be seen by them. They must have been impatient as the evening was drawing on without their being sent for. But there was still enough light to see how they had carefully decked themselves out, especially the mother. She had a thick, white, hand-woven *agbor* wrapper, tied high over her breasts and flowing down towards her ankles, with widely spaced blue stripes running cross-wise; a string of large, dull red beads around her neck, and a piece of the striped *agbor* cloth over her head; while the daughter had a long, ash-coloured gown with large sleeves, ending in a broad band, tightly buttoned at the elbows. Orimili thought that her brown sandals and her pink-and-blue head-dress went very well with the gown.

'Adoba,' resumed Amenogha, as soon as his wife and daughter had taken their seats, 'you know this man here, I presume, Ogbuefi Orimili Nwofia?' The girl nodded yes, and he continued: 'He has a son, called Osita. You must have heard his father and me speaking of him. He is studying overseas. Orimili has just been telling us that he wishes you to marry that young man of his, Osita.' He paused. All eyes were on Adoba. That was as it should be. Also Emenogha was enjoying the correctness of his bearing and manner in introducing the question. To him, this was the high point of the occasion, and he savoured it to the full. He resumed:

'Our neighbours were all here when Ogbuefi Orimili spoke on behalf of his son, but they will rather not say anything yet, until they know what you think of the proposal.'

He added, for its comic value, 'I assure you that we have not taken even a sip of the drink he has put before us. It is you who will tell us whether or not to drink it. You can see too that we have been drinking, and that the casks are not half-empty yet. Therefore, you will not be denying us anything if you tell us not to drink Orimili's wine. Feel perfectly free to speak your mind. Or, do you want to go and confer with your mother, before returning us an answer?'

'I'm sure,' the mother tried to be helpful, 'that Adoba is mature enough to know her own mind. I shouldn't think that she needs to confer with anybody since it is she who will marry her husband; her advisers won't do it for her.'

'Well, daughter, your mother says that the decision is up to you. So are we to drink Orimili's wine in your name, or…'

'Yes!'

The neighbours applauded.

Orimili beamed, relieved and grateful. Oh, what would he not do for that child!

Ogbuefi Obiefuna Emenogha reached for the gin, inspected the bottle closely, and handed it over to Ogbuefi Udeagu to uncap.

Ekwenze Orimili carried his wine very well. He and Emenogha were usually among the last of the townsmen to leave Amanza on the great market days. It didn't perturb them that some said that they stayed on so late in Amanza to see that there were no left-overs the wine-sellers would be obliged to take home. It was also said that it was natural that Orimili should be able to take in vast quantities of palm wine without showing the least sign of it. Was he not after all the namesake of the great river? And did not a name, all things being equal, endeavour to fit its owner? As to Emenogha, they found nothing in his name to attach the reason for his carrying his wine as well as did his friend.

As a matter of fact, Orimili put a lot of effort into making himself appear calm and self-possessed in company, even when he had begun to feel a certain flightiness in his head and bowels. He usually fought hard and held good until he was safe in his own house; then he did relax and let go.

Emenogha walked with him to Amanza; not indeed to

see him safely home, for he himself was struggling with his own giddiness. It was rather to catch up on the small talk they missed because of the company.

'I am glad that we have got this thing going,' observed Orimili. 'Your daughter is so very charming; I think that she and Osita will look well together. Wait until Osita comes and sees her; I'm sure he will call himself fortunate.'

Emenogha, at this, grinned self-consciously. He wasn't used to receiving such straightforward compliments from Orimili; nor did he give any. Their usual amusement consisted in teasing and gutting each other. He only said: 'We wait then until he comes and sees her.'

Orimili looked at him sideways. 'You don't believe he will call himself lucky? Well, perhaps he won't say so aloud, but I am sure he will think it.'

'My girl appears to be enthusiastic,' Emenogha conceded. 'If Osita should think himself lucky, I would call that making a good beginning: you see what I mean?'

'They will make a good beginning,' Orimili quickly affirmed; 'and they will be good all the way. Osita can't go wrong now.'

'No, there never was a danger that he would.' Emenogha had unwound. He too had compliments for his friend: 'Do you know, the more I think of this match, the more I am certain that we have done something uncommon. There must have been a little girl long ago, whom your parents knew, and said you were going to marry when you grew up; hadn't you such a one?'

'Several,' Orimili answered with a smile. 'They must have

meant me to be a polygamist – something at which I haven't quite made a success.'

'Well, I had one,' resumed Emenogha. 'But the point I was going to make was that it got forgotten or outgrown. It usually ends up that way: the young people grow up and go their separate ways. But in this case, we have done exactly what we have always wanted to do. The work isn't quite finished, of course. I am looking forward to the time when it will be all over, when we can sit back and relish what we have done. Don't think that there is anything else for a father in it. It is like fighting a war. For the men who do it, only the memory of their bravery or cowardice survives to be relived in the secrecy of their thoughts. The advantage now passes to the women, who tell the story of the war, and make a drama out of it for their own entertainment.'

This remark put Orimili in mind of Ekesi instantly. She was a friendly ghost, and her image played constantly in and out of his consciousness. If only the good woman had survived to see this day! Orimili pushed her gently aside, and addressed himself to the living man before him: 'Our own fight, then, has just begun, and the day of the women is a long way off. Several objectives must be taken before they may dream to entertain themselves. The bride-wealth, for instance. By the way, I very nearly committed a blunder this evening; not having considered that your neighbours would be many. I ought to have brought one or two of my own. It was pure luck in fact that I brought the gin with me.'

'Ah, today was only the first visit – er… to cut a pathway. Let them come next time as the way is now open.'

'Still, my people will hear of it and won't let it pass without comment. For they are prouder of Osita than even Ekesi would have been. I must make it up when we meet for the bride-wealth, and bring a good number with me. Shall we fix a date?'

'Are you in a hurry to pay the bride-wealth? I don't see why you need be.'

'No, I oughtn't to be… except that I was thinking to mention it to Osita. If I tell him that he and Adoba are now engaged, that mightn't strike him as *something*. He might just say: but hadn't they been engaged all the time? Whereas, if I tell him that we have settled a part of the bride- wealth… don't you see?'

'Still, we can take a breath before moving on to that' Emenogha quickly answered him. And he added, 'You have read his last letter, have you?'

'I haven't. Onyeme was going to read it to me this evening, but I had this engagement with you. Tomorrow I go to Okono, only after that… Oh yes! Tomorrow of course!'

'Tomorrow? What about it?'

'I mean Osita's letter. I'll take it with me to Okono tomorrow, that's what I mean. I promised Uderika Nwanne to pop in and see his son at the teachers' college.'

'Oh, good!' Emenogha had seen it. 'Get down a couple of birds with one stone.'

Orimili did get down two birds the next day at the teachers' college, and Kanene Nwanne did not know which made him happier: the money his father had sent him through Orimili, or the extra tip Orimili gave him for reading Osita's letter to him.

The letter itself didn't sound much to Orimili. Osita had enquired about everyone related to him: his step-mother, his half-brothers and -sisters, friends, mentioning everyone by name, as if to show that he had forgotten nothing, and that everything was as before. He mentioned the war 'in Europe', forgetting that his father knew nothing of the English Channel, but had terrible visions of him standing alone with war raging all around him. Also he hoped to have happy news for him in his next letter; it wasn't fully ready for telling yet. Orimili had quickly enquired what the news was all about, and Kanene had said that that was what would be made known in the next letter.

On the whole, the letter was encouraging. What worried Orimili a little was that in mentioning that he expected to finish his course on schedule next year, he had asked his father to be kind enough to save up a little more money, for there were a great many things to buy, and bring home with him – things he would need when he began to practice as a lawyer. As a matter of fact, he listed some of the items by name; which caused his father to enquire of Kanene what were wigs and gowns, carefully blending the tone of honest enquiry with one of outrage.

'Lawyers' things,' Kanene had replied.

Before the question of the letter had come up, what Orimili had been trying to get across to his friend was that there was a great pair of birds he was aiming to shoot down by means of the one trip to Okono tomorrow. Not only was there a deal of cargo to discharge at Okono (by the way, what a pity that there was no chance for him to see the boat tonight, and be sure that everything was as it should be!), but also he must get someone to look over the vessel, for he feared that repairs were needed.

'Repairs? I hope it is nothing serious.'

Ekwenze Orimili replied that it was something to do with the hold, and that it didn't look too bad. Still he would have it checked out, for even small faults could result in serious trouble for a boat.

'So you will do the repairs straightaway?'

'It may come to that, though I have a tight schedule which I'd rather see through before the repairs.'

The drunken feeling increased as Orimili came nearer home. He felt his knees a little weak, but the play of the cool night breeze on his hairless head was pleasant. This cool breeze must not be missed, even for the advantage of resting his tired frame on his bed. He stepped up to the kola-nut tree in front of the yard, and reclined against the trunk. It felt rough and hard. Ah, someone should have had the sense to leave a chair beside the tree for him to sit down and assimilate the breeze. His people had gone to sleep, of course; there was no light showing anywhere. He sighed and told himself that it would be too much trouble to go into his parlour and bring a chair. He put his weight on the tree, and tried to forget its roughness.

The tree had been inherited from his forebears, and he had completed his house before he realised that it blocked much of the view from the road. This was sad, for he was rather proud of the house and would have wanted it to be fully displayed. He let the tree stand, not because it was a legacy – it didn't occur to him as a reason why one should value an object. Rather, the tree was fruitful, and it supplied much of the kola that was used in the house from one end of the year to the other. The pods were harvested in one day, the nuts removed, and stored by his wife.

Orimili reclined on this tree, and tried to pay attention to the movement of the waves in his belly, which caused him to feel giddiness spreading through his body, and upwards towards his head, trying to make him topple over. But there was a quick eddy as the wave was chased back by the cooling effect of the breeze towards the area of heat and turbulence in his stomach. The contest was won, it seemed, by the cool breeze, for Orimili soon dozed off. And he had a dream or a vision – he couldn't make out which. What he saw, however, affected him deeply. For he saw his dead wife Ekesi, seated in the distance, with Osita, a five-year-old boy, upon her knee –exactly the age he was when his mother died. They seemed to be seated in a grey halo; he couldn't make out clearly what the background was, and whether she was sitting on a chair or on the little cloud itself. He put out his hands to the boy, who lifted both his own as if to be picked up and hugged, just like a bird, spreading its wings, ready to beat them, and fly off. His hands were still stretched forth towards the vision, when he awakened.

The first sensation upon awakening was, of course, disappointment. How real the vision had seemed – never mind the haze and the cloud. And to think that he had been within reach of the pair, and was just in the act of lifting up the boy: why, hadn't he held back, only one moment, to be sure of his footing, in order not to stagger when he took the boy's weight? Amazing, how strong women were. Imagine little Ekesi, carrying Osita without the least difficulty, whereas he himself had had to be sure of his footing, before making the attempt. Now see what he had lost in that single moment of trying to make sure. Joy had flitted away – well, not entirely, for he still had the son, even though he was so far away.

Orimili was now lost in thought, trying to work out the meaning of the vision: it had to have one. As it turned out, it was a dream he had to interpret again and again, and on one occasion, kick himself for the haste and the shallowness of his first view of it.

For the moment, however, Ekwenze Orimili Nwofia was fighting back tears. Quite clearly, the vision showed that though Osita never manifested his need, the death of the mother had left as deep a vacuum in his life as in his own. He hadn't realised that they had a bond so fundamental – a bond which was at the same time a vacuum. Orimili assured him mentally that he would do everything humanly possible to help fill up that gap for him. Now wasn't that the whole point about Adoba; about his taking so great a part in arranging the union?

3 | The Dark Bird

Edoko Uwadiegwu never recovered consciousness. The blow he had received had totally paralysed him. He continued to respire, but it was as if something else living inside him was manipulating his lungs. Perhaps it was the evil spirits doing it; which would mean that they weren't where the herbalist said they were. Whatever was manipulating his lungs was doing it at an uneven and extremely slow pace; yet with evident fury. Each breath seemed capable of suffocating the sick man, and was as if it was going to be his last.

His people nursed him as best they could. Only the more elderly neighbours and friends dared to visit him, as if the rest of the people did not care to be marked for having shown him compassion. Life was so precious, and the elementals so jealous and inimical to it that one was always well advised to keep as far away from them as one could. To the last man, these visitors had afterwards called aside Nduka and Nzeadi, the sick man's sons, to urge them to be strong. Sometimes it seemed to the brothers that the callers had judged the man done for.

The atmosphere in the house was heavy and brooding. Edoko's illness seemed to have seeped out of him, spread throughout the compound and suffused the very spirits of his wife and children; so numbing was the wave of death which seemed to ooze out of the sick-room that it overwhelmed his people with an asphyxiating silence. This numbness affected even the younger members of the family, though they themselves had not been allowed to visit the old man. Nor did the herbs which the herbalist ordered to be burned at the bedside fire help the dense atmosphere in any way.

Edoko lingered on for several days, tempting his people with the hope that he might recover; for they counted much on the one persisting evidence of life, which was that he had continued to breathe – even if mechanically. Edoko was doomed, however; and some were surprised that he held out for five days before giving up.

The news of his death seeped around the town in whispers. His people sent word to their relatives in different villages, and the nearby towns to let them know what had happened, and to tell them that the funeral would take place the next day. The grief in the house itself was silent on that first day. It would become uproarious the next morning, when his married daughters and female relatives would be arriving in loud lamentation. By this means the rest of the town would know that the obsequies had begun.

Ogbuefi Edoko's family were especially grieved that he had died before there was a chance for them to learn from him how to go about managing the affairs of the family. They did not know, for instance, whether Edoko was in anyone's debt, or whether he was owed money or goods by some neighbour or friend. They knew the boundaries of their lands only because they had been farming them. But if a case similar to that between Nwalioba and Ikedi were to arise, they would not have been able, for the most part, to swear on their father's authority where the boundary was.

Apart from this problem of not being able to swear that one's father had said so-and-so to one, Nduka was unperturbed by the fact that his father had not said anything as regards the disposition of his property. It meant that he had full authority as the eldest son over the family property and investments. The one investment Edoko had made, which was still valuable, was his *ozo* title. The right to assume this title belonged to the eldest son, naturally. Nduka was determined not to let the title go into abeyance, but the takeover was going to be very costly. The young man could see why it was not right that just because one's father had been a titled man, one should step into his place in the society of titled men without paying anything for it. For *ozo* would soon become everybody's plaything. How could one value a boon which one succeeded into, without paying the price? It was also reasonable that the successor should not make a cash payment to the society; otherwise it wouldn't be succession any more, but a fresh title. A live bull and a grand fete were not too much to ask, even though... Now, how was he going to find the money for a bull and for the *ozo* feast? Nduka racked his brains over this as the preparations for the funeral were going on. By and by, he should work it out. In the meantime, it should be wise to speak to Nweke Nwofia, and see what help he would offer.

Nweke Nwofia was the first neighbour to arrive immediately after Edoko died; and Nduka was afterwards thankful that he had had the presence of mind to send for him. For despite the admonitions of the relatives who had been visiting, his head had suddenly gone vacuous, all thinking ceased soon after the old man's passing away. Nzeadi had been even worse. Everybody had depended on Nweke; it was amazing how the brothers had completely gone hollow in spirit. Nweke had directed everybody, directed everything, and pulled the men out of their shock. He had put the corpse in proper form, and had quickly begun making arrangements for the lying in state. No one knew what would have happened had he been away when sent for, or if the shock had set in before they remembered to send for him.

As the preparations were being completed, Nduka had a conversation with Nweke to obtain further clarifications as regards certain aspects of the funeral rites which applied to the titled men. In the end, he said,

'Ogbuefi Nweke, can I just ask that you stay with us, and direct us so that we will have everything right. You see, you understand these things very well, whereas I'm sure I won't know how to go about them, if I were left on my own.'

'Oh, you needn't mention it,' answered Nweke Nwofia, 'for I feel the blow personally, just as all the people in our neighbourhood do. I shall be here all day tomorrow; and if you need me in the meantime, just send a child to my place. I shall come over immediately.'

'Thank you. There is one thing more, which I should like to understand clearly. You know that my father's title should be reclaimed. I don't think it should be good to let it go, or even to let it remain in abeyance longer than necessary. The obstacle, of course, is that it will cost a great deal to reclaim, and I am far from certain that it will be within my means. However, it shouldn't do any harm for me to know what the total cost is likely to be. Could you give me some idea?'

'You mean to succeed to the title?'

'Well, yes; I'd like to.'

Ogbuefi Nweke became thoughtful for a moment. Finally, he heaved a breath, and said, 'I am glad to hear you say that you wish to reclaim the title. I'm sure that your father wishes that, even though he never had a chance to tell you about it. Is it not an investment, after all? Of course, you should recover your title to it…'

'Yes, if it can be done,' commented Nduka, unsure that he would have the courage and the means to follow up the project.

'I suppose the first and most important business, when it comes to succession, is to ensure that the society welcomes the move. That, you needn't worry about, as I shall do whatever I can to see it through. As to the costs, they will be high: no doubt of it. You won't pay any cash sum, of course; which means that you are being saved up to one-half the cost of taking a title. You can save a great deal more if you tackle it at once during the funeral rites. Take the fourth-day memorial, for instance. Is it not really a fete for the *ozo* society? A fete in every way as elaborate as the original fete in which one took the title? To begin with, you must slaughter a bull for the *ozo* society on that day. If you will assume the title at another time, you will slaughter a bull too, and hand over a live one. That makes three. Quite obviously, it will cost you the least if you follow it up immediately.'

'Quite interesting.' Nduka paused over it, and then

pursued, 'Suppose I and my kindred decide to follow it up, say, on the memorial day, are there other things that will be required of us apart from the bull?'

'If you can provide the bull, why, there is little else – except the cash payment to the wives of the titled men; which doesn't amount to much. There shall be two or three rams – in addition to the two or three that will form part of the memorial rites. For certain villages have to be presented with one ram each: your mother's village, the peers of our village – it will be clear as we get into the details, whether there shall be others besides these two.' He went on, enumerating item after item, in the declining order of cost.

One might have expected Nduka's panic to diminish, following the decline in the quality and cost of the items enumerated. It moved in the opposite direction, and he was quite in despair by the time that Nweke had finished. He told the titled man that he was grateful to have got an idea what the succession entailed. He was worried, of course, he admitted, his voice tight and strained; it was all he could do to stay polite. He was worried that one had to pay so high a price for what was one's own! He would keep in mind, however, what the man had told him. Maybe by and by he would come out with a decision.

'It needn't frighten you,' Nweke made haste to reassure him. 'The thing can be done. All it takes is determination. You know the son of Makachi Ejezue? Well, did anyone imagine he would be able to redeem his father's title, when the man died two years ago? But he did it, and left everybody satisfied. I am sure you too can do it; that is, if you really care about the title.'

'Why, what you have listed sounds to me like taking the title from scratch.'

'Not at all. Consider what you will be saving; the bulk sum which unassociated members pay, the days of festivity during which both the associated and the unassociated candidates keep open house. If you put back the day of your initiation in order to be quite ready, you will have to observe those days of festivity, even though you are only redeeming what is in fact yours, as you say. For isn't the point of taking or redeeming a title that one is sufficiently well off to spare a little for other people? But you won't be required to show how wealthy and generous you are as everybody knows that you are in mourning.'

'Yes, I quite see the point. But remember that one has only three days to have ready all the things you have listed. I imagine that most wealthy people would find it quite impossible – and it isn't as if I am well-to-do. Frankly, I can see no way out.'

'You must know,' replied Ogbuefi Nweke, 'that very few people are able to cope with the burden of title-taking all by themselves – it is quite a burden, however you look at it. One always needs the support of one's relatives and friends. And that's what you should do: speak to your relatives and friends. You'd be surprised to see how you get on. Everybody knows that much is invested in taking a title. I don't believe they would stand aside and see your father's investment go unredeemed; and his seat in the high governing body of this town unoccupied.'

Nduka was not consoled by what Nweke had told him. The high demands of the society of titled men were simply absurd. Was it any wonder that very few people were applying for membership? In his entire life, he could recall only two people joining the club, who were paying the full cost of membership. All the others he knew were only redeeming their fathers' titles. Then it struck him that the titled men were depending on the sacrifices of people of his sort, who were reclaiming their family rights, for much of the yield of their own investment. It was natural, therefore, that the club should make high and unfair demands of people redeeming their rights. He was growing indignant. Was it possible that the society adjusted their demands every so often in order to improve their individual shares? It was shocking if this was true, because it sounded so much like nibbling oneself for one's livelihood. There was a nasty, boneless fish, Ekwum, said to feed on itself. Nduka never found out how the fishermen knew this. He knew the fish of course, but he had not seen one that was blemished as to suggest self-nibbling. However, was the *ozo* society no better than Ekwum? Well – he told himself – sooner or later another succession case would occur; then he, Nduka Uwadiegwu, should begin to get his own back!

He said to Ogbuefi Nweke Nwofia, 'Thanks again for everything, especially for the idea of consulting my relatives. I shall endeavour to get them together before they disperse after the funeral. Maybe we shall find a way out.'

'I'm sure that's a wise thing to do. You will tell me afterwards how you get on with them.'

Nduka made a brief speech to his relatives, in which he stated his desire to take over his father's title. He had been advised – he told them – that it would be best from many points of view to redeem it on the fourth-day memorial of his father. In fact, from what he had learned from senior *ozo* people, he should either redeem on that day or forget about it. So, did they not think it would be a good thing to take up the matter directly, and not allow a lapse of time since this would not mean the loss of the investment?

The relatives, speaking one after another, assured him that it was praiseworthy of him to desire to redeem Edoko's investment. What would console the recently deceased more than to see his son already taking charge, and showing interest in all aspects of family resources? It showed that the evil ones who had hounded Edoko to death had not really succeeded, since Edoko was living on. One of them, Ebeso, said at the meeting that he particularly connected Nduka's mentioning of the outstanding title to the saying that the longing for one's farm-house was as good as being in the farm-house; a deduction which was quite reasonable, considering that only a dedicated farmer would be thinking of his farm when he was somewhere else, probably in the lap of ease. So commendable was such a longing that no one cared afterwards to find out whether the man made it good.

Nduka was delighted to hear all that, especially the one about the dedicated farmer who longed for his farm. It showed that his people were coming along. He might yet get them to come with him to the farm-house itself, for, being a practical-minded fellow, he was sure that what proved that the farmer actually desired his farm-house was that he forsook the lap of ease, which was the village, and repaired to the farm.

'I thank you for your words of encouragement,' he told them. 'I am heartened indeed.

'The other thing,' he continued, 'is that in taking advantage of the season of mourning to put forward our claim, one has only a very short space of time to put together everything that will be needed. And, much as I would have liked to tell you simply to come along with me, at no cost to yourselves, unfortunately I can't because I have only three days to get the things ready. So I shall need your material support as well.' He gave to them, item by item, a list of what was going to be needed, inviting them to specify which item they would like to donate.

'I thought I heard you say,' someone remarked, 'that *you* were going to redeem the title. What are you yourself…'

'No, let's get it right. You see, a title is vested in one person. I happen to be the one in whom the present one is to be vested, but it is still the property of the whole family. It is our right that one member of our family should sit with the aldermen; as to my father, what does he want with that seat now? It is up to us who survive him to take it up. Why? Because the investment was made with the property belonging to the whole family. If my father was a great wrestler, that would have been a personal distinction, and at his death the reality would have died too, only its fame would have persisted. Nobody would ever say: Now that Edoko is dead, his wrestling prowess has passed on to Nduka his eldest son; nor will they say to me: Go and perform such-and-such a ceremony, and the prowess will be yours! They will only say: There is Nzeadi, whose father was Edoko, the great wrestler; there is Udechukwu, the nephew... That is the only way in which we share in his personal accomplishments. The title is different. Since he invested in it with the family resources, I think that we as a family should redeem what belongs to all of us.'

He ceased. No one spoke for some time. Then Udechukwu Nwibe, the nephew, spoke up:

'Nduka, you have given us all some food for thought. I'm sure that you notice the way we have reacted with thoughtful silence. Yes, it is true that your object is to recover a good owned in common. Isn't a title in some way like family land, which remains in the family, and which members of the family, if need be, would fight for even if they are not the one actually working it? One great difference, of course, is that one doesn't pay for one's land each time the current holder dies – to say nothing of the fact that control of the land may sometimes go outside the direct line of descent.

'Be that as it may, part of the reason for our deep silence is that having recognised the urgency of your appeal, we have taken a quick look at our personal goods – I'm sure that we have all reacted in the same way since what you say is so obvious. What did we see, however? That none of us here can boast of a bull or a ram, or any of the big items required. How can you blame anybody for not having a bull, since we have all done our best to contribute provisions for the funeral? The fourth-day memorial is yet to be held; have we not all set aside something, be it ever so small, to help to make it easier for you and your brother? Imagine the amount of water people will drink that day. Very little of it will be drunk in your house, but in the nearby ones; supplied by people who may not even be related to us. Each one of us here has made substantial contributions besides; and not because our barns are overflowing with produce. I think that the wiser course may be in the end to postpone the reclaim until the conditions improve.'

Nduka took this thinly veiled rebuke as if thoughtfully. He sat, handsome despite his shaggy beard, which he stroked – that beard was going to be uncared for throughout the period of mourning. His head hung stiffly low, as a stubborn ram might put down his head, his feet dug in, refusing to be led by the halter. Thereupon, his younger brother, Nzeadi, offered to make Udechukwu's case even more unchallengeable.

'I am quite enthusiastic about redeeming the title – we all are, as Udechukwu has already pointed out. But the conditions are not good at this time. It is nobody's fault that our father passes away so near the beginning of the rainy season, when barns are depleted, leaving mainly seed-yams and odds and ends for sowing. I think that it will be easier on everyone if we finish off today with the decision simply that the title will be reclaimed. We will start, then, after the mourning to save towards it, don't you think?'

A new thought was forming in Udechukwu's mind at this point, as if in response to Nzeadi's 'don't you think?'. Nduka didn't yet see how ridiculous he was making himself. So let him elaborate a little on what he meant by putting off the enterprise to a later date. However, Nduka himself had also been thinking, and before Udechukwu could say what he wanted to say, he broke in:

'I thank you all for what you have said. There is one small point, though. I have a very strong feeling; er... rather, it was what the senior *ozo* man told me – that the reclaim should be now, or never. The blow which cuts to the heart is frequently that for which no preparation has been made. I think that it will be best to explore all the sources through which funds may be had. Should not one borrow – at a reasonable interest – if there is no other way out? Personally, I see nothing wrong with borrowing for the good of the family. On the other hand, the idea of putting it back a little, for which, I agree, a good case can be made, is... emh... do you think, really, that that should be resorted to, without first examining all possible alternatives? For I'm told that the cost will be more than double unless we make use of this period of grace.' A pause, and a rally: 'That is, unless you are saying that we should let go of the title – I mean, investment?'

'By no means,' the younger brother quickly put in, his voice steadily rising as if in anticipation of a collision. 'It mustn't be said that we lightly let pass by an honour that has been bought for us at great expense. Rather we must keep it in sight always, ready to claim it at the earliest opportunity. We daren't shame our proud forebears; if we cannot add to their glory, at least we shouldn't fritter away the fruits of their sweat, handed over to us to preserve!' Nduka's stubbornness exasperated him, but he liked seeing him squirming and thrashing in the hot water he had boiled for himself. Looking at Udechukwu with a perfectly straight face, he added, 'I think that my brother is within his rights to borrow money, on interest even, to redeem the title. After all, it is he who will wear the white thread on his ankles.'

Udechukwu now found the opportunity to improve on himself; and he did this by loudly rebuking Nzeadi: 'What do you mean, encouraging him to borrow money on interest? Are you going to help him to pay back?'

Embarrassed, Nzeadi only cast about: 'Did I... Oh, I didn't mean... But we aren't quarrelling, are we?'

'Of course not. I am sorry. I was only saying that rather than incur a debt which one might have no means to pay back, what about disposing of some piece of property, and committing the money to reclaiming the title?'

Ebeso said, 'Do you want them to sell their house, or what? Or do you want them to redeem the thing, and perish as a result?'

'Not at all,' answered Udechukwu. 'I mean that the Uwadiegwus may see fit to dispose of some piece of land, or some such thing. Something substantial that will give us the money we need!'

'Udechukwu,' cried Nzeadi, 'that's not fair! Is not the problem how to save the achievements of our forebears? Then, why suggest that we should go about this by throwing away something of far greater value? How can one exchange a piece of land for a feather for one's cap?'

'I'm afraid,' corrected Nduka, 'that the feather-and-cap metaphor rather belittles the object of our discussion. What we are talking about is how to recover our investment and membership in the governing body of Okocha; what sacrifice on our part will be necessary to achieve this.'

That night Nduka paid a visit to Udechukwu Nwibe. Their conversation was brief. Still smarting from that failed attempt to get his relatives to speak with one voice – his voice, that is – in the matter of reclaiming his father's title, he addressed the man with little ceremony. His relatives were to be made to observe his protest in his actions. He had gone over backwards to be nice and polite; all to no good. Fine, he was going to show them.

'Had you anyone particularly in mind when you suggested that we put up a piece of property for sale, someone who will be ready with the cash?'

Taken aback by the visitor's brisk manner, Udechukwu cast about. 'Well, in fact, I had no one particularly in mind. But I don't think it will be difficult to find someone who will put forward all the money you want in exchange for a valuable piece of land, for land is in high demand now. Lots of people are buying up land; I haven't the least idea what they want that for. At any rate, you do wish to sell off a plot?'

'Oh yes. We have a good deal of land in the village and elsewhere. Um… don't imagine that I find this pleasant, even to talk about. But the proverb says that money is made through the expenditure of money. I think that this is true of everything thought to be valuable. Obviously, Nzeadi does not understand that; otherwise he wouldn't say that a sale is not to be considered at all, though it be in order to redeem our father's hard-won title.'

'All right, if you feel sure that you want to dispose of some land I shall make enquiries, and I'm sure to find someone who will offer us a good bargain.'

Ogbuefi Nweke Nwofia presumed the right to open the meeting of the titled men because he had called it. He stood up, and surveyed the group. His gaze rested briefly on Ogbuefi Ananwemadu, before it moved on to Nwalioba, and to Obiefuna Emenogha, and then to Oranudu.

He saluted a few of the men by name and title and called upon Emenogha to recognize all the rest on his behalf. The gesture was ambiguous as they both knew. It was something a man might request of his friend to show his regard for him, as well as a way to give notice to an enemy to prepare for a trial of strength. Blear-eyed, Emenogha only nodded; and Nweke continued:

'I sent out a call for this emergency meeting to let you know that all things being equal, we should expect a new member to join our society in a matter of days. It is my pleasure to represent the young man to you as he only wishes to step into his father's place in the fellowship of titled men. It is high-minded of him to seek this status; we are all in the position to appreciate this since it is the dear hope of each one here that his own son one day will arise and announce himself to be his father's living image.' There was a cheer from the titled men, after which Nweke resumed. 'What is the use of having children, if they are not man enough to stand up and answer the name of their father?

'Edoko Uwadiegwu's son has told me that he wishes to step into his father's place among us. I know him quite well; some of you probably know him too. He is cut exactly in the image of Edoko: the same face – if you look closely enough, you'll see that there is not the slightest difference, even though some say that the mother's features can also be made out in it. The resemblance is even more marked in the tone of voice. When he called me aside and told me what he had a mind of doing, I looked into his eyes. What did I see? Edoko's fire; that's what I saw. Nduka is very much his father's reincarnation – which is not surprising, for in the ordinary course of things a kola tree produces kola nuts and not oranges.

'Further, I did not fail to acquaint him with the costs to be paid. Of course, he understood what it was all about, and said he was ready to provide whatever was to be required. You will agree with me that he is strong-minded, and has high purpose. Do you not know that most young men in similar circumstances would let themselves be daunted by considerations of cost. But Nduka, as would have been typical of his father, did not brood over such matters.

'As we all know, having the firm purpose and the means to secure one a place in the *ozo* society is only one-half of the requirements. The individual must also be of a good character. Every care must be taken in selecting the people who are to be entrusted with public affairs. We cannot excuse ourselves from enquiring into the candidate's character on the ground that he is young, and not likely to take charge of things until much later. Is not the vulture a figure of the man of title in as much as both the baby-bird and the mother look equally elderly? Aren't they all bald? An *ozo* is before other things an elder, be he young or old. That is why a candidate should be thoroughly examined for fitness; the younger the candidate, the more thorough the scrutiny. So it must be with this young man asking to join us.'

He saluted his colleagues again and sat down.

Ogbuefi Oranudu was interested in the issue for reasons

of his own, and asked Nweke which of the deceased man's sons he meant.

'Nduka, the eldest of course. I thought I mentioned that in my speech.'

Oranudu nodded again and again, impressed that Edoko's son had acquired such wealth as to think nothing of taking the funeral rites of a titled man together with his own initiation rites into the *ozo* society. Would his son be able to do the same? No; not he. He'd wager his title was going to die with him. Something here to taunt the fellow with.

The silence of the company was rather prolonged. Then Ogbuefi Obinagu Nwalioba spoke:

'When does he mean to be initiated? On the memorial day?'

'Yes,' answered Nweke. 'He says that he should be ready by that day.'

'Well, I don't see anyone objecting to him,' resumed Obinagu Nwalioba. 'But I must say that it is a surprise to me that he feels able to meet the expenses of succession. I am sure that he will do well as a member for having so much more in him than meets the eye.'

Having something much more weighty to him than Nduka's bid, Obiefuna Emenogha, who spoke next, chose to ignore the insinuations of the last speaker. What did he care whether or not Nduka was doing as was expected of him? 'I believe,' he hastened to say, 'that we are seeing one of those rare moments when the gods become bountiful. It has been a good while since someone made an approach to us. Now suddenly, there is someone wishing to reclaim an old seat, and another desiring that a new one be created for him. And both are men of quality!' He now saw fit to return Nweke's dubious compliment earlier in the meeting: 'I am not well acquainted with Nduka Uwadiegwu, I must confess; but what is that to the fact that some of our number have spoken in his favour. Nweke swears that…'

'Nweke swore nothing,' cried the worthy in self-defence.

'Oh well, he doesn't swear it,' amended Emenogha, 'he only affirms it. In any case, let us confer his man with the sacred title, and do the same to the other man, Orimili Nwofia, who needs no introduction since you all know the sort of person he is – that there are few of his calibre in this town.'

'I have the impression,' observed Ogbuefi Ananwemadu, 'that Orimili would prefer his own induction to take place during the next harvest season; is that right?'

'That's right,' answered Obiefuna. 'But I am sure he will be happier still of a chance coming this season, which will be auspicious because of Nduka's induction. You see, he approached us at a time we weren't anticipating a meeting to discuss title-taking and succession. But here we are, doing just that. You may be certain that Orimili would be ready, if we were to say that his induction will be tomorrow!'

Ogbuefi Nweke was the next to speak, and was determined to return the meeting to order and due process:

'I am glad that you don't object to Nduka reclaiming his father's title. It is just as I had thought – is he not, after all, the son of a man of title? Would we have objected if his father had made him wear the white thread on his ankles without being inducted as a member? Still, it was good to subject him to a thorough examination, with all of you participating. We make no exceptions even for our privileged son, as a bush fire does not spare a tortoise despite his coat of iron. Should the fowl dare to hope that it would be spared, when it is all dressed up in a suit of dry grass as if in readiness for the pyre?' Nweke paused for the message to sink home. With a baleful look, he answered his own question, 'Of course not!' Triumphantly then, 'So, it is agreed that Nduka should be accorded the title and privileges of our society, and may be addressed as 'Ogbuefi' like the rest of us. That's the chief part. The second is that the conferring will take place on his father's memorial. We shall all be in attendance at the vigil of the memorial, and be there early enough to work out all the details of the induction. As to the other application – well, the comments which have been made so far have been of a general nature. We all know that there is a great difference between redeeming a title and taking one from the ground up. Let us not forget that the ancestors also participate in these deliberations; and whereas we know for certain that they favour a man redeeming his father's title, we have to ascertain carefully their views regarding the candidate for initiation.' He swept the assembly with his gaze, trying to catch the eye of each of the men in turn. Saluting them yet again, he told them: 'We cannot be too careful in this matter. Ogbuefi Emenogha has pointed out that Ekwenze Orimili is well known in this town. I quite agree; I do know the man. But I should think that the question is not whether we do know him or not, so much as giving due weight to *what* we do know about the man.'

Ogbuefi Udozo was on his feet instantly. 'On the

contrary, it is quite sufficient that we do know the man, and that we are sure that he is worthy of the title. What do you know about him that makes him unworthy? What character blotch? Unless you can spot a handicap of that nature, let's quibble no further, and go and feast with Orimili!' This drew a cheer from some of the men. Udozo was taking Orimili's case into a corner, where all would depend on the delicacy of the opponents as to what they might permit themselves to voice out about the candidate. Strangely enough, Emenogha, who next took the floor, was content to leave the case in that corner. He argued that the fathers obviously approved of their man, or he would not be the business magnate he was.

Nweke Nwofia interposed, showing impatience at Emenogha's ingenious logic. 'It is true,' said he, with a happy consciousness, 'that wealth is a favour from the fathers. But I don't see that a man favoured and blessed with wealth is for that reason also approved to become an *ozo*. Some of us here now would not be able to pay for our title, if required to take it afresh. You don't mean – do you? – that because they have become poorer, they are no longer approved to be *ozo*?'

'So, why don't we change the rules, and say that anyone who is approved by the ancestors, whether or not he can pay for the title, is eligible to join the club?' That was Edozie Nwanze, his cap pushed forwards and hanging at a precarious angle against his forehead.

'Need we go that far?' reasoned Nweke Nwofia. 'Mind you, it is an unpleasant business for everyone asking some of these questions. Still, we must be sure not to get ourselves into trouble with those who have gone before us, on whose pedestal we stand!'

'What's the use of the discussion, then?' Obinagu Nwalioba hotly interposed. 'Why not...'

'It was you who began... I mean, Emenogha...'

'Let me finish, will you?' his eyes aflare. With a visible effort he controlled his voice and became ironical: 'To be on the safe side, let us ask a seer to divine the will of the ancestors for us and tell us whether Orimili is part of Okocha or not. Yes,' he agreed with himself, 'that's what we should ask them. But if we are not too squeamish to tackle the case, let us appraise the evidence before us. I see nothing in it that makes Orimili less deserving of the title than you, Nweke, or I.'

'A seer, indeed!' hissed Ogbuefi Echesi. 'The quickest way out is to consult a seer, isn't it? Take care where you people are leading us!' Evidently, he was full of offence at Nweke Nwofia. 'Why is it that our decisions in this assembly have always been by discussion only? Is it not because the fathers are presumed to be with us even in the discussions? Let me tell you, then, that they will be equally pleased with our decision to confer the honours on Orimili. It is a good thing, as a matter of fact, that we are having this debate. What is more interesting still is that though it has been going on all this time, with moments of tension, no one has found anything to object to in Orimili. So, now that we have had the debate, let us grant the application and adjourn.'

'I don't agree with you,' objected Ogbuefi Nweke Nwofia, 'that the debate has yielded nothing to clarify Orimili's position. Can someone tell me why Orimili has waited until now to apply for membership?'

'Ogbuefi Nweke, *nwakaibeya*,' Ogbuefi Emenogha took leave to rebuke his titled friend, 'you are trying to block our progress! I don't know why you choose to do this. You seem to object to Orimili's membership; why? At any rate, you are forcing yourself in our way evidently to prevent us deciding in his favour. You owe this meeting an explanation. If you have an objection to Orimili, specify it; maybe someone here will be able to explain it to you. Otherwise, my motion stands that we accept him.'

Ogbuefi Obiefuna Emenogha hung fire, and waited for Nweke to make his objection known. But Nweke did not speak. So he said:

'We are all agreed that Ekwenze Orimili shall be conferred with…'

Ogbuefi Ugonabo sprang to his feet: 'What are you saying, Ogbuefi Emenogha? Is this still the *ozo* society of Okocha, or what? How can you speak as if you do not know what everybody knows?' If ever a man had a name that didn't fit him, it was this man, Ugonabo – a double portion of serene nobility. But he was mean as a scorpion, and it was as if the eagle (*ugo*) in his name was meant as a mockery. He wasn't the least delicate, and hated the very air of it.

Facing Emenogha, he charged on. 'It is you we should be asking the question, whether you have a particular reason why you want to rush Orimili's application through this assembly, without a thorough scrutiny. I won't let you sweep me along in that manner; never! I should like to ask you, in fact: do you not know that Orimili Nwofia is a stranger to this town, and that this is the reason why the debate has dragged on for so long? I am quite surprised that no one has brought up the fact. Do you know of any place in Igboland where strangers are given the *ozo* title? Every one of you is afraid of speaking the plain truth, and that is why you are trying to lead the *ozo* society of Okocha into an abomination. But I'm not afraid of the truth. If you are offended by what I am saying, it's all right with me; you can meet me at the cross-roads and we shall fight it out. We should be men enough to say "no" to Orimili. He is everybody's friend – agreed; he also has the means to take the title, perhaps four times over. You have told us that he is a reliable man – you are right; I know that much. Still we should say *no* to him; and I do say *no* to him. Why? Because this society belongs to Okocha, and not to Olu and Igbo!'

He closed and resumed his seat as abruptly as he had taken the floor. At the same time, Nweke Nwofia shot up, manfully repressing a burst of triumphant laughter. Orimili had the means to take the title several times over – trust Ugonabo to find the strongest phrases for anything. However, Nweke Nwofia had the means to block him indefinitely. His speech began, low-key: 'We thank Ogbuefi Ugonabo for his nice speech, and for bringing back the voice of reason into this assembly. If one does a good job, he should be commended for it, so that he will do even better next time.' Ogbuefi Nweke could be smooth and soothing, depending on the occasion, and he was shrewd in judging occasions and adjusting his tone to carry everyone along with him. He took great care not to appear antagonistic.

He spoke now, looking very earnest: 'As the objection has

been named, perhaps someone will be able to explain it to us; Ogbuefi Emenogha, for instance. For my part, I cannot pretend that I have the least notion how to do it.'

Emenogha hated this man, Nweke Nwofia, especially for being able every so often to put him on the spot. He wondered that the man had everthing going for him: wealth, power, a following. The only thing he obviously wanted was comeliness: consider his wide forehead, angular at the extremes, almost with sharp points; consider his high-arched eyebrows and blood-shot eyes. If this man were comely, he would have thought himself the king of men. As it was, he wasn't doing badly at all! Obiefuna Emenogha promised himself yet again that he would overthrow that man. He would bide his time. His speech was short and stormy: 'I ask you all to take note that Ogbuefi Nweke is claiming Ogbuefi Ugonabo's point as his reason for impeding our meeting today. For my part, what I wish to ask is why a man whose family has been with us for several generations has been called a stranger in our very presence. Has that man ever been heard to claim that he was from somewhere else apart from Okocha? Does he stay away from public works? Do we distinguish ourselves from him in our sorrows and joys? Is it not treacherous to be with him in work, play, and at the sacrifices, only to count him out when it comes to conferring honours? I think it utterly shameful that there should be found among us one who would stand up and voice out such dreadful things! Whoever heard such a thing as a man being called a stranger in the land of his birth! If you are afraid of Orimili, and want to stay as far away from him as possible, that's a different matter altogether, and

I can well understand that. But that's no reason why you should try to prevent him from receiving the honours this land offers its children.'

'I am not afraid of Orimili,' cried Ugonabo. 'You can go and tell him what I have said. He is welcome at the crossroads to fight it out! Is it a secret that his great-grandfather – or some remove of that sort – did not know our own great-grandfathers? Yet our great-grandfathers were here all the time. I should say that you are the one being irresponsible to represent Orimili in this manner in this assembly. You tell us why it is so important to you that he should join the society. Was it part of your agreement with him when you accepted a bride-wealth from him for your daughter?'

'You dare?' Emenogha sprang to his feet, jabbed a forefinger in the direction of Ugonabo, and took a threatening step or two. 'You, a mere lackey, who wears the white thread of self-sufficiency, only to do another's bidding!'

'Don't!' cried Ogbuefi Ananwemadu, glad to have a say. 'No, you go too far! I mean both of you.'

Emenogha had only waited long enough to see if Ogbuefi Nweke would take offence before sitting down to marvel at the speed with which news got around in Okocha, and how clever some people were in distorting it for their own horrid purposes. The present debate was to yield its own distortions in a matter of days; but what Emenogha cared for at the moment was that he was even with Ugonabo. Still he must take care not to be provoked by the man. Ogbuefi Nweke was the big fish. He must remain watchful for his opportunity to try to do as he had vowed.

Not since the early days of his appointment as a chief,

when the peers were still trying to understand his game, had Ananwemadu had the kind of attention he got at this timely intervention of his. He stood, his two arms stretched out sideways and pointing towards Emenogha and Ugonabo. Ananwemadu would give no quarter; this he signalled by holding his head low, his eyes shut. He was gathering his thoughts at the same time, and thinking that this was an opportunity to begin rebuilding his image. He adopted a high moral tone: 'What is before us is a matter of propriety; it is nothing personal. I must say that the troubles we have had here have been caused by mistaking such issues for what they are not, and making enemies over them. How have we moved from considering someone's suitability for *ozo* into offering to meet and fight at the cross-roads? Haven't we got Ogbuefi Oranudu with us? What could have been more helpful than to ask him what he knows about the man's background, and what advice he would give as to conferring the title on him? Who should know these things, if not he? I'm not saying that questions of that sort have ever been important in deciding who should be honoured with membership in this club. I have worn the white thread longer than a great many of you, having been initiated as a boy by my father.'

'So what!' shouted Ikedi.

'So I know what I am talking about, that's what.'

'In all that time you have been an *ozo*, how many candidates were found to be strangers in Okocha?'

Ogbuefi Nweke took Ikedi up on this: 'Haven't you heard, Ikedi, that the word "stranger" is offensive?' Having thus rebuked his crony, Nweke went on to ask Oranudu to give them guidance, commending Ananwemadu at the same time for reminding them that Oranudu was their man.

Ogbuefi Oranudu remained calm, his eyes to the ground, as if he had not heard the invitation to speak. When he finally did speak, it was very unlike what had gone before, when the speakers sought to hold each other's gaze and try to stare them down. Sitting, facing in the direction of Nwalioba and Udozo, and seeming to be looking directly at them, Oranudu nevertheless evaded all eyes. His game was not to stare anyone down, but to remain unseen and mysterious. There was no mystery, however, as to whom he ranked first among the aldermen. It was Nweke Nwofia. Oranudu opened the Initial exchange of greetings with Ogbuefi Nweke, recognising him by his praise name:

'Ogbuefi *Nwakaibeya*!' he saluted.
'Ogbuefi *Ugonnaya*!' Nweke returned him.
'Ogbuefi *Nnadebeluaku*!', he turned to Emenogha.
'Eh! *Ugonnaya*! I'm attentive!'

Oranudu saluted a few more by their titles, ending with a plural one to take in all the rest. He began with an invocation:

The dancing movements may seem to clash
But do in fact match the drum's rhythm.
Do we not talk because we disagree? And yet
Is not the common weal served by both?
Only be sure in all you do
To seek the truth and nothing more,

Since peace is not found but in truth's wake.
> Good health to you all!
To man and child, old and young,
Good health!
And success go with you in all you do!

'In the days of our fathers, a question of this sort could not arise. Why should it arise? Did not everything, man and beast, rain and wind, follow their own regular cycles? But now everything has been overturned. Only the great river, Orimili, I think, has kept its course – in that it is still flowing southwards as it did in the days of Omee-Ogwali. You are all very young, of course, else you would have noticed that the flood of the great river itself is not as full or as powerful as it was when I was very young. So, even Orimili has changed.' The peers, who never had the good fortune of seeing the great river in Oranudu's time, were impressed by what he was saying, marvelling that such a change should befall the great river, and wondering whether it would have diminished to a tiny stream by the time of their great-grandchildren.

However, Oranudu had resumed his invocation, speaking now to the ancestors:

> Though the calamity has come
> In our own age, yet, revered Fathers,
> No offence must you now take,
> Nor to us the fault account
> As it is not ours, but the outsider's age:
> Armed with gun and spear and sword,

> With face set to slay and overrun
> Unless he has his heart's desire.
> But you said we should not struggle
> And die; that Okocha shall flower yet.

He went on to explain that the overturning of things was such that children were being taken from their parents and made to work for other people, his own grandson being a good example. The good days were gone, when you knew a man's worth by looking at his barn; and when you would know upon seeing the white thread that one has made it, thanks to the machete and hoe. Now there were people who didn't own even a yam tendril, and yet were said to be able to pay for the title; wasn't that remarkable?

Oranudu surprised most of his listeners by letting them know that the reason why the outsider first came to Okocha was because he had been driven away from his homeland as a result of a great war, similar to the one which was now said to be taking place exactly where the former had been fought. Even fairly recent events had got mixed up in the old man's memory with very old ones. His hearers were patient with him though, especially as they saw that his intent was to point them a lesson. They were to learn to live peacefully with one another, he told them; and not be like the Europeans who had been fighting and fleeing their homeland. What could be worse than a man leaving his homeland? If the first Europeans had come as a result of the first war, what would happen at the end of the present one? Shouldn't there be many more? He recalled a war, years ago, between Ebonasa and Amofia, a neighbouring town. Ebonasa had had to fight alone because the other two villages of Okocha, Ugwueke and Amanna, had refused to support their sister-village. The war had raged for two years, during which there had been terrible suffering.

What one couldn't forget about the war was the sight of the great warriors of Ebonasa. He himself had been too young to fight, and was living with his mother and little brother in Ugwueke. For the Ebonasa people who had relatives in Amanna and Ugwueke had sent their wives and children to these relatives. He used to come to Ebonasa with other boys, bringing food to the warriors. That was how he had come to see the warriors decked out for war. How he had longed to be one of them! There were Uderika Onyekwe and his companions; the great Onyemenaka and Echabi, his own uncles; Okadigbo Azodo and his companions; Oranudu, his own father. The old man shuddered, evidently reliving the actual moment; and he pursued in a tone that was hardly audible:

> That which is large and mighty
> Has depths and secret energies,
> Which supply to counter movements of change.
> Thus will the greater river never be salted,
> Nor the dead be in want of space to sleep in.
>   So it is with you, great warriors.
> You have joined our Fathers in
> The land of spirits blessed; dead
> Yet full of power.
>   Haunt for ever your undoers all;
> Be they men or evil ghosts!

> Yet with undying care
> Stay your brothers here!

Clever old fellow, enthused Ogbuefi Nweke silently. Now it was dawning on him how far apart in age they were from Oranudu. The old man must look upon them as children to be attempting to use lore to make them forget their hostilities! But it was he who was being a child even to hope that. The hostilities were where they were – just under the placid surface at which he was inflicting lessons and lore. They would break out again; of that he was certain; maybe even before the present meeting was over. He nudged the old man gently: 'And Orimili Nwofia…'

'I was coming to that. Orimili's grandfather was in that war, you see? And that was when I first knew his people. Nwofia's people had come to Okocha a generation or two before that war; no one knew from where, except that it was somewhere in the north. I think it was Nwofia's father or grandfather who had made that journey. However, our people were good to them, and gave them land to dwell among us. One day I came down to Ebonasa to bring my father his food, but I didn't see him, nor any of the warriors. That must have been the worst day of fighting for our people in the entire war, in that they lost five warriors in a single engagement. It is still a wonder how they rallied from that dreadful blow, to win the war. They had sent a raiding party to Amofia, among them Nwofia; and the party had walked into an ambush. Only Onyemenaka and one other warrior escaped; the rest of the raiding party was wiped out. So all our warriors had armed themselves and returned to Amofia to recover the dead. I was waiting until they returned, and it was dreadful to see them march back into Ebonasa, bearing the corpses.' Ogbuefi Oranudu paused and shuddered, his eyes glazed as if they were altogether sightless.

When he resumed speaking, his voice was low, just above a whisper. To this, his hearers reacted as one man. They all leaned forwards almost mechanically, intent to miss nothing of this remarkable history. 'One could see how even the grasses of the field were affected by what had happened. It was as if the shade of night had overtaken the village in broad daylight. All that one heard was the terrified cackle of the hens. Messengers were sent to inform the families of the fallen heroes. They came; among them, Obiako Nwofia, Ekwenze's father, not much older than me, maybe one year; at most two. He was accompanied by his mother and both were calm, overwhelmed like everybody else. No one uttered a sound, while the fallen warriors were buried – I can see the entire burial party at Ama Ebonasa, just as if it were all taking place this instant.'

With a sigh and a shake of the head, he resumed. 'The war ended, and we went back to our homes.' There was more power in his voice now. 'Obiako had a boat, and was at the great river every day. Everybody pitied him, and said, poor boy, what could he do with himself, without a father to direct him? Well, didn't he end up owning a big boat, and ferrying people and goods to Okono? Is not that the meaning of the saying that there is no point worrying over a rat, and trying to make a burrow to protect it? It makes its own burrow, even if it looks weak and vulnerable.' He paused.

Ogbuefi Nwalioba took the opportunity to put a question to him:

'Ogbuefi *ugonnaya* Oranudu?'

'Eh! *Ogalanya ngada!*'

Nwalioba began by praising the old man for the power of his memory, pointing out that in narrating this history he made one see the meaning of the adage which said that one's ruined utensils increased in quantity the longer one had been using such utensils. He didn't mean this in an ironic sense. So, having scored the point, he made an invocation on behalf of the old man; that he might continue to enjoy good health, and that he might elude all his adversaries – the unseen ones, of course. If any of these should come with the idea of fetching him away, let them be rendered powerless through the power of the invocation; and, moreover, let them not be able to identify Oranudu. Thus they would be obliged to go back again to their evil place covered in confusion.

'Now,' he continued, 'I'm sure that you have given us a clear idea how to proceed in dealing with Ekwenze Orimili's request. I am particularly struck by what you have said about his grandfather's role in the war; the way he fought and got killed in battle, and was later recovered and buried with the other heroes at Ama Ebonasa. I think that this shows quite clearly that his people have always been one and the same people as our own people. Who then can have anything to object in such a one?'

Ogbuefi Oranudu remained silent for some moments.

Then he rejoined, 'Yes, it is true that his grandfather fought together with our people, died with them, and was buried with them. However, the strange thing is that Obiako his son did not on that account ask to be conferred with the title. Had he done this, the elders of Okocha would then have made a response and, in that way, left us something to go by. Nor has there been another foreigner on whom the title has been conferred.'

'I shouldn't think that that is a problem,' answered Udozo. 'Probably Obiako didn't have the means to pay for the title, but his son does have it; and moreover, he has applied to *us*. Another thing I'm sure of is that the land of Okocha has smiled on them. Is Orimili not the wealthiest man in Okocha today? Isn't his son now getting ready to come home from overseas? Who among us here is expecting his own son so to return?'

'Come to think of it,' rejoined Oranudu, 'is not Okocha itself the land of travelling people? Did not our people come all the way from across the great river to this land, and did not the land receive them warmly? But the other side of the story is that the land itself is a gift from Okocha, our great Father, to his sons. Since our Father arrived here, found the land pleasing to himself and took it over, our people have ceased to travel. They scarcely hunt now, even though that was the occupation of their Father, and it was in one of his hunting expeditions from across the river that he discovered this land. Didn't he go back home after discovering the place, and later returned with a great company of warriors to settle in? They began to take wives to themselves and to have children, who, in their turn, handed the land over to their own children. The difference is that no one knows from which country Orimili's people have come; except that it is somewhere in the north. And has not Orimili's son continued journeying in the same direction, beyond our shores to the land of the white man?

'As I said before, in this age of the outsider, would you be surprised if the white man at the river' (the manager of Guy & Son) 'comes to you with the demand that you tie the white thread round his ankles? How can you refuse, when he can cause soldiers to come and round us up for denying him?' He sighed deeply, and turned away.

'Things have really changed.' Ogbuefi Obiefuna Emenogha echoed Oranudu's theme with a great show of understanding. 'The pity of it is that we can't recover what is past; not even if we paid money for it! Fortunately, we are not required to go after it as the excellent Ogbuefi Oranudu has told us that one should do what one must in the light of new realities; which, to my mind, is especially relevant to the case in hand.'

'Yes, yes!' Nweke quickly put in. 'History is always relevant, isn't it? Ogbuefi Oranudu has given us quite an earful of it; and Nwalioba has reminded us how valuable it is to have among us people of such vast experience. One day people will look upon us just as we do Oranudu as funds of wisdom and history. I'd say that he himself has shown us how to prepare for that day: one must be alert to observe and remember everything as they are and as we have received them.'

'Quite right,' commented Obiefuna. 'He also told us – remember – that the reason we have this impasse is that an earlier generation had not taken a certain decision for us. The question didn't come up in their time; or they would have answered it. It has come up now; and we know how to answer it. For it is about Orimili, whose grandfather, we have now been told, fought with our people, and was united with them in life and death. Can anything be clearer?'

'No, nothing!' replied Ugonabo, sarcastically. 'Yes, he did tell us that Orimili's grandfather fought and died for Ebonasa – in a war which two-thirds of the town refused to join in! We are talking about the *ozo* society of Okocha, not that of Ebonasa!'

It was strange that Orimili Nwofia, who never recalled wrestling with anyone in his entire life, should be causing such deep divisions among his townsmen. He himself would have been struck by the queerness of it, and might have gone further and withdrawn the application if he had known that the division was to go still deeper.

One person who saw a little more clearly where this whole thing was leading was Ogbuefi Nweke Nwofia. The peers were sticking to their positions. An explosion was sure to occur if the debate were to continue. He might have deliberately steered towards that explosion, if there was a chance that it would knock out Emenogha. But that worthy was far more subtle than Ananwemadu, and was likely to hold his own. Things would worsen markedly if he survived the explosion. No, he daren't steer that way. But what confronted him on the other side was the prospect of having to withdraw at some stage his opposition to Orimili. It wasn't that he saw any merit in the case; it would rather be dangerous to have him. To be able to throw out his application, he had to have the unanimous support of the members. Ogbuefi Nweke finally settled for a change of tactics. He would pretend to show interest in Orimili, and then contrive to delay his admission, taking care not to give the impression that he was trying to keep him out for his own personal reasons. He stood up even before Ugonabo finished his virulent speech, and spoke in a measured tone:

'Judging from the way this debate has been moving, I'd say that we won't be able to reach a unanimous agreement today. But I must say that the debate has been very interesting and informative, and powerful arguments have been given on either side. But the difficulty seems to be that even though we all recognize Orimili as a public-spirited man, and everybody would gladly say, Oh yes, let Orimili be given the title, if only for this great quality he has; still concern has been voiced regarding his background. We cannot discount that, can we?

'I think that it will be so much wiser for us not to insist on reaching a decision today. We all know how hasty decisions often lead to regret. On the other hand, Orimili is not running away; nor is there a reason to fear that he might lose his money and no longer be able to take the title if, say, in a month, or a year, or two, we tell him that he is welcome to join us. So, let us take our time, and consider the matter fully, before making our decision.'

The night owl was a bird that seemed naturally to evoke dread and mistrust. It had a mysterious manner about it, being fully awake and on the haunt at night, when all other 'ordinary' creatures were taking their rest. It would sneak into the darkness of a tree's foliage close by someone's homestead, and commence to give out its terrifying, orotund cries. That bird was rarely seen unless it was in flight: then it appeared as a silhouette of darkness, with a certain perverse determination in the manner of its flight, such as one did not notice in the flight of the other more honest night birds, for example, the bat. The one characteristic, apart from its stubborn manner in flight, was the sound of its cry, which could bring a chill to the heart of even a brave person. It was for them an evil omen; and if it took up its station near someone's homestead, one knew that evil could not be far away. It was as if such a one had been marked, and one's equanimity hardly returned for driving it away. The night owl aroused in the people of Okocha feelings of helplessness, and sometimes rage – the same sorts of feeling they had towards death. Thus did they see the bird as an image of death.

Death itself was a self, mysterious and demonic. It seemed to select its victims with care, evidently aiming to shock and wound; which is as much as to say that its real target was not the victim who is laid low, but the proud and living spirit of the people. Death demoralized the people of Okocha, and their funeral rites reflected their helplessness and rage.

Edoko Uwadiegwu's funeral was overcast; the atmosphere was heavy. It was as if Death had attended the rites in person and made everyone in the crowd of mourners feel its cold essence. Ogbuefi Nweke Nwofia had often experienced this chill at the death of influential people, and didn't feel himself again until after the burial. So funerals were like trials to him, each one lasting a whole day. As he was a significant figure in his neighbourhood, he often found himself virtually in charge at social events, not least funerals. Still his wealth of experience in these matters did not help him to understand what he usually felt. Perhaps this was because he tended not to reflect on it once the oppressive air had lifted from him. So it was at Edoko's funeral. He didn't know how the presence got to him, whether it settled directly on people's minds or whether it settled in the air and was felt as an exterior influence. However, the very air which enveloped the compound and the entire area surrounding the compound seemed peculiarly dense, and the density increased as one approached the spot where Edoko lay in state – which was what made it appear as an exterior influence.

> One of the dirges that day, however, gave him pause.
> Safeguard the child, the grown-up,
> The aged, when night-bird's abroad
> That's hostile to life, the same to
> Joy; whose voice does resound,
> And felt in the heart in the dark;
> But form unseen.
>
>   Safeguard the child, the man, the
> Woman, sheltered and safe
> In the land, where homesteads
> Are built, and crops flourish,
> Wherein the eyes of the Fathers
> See unseen.

It was a familiar dirge, only that it seemed incongruent today. It was as if death was encountered only in the night, forgetting that its most recent victim had been taken in broad daylight. It was a form of assertion against death, but the mourners didn't take it up enthusiastically: they never did on the funeral day – as if they wouldn't dare that mortal enemy while he was still brooding and throbbing in the very air surrounding them.

The story was entirely different on the memorial day. The mourners assembled in force. They came from all corners of Okocha, as well as from the neighbouring towns. The townspeople in particular were all clad in battle gear: eyelids whitened with chalk, and cutlasses stuck into their belts. A number of ceremonial masquerades also attended; some armed with a shield and spear and cutlass. The people were making their demonstration against death, despite the element of festivity that had entered the memorial observances because of Nduka's accession to his father's title.

They put on show a great number of warlike performances, and the songs were the sort which inspired courage in the brothers-at-arms and intimidated the enemy. One song went:

> The iron-bar is snapped in two,
> And this to us is a call to arms.
> With mighty arm and stout heart
> Off we march against the foe.
> That iron-breaker he might see
> We let pass no thrust or insult

> Against Okocha, noble and mettlesome;
> Legendary hunter too, and forest's terror.
>> So to battle marched the hosts
> In scores they fell to edge of sword
> Which we with might and vigour wield.
>> The watchers they saw,
> The field doth recount
> A city laid waste.
> They saw a scene of ruin.
> What a scene of blood!
> What a scene of ruin!

The atmosphere was no longer heavy with death; it was teeming now with dust. No real harm came from dust; at the most, it gave one a head-cold. They performed their warlike exercises, cheered themselves up and departed to their homes. There were in fact moments when the cutlass had been drawn by their wearers, and brandished; but there had been no enemy to menace with it.

Towards the close of the day, the women gathered together at a corner of Edoko's compound to share the carcass of the sheep which the Uwadiegwus had presented to them to show appreciation for the part they had played in helping to lift up the people's spirit from the depth it had retreated into as a result of recent oppression by the nearness of death. The carcass had been hacked to pieces and divided up on a mat of banana leaves in as many parts as there were women present. Okuata Orimili waited among the women till it was her turn to select a portion for herself.

They took turns according to seniority, and this was

worked out on the basis of when one got married. There were among the women gathered together in Edoko's place that day some who were young, compared with their neighbours, but they ranked before them because they had married earlier. This method of determining seniority had been working smoothly for the women because it was as though they were beginning life anew when they married. In fact some of the elders of Okocha said that the women finally became themselves when they left their parents and became mistresses of their own homes.

It fell now to Okuata to select a portion of meat. She bent over it and was on the point of picking up one when she heard a voice from behind her command with evident contempt that she should desist. The voice went on: 'You ought to know better than to choose before it is your turn.'

It was the voice of Okwuese, the younger wife of Ananwemadu; and it flashed through Okuata's mind that she was up to something. She straightened up, faced about, and quietly asked Okwuese, 'Has not Obiageli Nnaemeka taken her turn? And is it not mine after her?'

'You wait until your betters have had their chance!'

'All right, if I have somehow confused the order, do tell us whose turn is next.'

'Give way then, so I can have my share.'

This turn of events came as a great shock to most of the women present. They all hung back, startled, just as Okuata herself was staring at Okwuese, mouth agape.

Both Okwuese and Okuata were of Ebonasa, into which Okuata herself had also married; and they were roughly the same age, although Okwuese was slightly older. But everybody knew that Okwuese had married years after Okuata had had her first baby. So what did she mean by trying to reverse the proper order? Gathering her senses about her, Okuata decided to assay the matter further to see what it meant.

'What do you mean, Okwuese? Since when have you had precedence over me?'

'You won't admit of course that you understand. Anyway, give way for me to have my portion!'

'And you imagine that I shall let you? You must be dreaming, for I can't see how else to make sense of what you are saying!'

'Who is dreaming? You or I? Who do you think you are?'

'I wonder... Maybe you are right in saying that I am not who I think I am, but I'm distinctly aware that I am senior to you – by a good many years too!'

'What sort of seniority is that? Marriage? Who are you married to, anyway?'

'This is most extraordinary, Okwuese. There must be something wrong with you; there has to be. Well, in case you really need to be told, I am the wife of Orimili, and had weaned a baby before they even proposed to you! Now, will you stop this nonsense!'

Okwuese threw up her nose: 'Is that all? Quite impressive! And *what* is Orimili? You tell me that. Who in this town knows where he comes from, if he comes from *anywhere*?'

This was a great new shock, more powerful even than the first, which had so startled the women. This one restored them to their senses at last, and confusion ensued.

As to Okuata, it was as if she had been struck deep in

the bowels, for she felt her very entrails surge towards her throat, and she was suffocating. This girl – she thought frantically – deserves to be chewed up, and spat into a dark pit! What can she mean? My husband… Me… My… get my fingernails on her blasted face – scratch it up for her – get hold of that tongue of hers – tear…!

All the women were speaking, shrilly castigating Okwuese.

Okuata melted into tears. She was bitterly sorry that her husband had not attended the memorial, not knowing why she should feel this way.

It was probably fortunate that Orimili was not present when the incident happened, for in a memorial rally which had been remarkable for its warlike displays, Orimili might well have found it in him to lay violent hands – or even something still more lethal – on a woman.

Okuata permitted herself to be led away by her neighbours who surrounded her. She felt, as she walked away, the yield of something wet and soft under her feet. She was treading the meat.

4 | *Highroad Okocha*

Ekwenze moored his barge at the Guy & Son quay for the day. He had brought home a full load of company goods from the warehouse at Okono. Those were to be unloaded the next day. His men were going to be fully occupied all day tomorrow, for directly after unloading the manufactures and building materials they had ferried up, they would pile on the palm-kernel sacks and oil barrels for delivery at the warehouse. It was essential that all the arrangements be completed tomorrow, so that Orimili would sail down-river on the day after.

It had been a very good day altogether, and he anticipated a few more of the kind during the season. Things were moving briskly for him, and he was glad. He could look down the road to the planting season, and see bright sunny weather all the way, broken up by patches of bleakness; just like looking down a stretch of a sandy road on a bright sunny afternoon, and seeing the pale and greyish whiteness of the washed, dry sand, broken at intervals by the shadows cast across the road by tall and leafy roadside trees. Ekwenze Orimili looked upon the market-day which broke the week into two halves as if it were a shadow across the roadway. The only difference was that when walking down the sandy road on a hot afternoon, the sight of such a shadow would have encouraged him to walk faster, and in the shortest possible time, to avail himself of its congenial influence. Seeing them down the road in his business calendar was something else; they discouraged him. They were more like the shades that fell across the water, which were chilly even in brilliant sunshine.

The dry season was reaching its most critical period, and food products were becoming scarce. The farmers had much less now to sell than they had a month or two ago. Now, it was mostly seed-yams and cassava. But even in the best of times, at the harvest season, Orimili saw his work on this midweek market-day as a chore. Not only was it chaotic from beginning to end, but also many of the market women strove to save a penny from the fare. They would present three pence, instead of the full four pence, and insist that it was all the money they had. But Ekwenze knew that each one of them had a deal of money tied up and hidden in the *ear* of the very dress-wrappers in which they were clad. Although he never really worked out what the individual trips cost him, he felt sure that he made no profit on his market-day trips, and that he probably lost money and took far more trouble than came his way in a whole week working for Guy & Son. He had often thought of raising the fare to five pence, but never gave it serious consideration. Not a chance in that. Oh, there would be an outcry, if he dared; and it would be deafening too. At any rate, not so late in the season would he dream of suggesting it – and not even during the next harvest season, since he should be taking his title then; if his case got through in the club. And after that? Why, the people would say that he was only trying to recover what he had spent taking the title; that he was bleeding them to pay for his title!

He was beginning to feel the oppressive heat. That was the harbinger of the rainy season – which didn't seem to make sense: more apt, if the harbinger had been stronger and cooler winds, thunder even. He brushed away beads of perspiration from his brow, sweeping his index finger across his face and flinging away the sweat. Then, transferring his grip to his left hand, he took hold of his large, green cotton jumper down the front mid-section, with his index finger and thumb, and worked it rhythmically in and out like bellows, to get up a circulation of air under his clothes. It helped a little; but when he left off working the bellows, the heat under his clothes rose abruptly, and he felt the perspiration running down his belly, and soaking into the waist-band of his thick khaki shorts. In his subconscious was the thought that the sun had reached a state of frenzy in its present performance, just like some old man, sitting and watching younger men performing the *ijele* dance, tapping his foot and shaking his head to the rhythm. Then he gets up, cupping his left hand to save his precious snuff from being knocked off his hand, while he performs a couple of steps; and finally, throwing away the snuff, and giving himself over entirely to the music. That was the stage the sun had now reached. However, the rains would soon arrive, and force it to… ah; the rains meant less cargo to ferry to Okono – and rougher passages upon the river too. As a matter of fact, he ought to be going down now towards the river, instead of going up into town. If only he hadn't been away so long from town – two days; he felt as if he had been away for one week, or two even – yes; if he hadn't been away so long, leaving himself arrears of social calls to make, the best way he could be heading in that weather was back towards the river. The sunny season was the most agreeable time on the river. It was so much cooler out there!

In this, Ekwenze Orimili was telling himself only the least important reason why he would rather be on the river than on dry land any day of the week. He felt a certain rapport with the river. Ever since the rites with which his ties with the elemental river-spirits were severed, Ekwenze had known this feeling of oneness with the river. That, of course, was a curious way to start up a relationship of kinship. One would have expected a parting of ways, as the rites were really for that purpose. A seer had found out that the young Ekwenze was cheating his parents, for he secretly belonged to a company of river elementals, had reincarnated a number of times into his parents' anguished home, and was preparing for yet another round of death and return, when he was found out by the powerful seer. It must be said for Ekwenze that he didn't know what he was doing to his parents; and yet this is not to say that he was in the least surprised by the revelation. What the man said seemed so utterly true that he gladly performed his part of the ritual. The seer himself had prepared the offering, and Obiako had carried it in one hand, holding his boy's hand in the other; and in this fashion the three had walked together across the town on a moonlight night to the river. There Ekwenze was to wade a short distance into the water and deposit the offering on the river-bed, while Obiako trembled at the shore: what if the boy decided not to break with his invisible friends and plunged into the water after them, throwing away the offering?

The moonlight ritual had affected Ekwenze in an unexpected way. He had hesitated at the shore for a moment, checked by the memory of the accident a few days before at that very spot, in which he had narrowly escaped drowning. However, another memory had also come to his consciousness at the same time, which completely overshadowed the dread arising from the accident. His father had a fiery temper, and Ekwenze had visions of being picked up in one hand and hurled into the river for seeming to draw back. Therefore, he quickly overcame his dread of the river and waded into the shallows, causing modest waves to break forth. These thinned into mere ripples as they fanned away from him and went chasing the opposite bank. Ekwenze was struck by the way in which the ripples had set off the white disc of the moon reflected in the water, causing it to break into an agitated dance. He waited for it to settle back into a steady position, and he found the sight which spread out before him, deep under the water, to be deeply stimulating. There was a sky high above him, and another deep below, with its shaky moon and stars; between them a sheet of clear, slightly ripply water, and himself a stump of crouching shadow. He looked at the earthen bowl he was holding in his hands, wondering whether it was big enough to cover the deep moon, for he wished to place the offerings over against it. In turning back to look at the deep sky again, he had disturbed the water surface, causing its agitation to increase ten-fold. He waited for it to settle.

The seer whispered to Obiako: 'See? He is arguing with them. They don't want to let him go!'

Obiako did not need to be told that he meant the river-spirits, for he himself had been thinking much the same thing. 'Do you want me to come to you this instant?' Obiako spoke in an intensely muted tone, so loaded with violence and menace as to cause a considerable strain to the speaker in getting it out. He finished off in the same violent tone: 'Put down that *thing* immediately, and… or else I'll come down to you with a stick!'

Startled, Ekwenze quickly lowered the dish, breaking the surface and shattering his deep sky and its moon and stars. How shocking that the beautiful under-water horizon – certainly more beautiful than the one above – should be so fragile. Maybe it only showed that the high one was equally fragile, and that one should be able to make it to break up; that is, if one really wanted to be naughty.

Without more ado, Ekwenze had placed the dish on the river-bed and waded ashore, wondering if he had been lucky in positioning it, so that when the deep moon eventually settled it would find itself looking up at his offering. His father came to the water's edge and took his hand as he came up, greatly relieved that he had been prevailed upon to give up his friendship with the river-spirits. He was taken home to a modest celebration.

However, that moonlight ritual did eventually become a key event in Ekwenze's memory, and all other memories seemed to arrange themselves in relation to it. The older the man grew, the more the incident gained in stature and significance, until it seemed to him the oldest memory – the first since his passage from infancy; the one marking his break with childhood. Ekwenze had worked with his father upon the river long before this event, but since the reincarnation ritual had been sliding back as time passed, it gradually began to seem to him that his work on the river came afterwards. It seemed to be reasonable that he couldn't have been working on the river unless a ritual had been celebrated as an inaugural event.

Ekwenze grew up to love the river. As he grew older, and the ferry business prospered, he came to be known by the nickname, 'Orimili', which was the local name of the great river. The name had stuck to him, and was used, as if it was his proper name, as well as his surname. Now that his age-mates had become part of the ruling class of elders, more and more of the townspeople were referring to him as 'Ogbuefi Orimili' or 'Ogbuefi Ekwenze Orimili' – as if he had taken the *ozo* title. Orimili appreciated this greatly, for it sounded to him as the people's voice signifying their recognition of his social worth, and assigning him a place which was his by right.

The nickname gained currency in the town mainly on account of the man's association with the river, even though most of the people thought that it referred to the supposed vastness of his wealth, namely, that it was inexhaustible, just as the great river did not shrink nor slow down, despite its having been discharging water since time began. For most of the people wouldn't have credited old Oranudu's discovery concerning the shrinkage of the great river to such an extent as to lose faith in the power of the analogy, the essential part of which was that their river was inexhaustible. However, the man himself had his own ideas about his wealth. It was all right for the river to be discharging water endlessly; he himself did not intend to be discharging money, but to be accumulating it. There had in fact been more discharge than he imagined would be absolutely safe, especially since Osita manoeuvred him into having to pay out huge sums of money every year. Because of this difference in outlook between Orimili and the great river (men were often so different from their close relatives!) he answered to the name quite straightforwardly as a man might answer his surname, if his friends preferred to address him that way. He was the offspring of the god of the river, being a river-spirit as the seer had divined, and formerly part of the retinue of the river god. The river was his element. He found such great pleasure in being in the river and sailing upon it, that he thought it was there, alone, of all places that true peace was to be had. Ekwenze felt himself to be totally at his ease, and free of all worries – certainly free of the frustrating sorts he frequently encountered in his home and among the people of Okocha. The river was a place where one sailed, silently, thoughtfully; where one heard the sounds of myriads of birds, and saw great numbers of large and multi-coloured birds; where the boat-hands talked in even tones, often not loud enough to be overheard, and then, of course, the occasional outbreak of loud laughter. When the boat was fully loaded with freight there was little space for movement and therefore, if one moved about one did so in a purposeful manner. During daylight journeys, Orimili whistled a great deal, mostly quietly to himself, feeling the atmosphere of peacefulness everywhere: in the air, in his heart, in his limbs even. One of the great reasons why he hated the mid-week market-days was that everything that made his day on the river pleasant was missing. In its place was the disconcerting play of noise and disorder.

However, for the next two passages he was to travel without passengers. And he wasn't going to have to spend a tiresome evening, before the passage itself, taking on board yams, cassava and vegetables of all sorts. What was more encouraging still, he had a contract to fetch up a huge consignment of company goods stockpiled in Okono, and each trip on this business was to be worth to him at least three market-day trips. Now, how about that? The thing was for Guy & Son to keep it coming. Should he then think of buying a larger vessel? For the sake of argument, suppose he bought a great boat that would be able to carry all the goods in the company warehouse in a single passage, what would he be doing during the interval it would take for the stores to build up again? He thought that his barge would be able to handle two times the volume of business it was doing now. Trust the old floater to take on anything and see it to a successful term!

Guy & Son was a windfall which had come personally to Ekwenze Orimili. Where would he be, he had often marvelled to himself, if he had been relying entirely on the four pence per head for the round trip to Okono, which the townspeople paid with much reluctance? Anyway, he would try to save up every penny he could from the present contract. He needed the money; after all, hadn't Osita warned that he would require a lot of money next year? How strange that he was giving him the hint exactly when the contract was being worked out, just as if he had smelled it from a long way off! Be that as it may, he wasn't going to spare a thought about that until the time came for him to do so. What, as a matter of fact, did Osita take him for? Could he be thinking that Orimili's sole mission on earth was to slave for him? Oh no; it would be a mistake to think so. No; what he must fix his attention on was the title – in case the club favoured him. If he could achieve that, he would firmly establish his family as a full member of the community. Such an achievement would be worth while in every way as a man's life's work.

He tried to figure out in his head how to deploy his funds to the utmost effect during the title conferment. It had quite become a pastime with him to reflect in this way since his friends promised to argue his case for him in the club. Starting with the down payment which was to be made in cash to the society, he passed on to the bulls both for presentation and for slaughter, then to the *okike*, the elephant tusk which was to be carried and used on ceremonial occasions as a trumpet; as he moved from one item of expenditure to another, and the total grew, so did it all seem to become more hazy in his head. So he abandoned the effort, assuring himself that he would have no difficulty adding up the total after the title had been taken, and the expenses all met. He didn't see that one could save money when one was taking a title. Could he, for instance, go without the ceremonial tusk, which was undoubtedly an option? Of course not. On the contrary, he should be prepared to do a little more than the best that had been seen so far. For example, when it came to the *okike*, should he aim at anything short of the very tallest that could be found in the market? His title was going to cost him a lot of money; no doubt of it. Also, he reminded himself, everything had to be paid for with hard cash. He could not supply even the provisions for the feasting, which lasted for weeks together. What sustained his resolution in the face of such hard thinking was the idea that this was what he was doing for his family, past and to come.

He had to do it extremely well. One of the things that came out clearly, when *ozo* was being celebrated, was the network of kinship. Everyone who was remotely connected to the man receiving the title rallied around their champion with provisions, especially raw food which was to be used for the festivity. Who had Ekwenze Orimili? Friends mainly. It didn't matter, however. Nothing must deter him. As a matter of fact, wasn't part of his scheme to show that he was more than equal to whatever demands the taking of the title would impose on him? What his townspeople must be made to perceive was that he was the one giving the feast; he, and no other. So it should be best if no one came to him with aid; best, if they were discouraged from bringing him aid.

As was the case often with Ekwenze Orimili, the ranging of his mind over the things with which he was preoccupied rarely led to any decisions. In this matter of receiving donations, for example, could he have found a way to avoid receiving help from Emenogha? Or even from such other friends as Nwalioba and Okandi Echebido? Or take the essential function of these donations as a strengthener of social bonds. To refuse gifts from anyone in such circumstances would be to undermine his real quest, which was full integration with his people. The title, after all, was also a way in which one associated oneself with a system of bonds, which reinforced the natural and friendly ones. However, Orimili had practical sense, and would have done what was expected of him at the title-taking, whether or not he understood its full significance. Was not this practical sense the very reason why he was well respected in Okocha? His never stepping on anyone's toe? No one understood better the little moral tale which his people had, about a man who had boasted that he could inter himself, without help from anyone. Challenged to show that this could be done, the fellow, being a very hard-working fellow, had quite easily made the appropriate hole in the earth, climbed in, and scooped down earth over himself. The man's boast came to nought, however, because after covering up his entire body with earth, his hand had remained upstanding over the grave. Were Orimili like the man in the parable, he wouldn't have let his unburied hand be seen so early in the game, by so openly depending on his titled friends to fight his case for him at the club.

The oppressiveness of the late afternoon heat remained at the outskirts of Ekwenze Orimili's consciousness, though it edged occasionally towards present awareness when he kicked up the hot sand, or dug his sandal into it, wedging it beneath the sole of his foot. He let his mind drift as he walked along the dusty road towards the town. He didn't need to keep his attention on the road, for he knew it so well that he was sure he could walk home without missing one step, if he were to be blindfolded. He was sure, moreover, that he would be able to remark every feature along the way, the blindfold notwithstanding.

The road formed a V with the river, having a shorter branch to the Guy & Son trading post, which met it almost at right angles. The old waterfront had been losing much of its traffic; so it was now little more than a pathway; while the Guy & Son branch seemed as if it was the main. The road ran through the centre of Okocha, and continued in a northerly direction to Amofia, where the European district officer lived. Along this road, an occasional motor car from the district office or from the Guy & Son Trading Company traversed the town, on their various errands, trailing a great wake of dust. At other times, it was the European priest, who also lived in Amofia, who thundered down the road on his motorcycle on his way to visit the school or his congregation, looking weird enough. For he always appeared in exactly the same get-up: a white helmet upon his head, his white robe gathered about his waist, revealing his black trousers, which merged with the charcoal-black machine on which he perched, the roar of which never failed to attract the children to watch him speed by, until he became a mere spectre in the distance, at the same time that the sound of his machine died.

Of all the forms of traffic on that road, lorry traffic, which was far less frequent, was the one in which Orimili took interest as most of its cargo fell naturally to him. But this afternoon, under the blazing sun and sweltering heat, he would have called a fully loaded truck a great nuisance, if it should come upon him on that dusty road. Anyway, afternoon wasn't a good time to be walking up the road. Early morning and evening were best in that one could think and consider things as one saw them, spread oneself out and welcome everything into oneself, just as a householder lounging in his parlour would welcome any one who came calling.

He brushed away the perspiration that coursed down all over his face like so many rivulets, emanating from the shining top of his head. The town was nearer now, for there was the primary school to his right. He glanced towards it. It was deserted. Soon the children would be returning for their evening catechism lessons, or to play football in the school playground. He recalled that Osita once got an ankle injury in a football match, playing for this school against Amofia. Osita had hidden the fact for two days, until his ankle was so badly swollen that he could not stand on it any more. Only then did Orimili get to know what had happened, and he had taken the boy to an orthopaedist at Amofia. After that incident, he forbade Osita to play soccer, threatening *to make him see his own ears*, if it ever came back to him that he had been seen at the game. Osita was rarely beaten by his father; in any case, not in a way to make him see his own ears. He didn't, for fear of being made to see his ears, give up playing his favourite game. He only played with greater care to avoid injury. For his part, Orimili declined to notice that his order was being disobeyed.

Fortunately, there was no further incident until Osita finished and passed out of primary school – nearly ten years ago, really. Orimili could hardly believe that it was so long ago. How quickly time passed! But he drew reassurance from the fact that in those ten years Osita had been growing into a man. Wasn't this why it was all the more natural that he should be arranging for him to settle down with a family of his own to look after?

He glanced again in the direction of the school, and was struck by the arrangement of the school-church complex. It formed a great inverted C, facing towards him. He slowed his pace to scrutinize it further. The arrangement had taken this shape only since Osita had left. For, while he was attending the school, it was a mere I-figure, lying more or less parallel to the road; then a leg was added, making a great L of the figure. Later still, the church building was set up, detached from the school at the top end of the L, jutting out, however, so that the complex acquired the C shape. Orimili now saw how clever the church people had been in locating the teachers' quarters behind the school building itself. Thus the tiny village of teachers and their families was protected behind the school-church complex. But then, that showed that they had something to hide, and they were like women, needing protection. Let them go to his place and see how things stood: his house stood facing the roadway in front. That was how a man's house should stand: with the kitchen, which belonged to the woman, hidden away and protected behind the man's house. Orimili never thought of his house without feeling a strong glow of pride warming his heart. For it was one of the largest in Okocha. He took every opportunity to show it off. Even the arrival of his son's letter was as good an opportunity as could be, and this was why he preferred that Onyeme should come to his place to read him Osita's letters.

What would happen, wondered Orimili, if the teachers should wish to breathe freely as men ought to – that is, if they were men, to begin with? The church and school would have to go. He decided to chart an imaginary line running from the outer corners of the complex towards the road. Then he became conscious that the lines were in no wise imaginary, for the entire area stretching from the school to the road belonged to the church people, and they had in fact planted a hedge to enclose the open space in front. He ought to have noticed that. The properly imaginative exercise should be to trace the lines to the waterfront. Then he saw the picture: the entire structure was gliding quietly towards the river, guided by his two imaginary lines; and then, crash! All disappeared. The river: indeed the proper place for the school to be! However, he quickly recalled that the school was actually Osita's, and also that of all the little schoolchildren of Okocha, who, as he pictured it, had been following in Osita's footsteps – all his children, really. So he relented, and permitted it to remain where it was.

He walked on, leaving the school behind. There was still a long way to go before he reached Amanza. Lifting up his eyes, he saw in the distance homesteads dotted along the road, which rose gently into the distance like a wood-brown shaft, running straight into the heart of Okocha, and beyond, into Amofia. He marvelled at the straightness of it. It was as if it had a certain purpose behind it. This road reminded him of the great river, which divided asunder what ought to have been a single land mass. Orimili rejoiced to contemplate the power of the river to prevail in keeping the two land masses separate. However, the river was not as straight as the road which rose before him; and also it was so wide that he could scarcely image it as a shaft. But the road was a long, broad lance, a powerful lance, driven into something far ahead. Orimili was standing on one end of that lance, or behind it – depending on how one looked at it.

Ekwenze Orimili made a mental map of the journey before him. He would soon begin to encounter the homesteads, and their number and density would increase as he came nearer the market square. It was at the market square that the sense of having come home to town always pervaded him. It wasn't a great distance from here to Amanza, the central square in which the great celebrations of Okocha were held. His house was a little further north of the square, along the Amofia road, but he was not going to take the risk of passing on directly to his home. For, just as it was with him when he had had a good measure to drink, he rarely felt tired at work, nor at any stage, while he was away, and was looking forward to going home. Not until he was actually home did his fatigue get the better of him. He was afraid that if he continued his journey directly home, he might find himself too weary to leave the house again. There were things yet to be done before going home, the most important of which was to call on Nduka Uwadiegwu and renew his condolence with him. That was something he should have done yesterday at the memorial, but he had missed the event. He permitted himself a smile on recalling that Nduka was now Ogbuefi, and he should get used to referring to him in those terms. Not that he anticipated meeting the young man often; quite the contrary, he scarcely knew him, and did not expect their paths to cross often unless – or rather, shouldn't he really say, *until* – he himself gained the title. It was important to get used to that manner of address, because he thought it wouldn't do at all to fail to use the proper form when their paths did cross and they had to have an exchange. He wondered now what excuse he was to offer to explain his absence at the memorial and accession. He had of course been detained at Okono for two days, repairing his barge. What made this excuse rather unsatisfactory even to Orimili himself was that it wasn't entirely accidental that the repairs took place exactly on the day the Uwadiegwus were keeping their memorial, with Nduka acceding to his father's title. He had coolly calculated that the repairs would take half a day to complete; and so he would have been able to return by nightfall yesterday, and go and see the Uwadiegwus the same evening. But the repairs had taken the whole day, and since he was to bring home a full load of company goods, he had stayed the night and had taken on the goods in the morning. Orimili had further misgivings that the towns people would sneer at the notion that he was mending his barge, saying that it showed he cared less for Okocha's communal affairs than for his own business. Some in the *ozo* might even use his absence at Nduka's induction against him. They wouldn't see that he must have been held up by something urgent: he worried so about what might be said of him. And he wouldn't let them get away with it; so, absent though they were, he nevertheless let them have it, muttering some of the words out loud; what kind of ferry would he be running anyway, if he couldn't keep his schedule? Did they think that the people down at Guy & Son would be impressed if he were to tell them that the reason he didn't bring up the stores was that he was attending an induction?

He met some of the townspeople as he came along, with whom he exchanged cheerful greetings. Approaching the square, he noticed a knot of men standing near the sacred tree at the centre of the square. This tree was an ancient landmark. It was believed to have miraculously sprung up to mark the exact spot where the founding father of Okocha had first set foot on the land. The people of Okocha did not wonder whether their father had been transported to that spot by a miracle as well, as it was difficult to see how he could have got there without traversing the space which separated it from the waterfront, perhaps along the very track on which Ekwenze was now walking. None the less, it was believed that the patriarch had come from across the river. What bothered the people of Okocha a little with regard to the sacred tree was the fact that it was believed to have been accepted by the three sons of Okocha as the point from which the three villages they founded fanned outwards, each one facing away from both the others, and sharing a common border on either side with one or the other of the sister-villages. Ebonasa, the oldest, took over the region to the north of the tree; Amanna, the region to the east and south-east; and Ugwueke, the region to the west, and south-west towards the river. In spite of this ancient arrangement, one had a fair distance to go, east or west of Amanza, before one encountered the first homesteads of Amanna or Ugwueke. The entire area surrounding Amanza *was* Ebonasa. Ogbuefi Oranudu had been applied to on a number of occasions to explain the oddity. His answer was always the same: that things had been that way from the time of Omee-Ogwali; that is to say, way back before memory began-a time which must predate the Patriarch, since history was taken to begin with him. The fact, however, was that Ebonasa constituted a good half of the town, in numbers as well as in the land area it occupied; and no one knew how this came about.

Orimili hastened his pace somewhat, to meet the people now gathered at the ancient tree, for he thought that they were speaking in earnest tones. Could some calamity have overtaken the town while he was away in Okono mending his barge? His anxiety grew as he came nearer towards the men. Soon he could hear their voices distinctly, and could detect no sign of agitation in them. But he kept his course; he could hardly turn back now after some of the men had noticed him hurrying towards them.

One or two voices saluted him as soon as he was within earshot. His spirits rose at the sound of the greetings. He called back his own greeting. One of them, Ikenna Nwozo, feeling especially cordial towards Orimili, endeavoured to engage him in a separate parley:

'In-law,' he voiced, loudly and self-consciously, 'are you working today as well? You seem to be tireless as the soil itself!'

'Not really,' replied Ekwenze; 'I got tied up at Okono; that's all. I hope that all is well in town.'

'Oh yes, of course. All is well.'

'Oh good. I was wondering that you were meeting here…'

'This? Oh, we're only trying to agree which village's turn it is to weed the square.'

'That's fine, then. I hope your people are fine; do give them my regards.'

'Yes, they are fine. Thanks. I need not ask about your own; I should say that we are the ones to answer for them as you are only just coming from Okono.'

'What's the news from Okono?'

'Nothing! Matter of fact, does anything ever happen there? Just buying and selling day in, day out. And I never see them meeting to decide whose turn it is to sweep the market square.' Laughing at his own joke, Orimili turned towards Amanna.

'You seem to have yet another business to do this evening,' Ikenna called after him. 'I'm sure I'm right that you are tireless as the soil; or should I say, the river, your namesake!'

'It isn't business, really,' answered Orimili, turning round to face Ikenna. 'I want to hurry over and greet Nduka, Ogbuefi Nduka. You probably noticed that I was absent from the celebration yesterday.'

'Oh indeed, you were missed. Have a good evening.'

Orimili turned again towards Amanna, but he had not taken a few steps before a well-known voice stopped him in his tracks. 'Father', the voice said. He swung round and saw his son, Ejike, running towards him.

'Did your mother send you on an errand? Oh, I see; you are going to the catechism class!'

'Yes.'

'That's all right then. I just wondered whether you had

turned into a young loafer, instead of helping your mother with the work at home.'

'But I did help with the work,' answered the youngster, who would have had trouble specifying the nature of the work he had done. However, he went on to explain to his father that he was indeed going to the catechism class.

Orimili was satisfied. 'Fine! Good boy!' he congratulated.

'Have you only returned from Okono just now?'

'Yes, but I must see Edoko's people before coming home. Were there any callers at the house?'

'Yes, Ogbuefi Emenogha asked us to tell you that he called to see you, and that he wishes to talk to you as soon as possible.'

Orimili made a mental note to go and see Emenogha the next day. Then he said, 'All right. Were there other callers?'

'No.'

'Fine. Hurry on to the school, so you won't be late.'

Ejike moved off towards the school, and Orimili resumed the walk to Amanna to see the bereaved family. By slow stages, his mind wandered back to the title bid; and it was in the form of a question that it broke into his consciousness: what if the titled men should turn down his application? With this, his heart gave a loud thud, which Orimili distinctly heard, feeling its pain sharp and deep. His heartbeat had quickened greatly, but it gradually slowed and returned to the normal speed, causing the pain to diminish accordingly.

He expected that the society would meet in a matter of weeks to consider his application. His anxiety should end then. He hoped that this would not be succeeded by a consciousness of defeat, which he feared would be ten times worse than the anxiety. No, the thought of a defeat could not be borne; not now that he had begun to see the title as something to give meaning to his entire life and pursuits. It seemed to him that his whole world would fail to pieces if he were to be denied. Oh, he wished he were gifted to see into the future so as to know what the peers would decide; and if it would be a nay, to know what to do to prevent it, and cause them to give an aye! That was what he needed now to make sure he wasn't denied and defeated– to defeat the very idea of defeat! Would that a miracle should happen, causing the debate itself to be overpassed, so that it would simply dawn on all concerned that Orimili was in fact a member of the club. How nice then, if the titled men returned him an answer saying that they were surprised that hitherto he had failed to take his rightful place among them! Ekwenze Orimili called upon his ancestors to help him now. This quest for the title was something he was doing not just for himself, but for them especially, and for the future generations of the children of Nwofia. They couldn't stand by, could they, to see him defeated?

Suddenly, he remembered Ejike's message that Emenogha had called to see him. How did he recall that just this instant, if it wasn't something connected with the tide? He felt that there must be a link, and was thrilled that his mind had done something uncommon, something akin to seeing into the future! But he didn't let himself be carried away by this strange trick of memory, being too preoccupied with his peril.

Was it possible that it had already been discussed at the

club? Why, had they not met to discuss Nduka's notice of accession? Of course, the young man had had to warn the titled men that he intended to join them, and since his application had been with them long before Edoko's death, they must have used the opportunity of Nduka's to discuss that as well. And hadn't they accepted Nduka? Fortunate young man! Well, wasn't the moment of accepting one candidate the most auspicious for accepting his neighbour? Dared he hope that without his suspecting it, he had been a titled man all this time he had been in Okono? How could he dare to hope? Such good things never happened to him! The joys that came his way were usually loaded with pain and suffering. Look at what he was suffering on Osita's account; yet he was the best thing that had ever come his way. How sad that he had missed the opportunity to find out whether there were grounds for hope. It was his fault, not having his senses about him, else he would have asked Ejike the mood in which Emenogha had come. Had he looked as if something bad had happened, or had he looked cheerful? There you go again, Orimili reprimanded himself; that was no question to put to a child. His best bet was to hasten his visit to Nduka, and go over directly for a chat with his friend.

Worried as he was, Orimili was determined that the people whom he met and greeted should think him his usual self, with not a worry in the world. So he always looked up with a smile at the sound of a greeting, and endeavoured to exchange pleasantries in a lively manner. He turned away from the main Amanna road into the bypath that led to Uwadiegwu's place. Soon he was within sight of Obikeze Uwadiegwu's hut. He was quite sure that he hadn't a moment to stop for a chat with the old dweller-alone, Edoko's elder brother, who made his living as a diviner. Ekwenze had things on his mind about which he must consult Obikeze. Quite obviously, this was not the time for such a consultation. Maybe after his next trip to Okono? Yes, just as today – come straight from the waterfront to have the consultation. There should be sufficient time then, since he knew from experience that Obikeze's Arobinagu, the god of divination, took a whole evening to consult. He did not like hurried interviews. Having been dealing with his Arobinagu for a great many years, Obikeze had imbibed the same unhurried manner, and conducted friendly chats in such a way that it appeared that there could be no other business which had a claim on the well-wisher's time. Therefore, Orimili had no desire to encounter the old man this evening. As he came closer to the old man's hut, he fixed his gaze straight before him, as if a glance in the direction of the hut was all that was needed to call the old man's attention to the passer-by. However, Obikeze did not need Orimili's glance to see who was passing. Since he happened to be in his front yard at the moment, all he needed to do to make him look his way was to shout a greeting. Obikeze did this the moment he saw Orimili.

Upon hearing the old man's greeting, Orimili felt momentarily vacuous in the bowels. Nevertheless, he contrived to swing round as if spontaneously, and to respond to the greeting with a show of surprise: 'Ah, Ogbuefi Obikeze, it's you indeed! I'm sorry I wasn't attentive. I had half expected to see you at Edoko's place. Tell me, how are…'

Obikeze did not hear the rest of the question, for he was mildly stung by the suggestion that he might be seen at his brother's place: 'Ah! You were going to Edoko's place to see *me*? Strange – and disappointing! I should have thought that you were one of my well-wishers. Is it not sufficient that, like everyone else, I attended the funeral and memorial observances? Why should I move my dwelling to Edoko's compound?' He sighed, looked away briefly, preparatory to changing the subject; then he rejoined, 'Why should we talk about these things, when there are a great many other things which are so much more interesting? Tell me how you have been. How was work today? Did you travel?'

'Oh yes, I did. In fact, I am just on my way home from Okono, having been delayed there for two whole days.'

'Delayed? Yes, I thought I didn't see you at the ceremonies yesterday, and it would be unlike you not to attend.'

'That's right,' answered Orimili, gratified, and moving a little closer to Obikeze. 'I had expected that at the very worst I should be able to return to Okocha by midday yesterday, and be here for the main part of the action in the afternoon. As it turned out, however, I couldn't get back to town until this very moment.'

'What happened?' asked Obikeze, interest mounting.

'It was my boat, and it was giving me trouble. I just had to get it checked out and repaired.'

'Is it all right now?'

'Oh yes. I got it fixed.'

'I'm glad that it is all fixed. Why don't you come inside so that we shall break a kola over that?'

Ekwenze was sorry at this, remembering that he had to

call on Nduka as well as Emenogha. Still one could hardly decline Obikeze's invitation. What explanation could one give? That one had something more important to do?

'All right,' he answered, 'if you insist.'

'Yes, I do insist. Come inside, and rest a while. Didn't you say you had just come from Okono?'

Orimili seated himself on a goatskin mat upon a narrow mud bed which ran along the wall on the far side of Obikeze's sitting room. Obikeze took his seat in his favourite place beside his diviner's gear and reached for his goatskin bag, into which he dug his hand to rummage for a kola nut. He found one, and presented it to his guest. Orimili expressed his thanks, and asked him to say the grace.

Obikeze picked up the nut, and called upon the god of divination, Arobinagu, before whom both the past and the future were spread open at all times, requesting him to look kindly upon Orimili, who had come to pay his respects. He might find it useful to grant him a glimpse into his future course – was there a human being who didn't at all times stand in need of such guidance from the god of divination? For what one needed to lead a happy life, the seer pointed out to his god, was the vision, by means of which one made the correct choices that kept one along the path already marked out for one. Was it not the Arobinagu himself who had taught them that 'Iruka' was a fitting name for a child, reminding them to look ahead at all times? And did he not also teach that a single day yet to come was everything, while four hundred years already come and gone were nothing? Orimili already knew a good deal about his past; what should be of benefit to him now was to show him something of the future – something towards which to plan or strain. What was life, if not that strain towards the future?

He went on to pray for the well-being of Orimili's family, mentioning Osita in particular, who had travelled abroad. For Osita was as an orphan out there; and it was part of the Arobinagu's solicitude for the people of Okocha to care for the lonesome and be a parent to them. (Orimili nodded his complete agreement.) Obikeze also commended the rest of the family to his god, to care for, and to protect; so that on his rejoining them Osita would find them no worse than they were when he left them.

Ekwenze Orimili smiled with understanding when he heard the kindly old man pray that the Arobinagu should accompany Orimili in all his journeys upon the river to be his pillar of strength, should the river god turn treacherous, as he often did to swimmers and boatmen. He must be ready at all times to baffle Orimili, the river god, and ensure that Ekwenze Orimili had nothing but good fortune, wherever he sailed, up or down the river. Obikeze was also mindful of the young schoolchildren of the town, calling on the Arobinagu to be vigilant over them, and be sure to erase from their minds anything they learned in the school which would not conduce to their good. The Arobinagu should instruct them ceaselessly, using dreams and flashes of insight, to show them the way to success.

He broke the kola nut, took a piece of it for himself and passed the rest to Orimili. They both tore off a tiny piece from their share of the nut, which they threw outside, with invocations murmured to the ancestors. This must have made up for the old man's neglect of the ancestors in his prayer.

They ate the kola in silence, while Orimili wondered whether the Arobinagu had revealed something about him to Obikeze for which he was pressing him so hard to make an enquiry.

When the old man finished his kola, he arranged his diviner's lots which lay before him. Orimili felt entrapped. Surely, the Arobinagu could see that the time wasn't right for that business. What might help him now, he considered, was to declare himself in need of the Arobinagu's guidance; then bid for time. So he let Obikeze see a little into his mind:

'There are a few problems nagging at my mind. I must sort them out with you some time, perhaps tomorrow.'

'Yes, of course; any time. It isn't something to do with your boat, the one over which you got held up at Okono?'

'Oh no. That was ordinary maintenance. Part of the cargo hold had to be replaced, that was all.'

'The cargo hold?'

'Yes,' Orimili casually said. 'Of course, the boatyard people always contrive to drag out even the minutest repair work, so that it continues for days on end.'

'Do they have other business apart from mending boats? Why shouldn't they hang on to one that comes their way? There aren't so many boats around, are there? In this whole town, after all, there is only yours to speak of.'

'I suppose that that's what it is,' answered Orimili, flattered. 'But there are lots of boats in Okocha, I can assure you.'

'Did they tell you why the bottom of yours was decaying?'

'The wood, of course; you know, being in water day in, day out. That sort of thing happens every so often.'

'Did they tell you that boats were meant to be left hanging in the air? Of course, they have to be in water, if they are boats. You mean, that you didn't think that there was more to the decay of the bottom of your barge? Then why did it affect only a part, and not the whole? I should say that it is odd, my friend. You think that a disease which takes hold of a man's heart could mean it as a joke! Sometimes, there are signs hidden in things that seem perfectly ordinary. You know, a woman came to me the other day, lamenting her ill-fortune and blaming it on her guardian spirit. Her daughter had convulsions, you see. But this woman had earlier dreamt of a kite carrying off her hen – a hen, mind you. She did nothing about it until her child became ill. I told her that she was the one betraying her guardian spirit. Hadn't she been given enough warning?'

Orimili agreed that the thing was worth looking into, but that there was no point in taking his problems piecemeal. The best thing was to bring the entire thing in a bundle, as it were, to Obikeze tomorrow, and he would see what he could do to sort it all out. He had been distracted these two or three days and hadn't collected his thoughts together for the interview he knew he must have with the diviner. He was also pressed for time now.

Obikeze didn't take him up immediately, but watched him for some time, and then said, 'You know, you look worried!' He leaned forwards as if ready to sally into Orimili's very soul. However, his first question didn't look like the feared probe: 'You are happy with the other aspects of your business?'

Not wishing his worries to be looked into just yet, he

was glad enough to give his host a well-rehearsed answer about his business: 'There isn't much to complain about, except that things tend to be unsteady; you know, up and down. So, one is not always as happy, all the time, as one would like to be. It is in the nature of the business, however,' he made haste to point out. 'One has to wait for a market-day and, if one is lucky, one may have a reasonably good day. For the rest, it is a matter of picking up an odd contract here and there, trying to fill in what will otherwise be empty days. All went well yesterday at the memorial, I suppose? I couldn't attend, of course. It must have been a deal of strain attending to all the mourners.'

'Yes, yes,' said Obikeze, 'it was quite hectic. As to the strain, well, we all do what seems right to us, whether or not it is noticed. That is how it is between me and my relatives. What am I to them, after all, except a nuisance…?'

'No, they can't think that!' Orimili interrupted, with a show of being shocked.

'Oh yes, they do. Yet I'm sure that I owe them nothing. Nor have I ever asked any of them for help. It is all hatred; pure hatred. Many of them must wish me dead! And one of these days…'

'No, don't!' Orimili broke in again. 'No one could wish you such evil.' It was not only the appalling supposition that he wished to discourage his host from entertaining, but also he was quite frantic to save himself from being dragged into listening yet again to Obikeze's misfortunes: how his family of three sons had been wiped out by smallpox, together with their mother; how his relatives seemed to suspect him of protecting himself with magic, while giving no thought to his dependants. How it was that to fail to have children of one's own was to count for nobody in Okocha. Orimili was anxious not to hear of these things because he didn't know what to do to help. He didn't see how it could help merely to listen. It would be mean to listen, but do nothing afterwards; as if in listening, one took an indecent pleasure. Obikeze's experience with his relatives was like inflicting punishment on someone for surviving an epidemic. The destruction of an entire household in one epidemic was a terrible blow indeed. Did it not follow, then, that the entire neighbourhood should rally round the sufferer of that dreadful blow? Well, not in the thinking of Obikeze's relatives! Orimili was sorry for the man, and shocked to think how unfeeling the people were.

Apparently, Obikeze had been rejected to show their disappointment that he had lost his dependants. Now, if one did not look too closely at the circumstances of the case, allowed Orimili, there was no question, the relatives had a point in their favour. For they were showing how they had prepared the ground for a harvest of a large kindred, and showing further that Obikeze's family was not strictly his, but theirs. Orimili understood this very well on account of his own experience; being the sole roof over the heads of everybody that belonged to him, instead of being one of the roofs, protected in his turn by a series of other roofs, each one larger and less prone to springing a leak than the one beneath it. On that same basis of their communal sense, weren't they outdoing themselves to make one of their own virtually kinless and roofless?

Here was a man who helped others in their troubles and

fears– and made a living out of that, one must add – but then couldn't find a single soul to help in his own trouble. Tragedies such as Obikeze's should not happen at all; and if they did happen, Orimili felt it would be better for everyone to know nothing of them. What could one do when one knew? Grant the old man a new set of relatives? Make the old ones kinder? He himself might do with some fine relatives; at any rate, he stood in need of kindness from the *ozo* people. But would they show it? So whenever Obikeze sauntered into that dismal history, Orimili made haste to drag him out of it. The result was that he never came to know the full story. Had he let Obikeze ramble off for once unchecked, he might have learned that the man's punishment for losing his family had originally involved a total excommunication; and none of his relatives could speak to him nor help him in any way, nor yet receive any help from him. He had been forced out of the common property of the family, and had had to move his dwelling to the farthest part of the property, where he had been allowed a tiny portion of land on which to build his homestead. Further, when he had attempted to remarry, his relatives had hastened to inform his prospective in-laws that they themselves would not trust their daughter or, for that matter, any living human being, to that relative of theirs. They also let fall a hint to the effect that the innocent young wife would be hardly freer to come and go among the kindred than Obikeze himself. That decided the issue. The young woman's family would have nothing further to do with Obikeze. He had gradually regained some of his rights in the family, largely because he was said to be highly favoured by the god of divination and had continued to be patronized by the rest of the village.

Orimili could look upon himself in his own troubles and judge himself happy, compared to Obikeze. What could be worse than having no successor? Suppose some accident were to overtake Osita (he deprecated the evil spirit who had brought such an idea to his mind, however), would he dare, upon his death, announce his arrival in the land of the ancestors? He shuddered involuntarily. Nevertheless, he strongly admonished his host not to be resentful, since that was like eating oneself. And he pursued:

'You cannot blame those who have passed away for passing away; it was not their fault – and it was nobody's fault. Should you then be resentful on their behalf? Are they not the more fortunate for not being here to contend with these hard and changed times? Just mind yourself; and do not allow the past to weigh you down. As to your relatives, I assure you that it is a renegade who would have nothing in common with their own relative, and such a one should be treated with scorn!'

Orimili's closing proverb might have been ambiguous, if the man to whom he was speaking wasn't sure of his being partial towards him. There wasn't the least doubt in his mind that Orimili was saying that the Uwadiegwus were guilty of neglect of Obikeze, and that in this they had forfeited their right to be thought well of. Were the other Uwadiegwus present, it would have made perfect sense to them also, as nothing could have shown more clearly how well they got on than that they didn't discriminate against him at the funeral and memorial observances; thus Orimili's proverb would have made them even more dignified than before.

Obikeze took admonitions very well – a good thing for one who lived by advising others. Of course, his tormentors were beneath his notice, he assured Orimili. He went on then to enquire about Osita, 'his' favourite child. Had the young man been heard from in recent times? And was he continuing to do well?

Orimili confirmed that his son had in fact been heard from quite recently.

'Good!' Obikeze exclaimed. 'Did he say that all was well with him?'

'Yes, he says he's fine, and sends his regards.'

'He will finish next year, isn't it? He must make haste and come home, so I can see him before I go to the fathers.'

'He'll come, don't worry. And you needn't be in a haste to go and see the fathers. Have you considered what we will be doing for divination, if you were to hurry off?'

'So you think I should go on living?' Obikeze beamed back at his visitor.

'What do you mean? Why shouldn't you go on?'

'Yes, because of the young; such young ones as Osita; yes. I don't know whether they would want anything with people like us; but I do want to see what they will do when they look around and see that they are the only ones standing, and that the moonlight is entirely for them, beckoning them to do their dance! You are a happy man to have such a fellow as Osita in the forefront.' Entranced, he made an invocation: 'No harm shall ever touch him!' (The people of Okocha uttered a great many of their blessings in the negative.) 'Higher and higher he shall climb, and never fall! The ancestors of Okocha are sure to be with him wherever he is, and whatever he is doing!'

'So be it,' cried Orimili, increasingly light-hearted with their talk centring on his favourite theme. 'We all pray that he may hold firm. Be sure that I shall mention you to him in my next letter as a special well-wisher.'

Orimili's words did not half-convey his gratitude towards Obikeze for blessing his son. He felt so uplifted that the cares which previously weighed him down were all forgotten. Even his sense of haste was gone. He reached abruptly into his pocket in search of a coin, hearing the jingle of which, Obikeze looked away. Orimili drew a few coins from his pocket, selected one, and placed it on the ground before Obikeze.

The diviner raised his eyes towards Orimili's face in a questioning manner.

'About my son,' said Orimili simply, in answer to the unspoken question.

'You mean Osita?'

'That's right. It is said that one does not forebode a misfortune happening to another unless one is closely related to that other. So I suppose it is natural I should worry about him. But as you say, one can never be sure of these things. He tells me in every letter that all is well with him. I want to be sure that he is not merely being dutiful, and trying to save me from worry. For example, he says in his letter that he has something interesting to communicate in his next letter! Why not communicate it straightaway, if it was interesting indeed? Mayn't he have been sick all the time he was assuring me that he was well, and is now beginning to feel the danger past, and ready to talk about it? I hope that my fears are groundless; and that is what I wish to make sure of.'

'The gods and fathers of Okocha will keep their favourite son from harm; be sure of that. However, it is good to keep in consultation with the Arobinagu so that should there be anything required by the gods to help them, so to speak, in doing what they do naturally, one should know that and make haste to supply what is needed.'

Obikeze shifted in his seat, to adjust to a more comfortable position. Whatever was in the interest of Osita Orimili had to be dealt with, allowing not the least delay that could be prevented.

He cast the lots and scrutinized them for a while. He repeated the operation, and then lifted up his eyes to study Orimili's countenance, as if some of the mysterious information which the Arobinagu vouchsafed was displayed to the diviner upon that face. Orimili returned him a questioning stare, wondering whether he was being called upon to put down another coin. The mute exchange lasted only a moment. Then Obikeze resumed casting the lots.

Obikeze looked up again, after some moments of intent gazing upon the lots before him. 'Osita's reincarnation rites, were they performed?'

'No,' answered Orimili, holding his breath in sudden alarm.

'Were they not?' repeated Obikeze, gazing intently upon

Orimili. He was quite a different person from the chatty and complaining old man that had been talking to Orimili all evening.

'No,' Orimili tried to be firm. 'The rites were not performed, for Osita was a strong and healthy child. There didn't seem to be any need to enquire whether or not he had use of the rites.'

Obikeze nodded mysteriously, cast his lots again, studied them briefly, and looked up again with a frown: 'Look, Orimili, cast your mind back to Osita's earliest days. Can't you recall such a rite being performed for him? You can't be so forgetful as to recall nothing of it.'

Orimili directed his gaze to the ground before him, as though his memory were located there. But there was nothing to decipher on the spot, just as there was nothing in his memory to recall. There had been no reincarnation rites for Osita. Orimili was becoming panicky, and his entire body jerked convulsively with the quickened beating of his heart. He had failed in a capital duty. Had some harm overtaken the child as a result? Or was it lying in wait like a serpent, ready to strike?

He looked up again, and answered with a remarkably parched throat, 'No! No rites of that sort were performed for my son. Er…' He stopped and considered. No, Ekesi wouldn't have done it without letting him know.

'Yes?' prompted Obikeze.

'Er… I was thinking of his mother. But what mother would do a thing like that, without her husband knowing? Certainly not Ekesi. No, there was no reincarnation ritual.'

'All right,' conceded Obikeze. 'You do not know that

Osita is a water-spirit, and of the party of the god of the mighty river?'

Orimili's eyebrows ascended by another fraction to what was probably the highest level they could reach. There was surprise in that expression, as well as relief. For he saw how true it was that his son should belong to the party of the river god. How could it be otherwise? It was quite impossible – the metaphor leapt effortlessly to his mind – that the issue of a mother snake could be any other than a worm-like creature. The wonder was that it never did occur to him that his son belonged with him to the party of Orimili, the mighty river god. Be this as it may, the kinsman of the god of the great river did not jump with gladness that Osita was also a kinsman of the god, and was thus a privileged person; nor did he render thanks to Obikeze and his Arobinagu for bringing him the rare intelligence. Orimili did none of those things; he didn't even announce that having got his fill of good news for the evening, he should now proceed to Edoko's place. What Orimili did was to reach into his pocket for another coin; placing it before Obikeze, he requested him to investigate the matter a little further, and tell him whether his son was in any form of danger as a result of his having failed all those years to perform the proper rites on his behalf.

Obikeze was glad to oblige. It did not take him much effort this time to discern that Osita was in no danger at the present, but that sacrifices were to be offered to the river god, and to the ancestors, so that they may not become hostile when they saw the young man return to Okocha.

'Are you sure,' insisted Orimili, 'that he is safe this moment?'

'Ha! ha!' laughed Obikeze, in triumph. 'Can't you see how the lots are disposed? It's so plain! I told you that our gods and ancestors are very proud of him; and, were they to become hostile at some stage, their object would not be Osita, but you yourself. Are you surprised at that, Orimili? Are they not right to expect you to know better?'

'Something can be done about this?'

'Certainly, every illness has a…'

'Fine!' cried Orimili. 'It is a small matter to arrange sacrifices. I shall see you again soon for that.'

It was getting to sundown when Orimili finally left Obikeze. Now, with a great piece of work behind him, it didn't seem reasonable to insist on pursuing his fixtures for the evening to the very last – right up to seeing Emenogha. There was a limit to the amount of work one could do in a single day. What he ought to do was to end his day out after seeing Edoko's people.

Orimili was thinking as he regained the pathway to Edoko's place how fortunate it was that Obikeze had been in his front yard and had seen him passing. He grinned an absolution upon himself for his (fortunately unsuccessful) attempt to pass by the old man's house without stopping to exchange greetings. He shouldn't blame himself for trying so hard not be seen by Obikeze, because if he had a schedule, it was only right that he should strive to fulfil it. The schedule! Pursue one's schedule, never looking sideways, until one ran one's right eye into the pointed end of a bamboo shaft that had snapped free of a newly made fence and was pointing directly into one's face as one came up the path. Orimili had become fully conscious of such a lethal-looking protrusion from a fence running along the side of the pathway. He gave it a wide berth. What would happen if someone was coming up the pathway in darkness? He stopped; went back to the fence, and broke the bamboo back in.

Another thing was his reply to Osita, which he was going to dictate to Onyeme Umunna at the earliest opportunity. Osita would probably think nothing of the revelation he had received from Obikeze's Arobinagu: typical of young people today not to care about such fundamental things. Anyway, that was their privilege for having fathers who would look after that end of things for them. Suppose he refused altogether to carry out the reincarnation ritual on his return? How dare Osita? Well, Ekwenze Orimili would make him! What he must bear in mind to tell in his next letter was about the war the white people were fighting. He visualized it as a dispute between two English kings, one of whom, he had learned, was called Hitler. Orimili was terrified to think that being the adventurous fellow he was, Osita might get himself mixed up in the war – to his own cost, and to his father's everlasting curse! Osita must be warned to steer clear of that war.

Orimili began to wonder, earnestly, what must be the cause of the war among the Europeans in their own homeland. Perhaps one city had been outraged by the killing of one of their own people by those of another city, causing the aggrieved one to retaliate by killing off a citizen of the other. Perhaps the victim this time was found to be too important a person to be lightly sacrificed for the first. The sort of thing had once happened in Okocha itself; wasn't that how the war with Amofia had started, in which his grandfather...? However, the European war was said to be a great war, and similar to the one which they had fought a generation previously. He shrugged. Weren't they satisfied with one great war in a lifetime? Why start all over again after every generation? He saw them now ranged in the grassland border region between Okocha and Amofia, in two great formations facing each other, in white topees and starch-stiffened, white khaki jackets, shining with extreme high temperature ironing, the folds and edges pressed straight, thin and sharp. Oh yes; now that he had placed the battle in a definite scene in his own mind, he was sure that he knew what the trouble was. They must have been struggling over land, just the same way Ogbuefi Nwalioba and Ogbuefi Ikedi might have to fight it out, if they didn't watch out. Orimili's eyes were now blinking repeatedly. He knew then that he had been staring with great concentration into nothing, while his imagination elaborated the images of conflict. Quickly, his mind flashed back over the last few moments and reassured him that he hadn't encountered anyone since leaving Obikeze. For he thought that his attitude in meditation must have been weird enough to cause anyone who encountered him to wonder whether all was well with him.

He returned to the letter which he must send out to Osita, and it made him glad to think that he too had something very interesting to mention to him. He was now disposed to smile that he and Osita would be swapping happy tidings in their next letters. Well, he would see what Osita should have, to beat what he himself had! What could possibly be nicer than Adoba, or equally nice even? Yes, why not? Make a competition of it, since he was sure to win! So, boy, you'd better be good with this wonderful news of yours, or I'll knock you flat with mine!

By the way, Adoba, and her mother… what was he saying? Of course, the whole family; just ask Emenogha to bring his family to the festive sacrifices to be celebrated for Osita. Perhaps by that time he would have got off his letter, and let him know that he now had a great responsibility and – with a baleful frown – that the days of adventure were over. Ekwenza Orimili was pleased to think that Osita would be proud of him for taking so keen an interest in his well-being. What young man would not be grateful to a man taking upon himself the task of finding him a suitable partner? And he had found for him the very best possible! Adoba was so full of life, so charming and well-behaved! He even ventured to hope that she would be to him nearly as Ekesi had been to Orimili himself.

So Orimili's thoughts had returned to Ekesi, another of the great themes of his reveries. The woman had died over fifteen years previously, while Osita was a little boy.

During all those years, her image had grown in his mind until he was certain that she was everything he ever wanted in his helpmate. At some of his more serene moments he had tried to reify in his consciousness her gentle ways. He was never completely satisfied with the result. Whether this failure was owing to the fact he did not appreciate her sufficiently while she had been alive, or because the woman herself was too full of goodness for any mind whatever to be able to recreate, for its own contemplation, her perfection,

Orimili could never make out. Sometimes it seemed to him that it was the one; at other times, that it was the other. Thinking of her now, Orimili shook his head gravely, overcome with sadness as he recalled the curious dream he had had some days before, in which he had seen Ekesi sitting in the distance, with Osita, a five-year-old, upon her knee. Ah! If only the recollection had come while he was with Obikeze. He wondered why the Arobinagu had said nothing about the dream. Perhaps it didn't augur any evil for Osita.

What a vision it had been, really! How clearly it had portrayed Ekesi as a mother! Striking – and quite natural too – that she should appear with the only child she ever had. How hard she had desired to have other children; but the gods had not gratified those wishes. Orimili felt himself to be in the mood to say to the gods, fine, if Osita was all that they were disposed to give. But, ever-living gods, why strike her down? What fault had she committed? Or rather – lest the gods take offence – Ekesi! Why didn't you remain, then, eh, Ekesi? Two of them together with Osita were happy enough together. They shouldn't have needed all those babies who never saw the light of day, and yet drove her to an early grave! His sadness became tinged with remorse. He shook his head again. Then he had a private revelation from Obikeze's Arobinagu. He was sure that there was no mistake about it. Hadn't the Arobinagu seen through Orimili's forgetfulness, into what was actually bothering him? Quite obviously, Ekesi would not be appearing with her child if she didn't mean it as a warning to him that there was something which might hurt the child. Hence she was holding him in a protective manner. It meant that there was something menacing him, which he had to be shielded from. Orimili berated himself for not hastening to consult Obikeze as soon as he had had the vision. He also murmured his thanks to Ekesi for remaining watchful over Osita, beseeching her not to take offence at his failure to take the apparition seriously. He thanked her especially for imparting some of her goodness, just a little bit, to Osita, assuring her that this act of kindness was in fact his mainstay.

Orimili was in the mood to atone for all his failings, of which he had recalled a recent one. Didn't Okuata ask him to buy her a head-cloth? Now, where was it? What excuse was he going to make for failing to buy it this time, after spending two whole days at Okono? All right. Next time; unfailingly. Having made this resolution, he endeavoured to rally his spirits by dwelling on the delightful twilight, which he had just noticed. He took a deep breath in the mild evening air, and felt happy and renewed. How different from the terrible heat of the afternoon; he felt he could keep walking for two days more, if the atmosphere remained exactly as it was now.

He entered Edoko's parlour, which Nduka had now taken over, and he found the latter seated before a low table, on which was a vessel containing some money. Evidently, Nduka had been receiving visitors all day, and they had been giving him presents in the form of money. So everybody was showing him good will. That was as it should be. Nduka also placed his chalk-caked feet in such a way as to be easily noticed by the visitor, the chalk being a symbol of his recent induction into the fellowship of title-holders. About his ankles were thick white cotton threads – he would wear such threads at all times, even on the farm, to remind him of his status. Behind him stood his father's enormous elephant tusk, beside which was his crimson cap, to which was attached a tall white eagle-feather; and he himself was dressed in flowing white wrappers. He appeared magnificent in the get-up. Rather young-looking, now clean-shaven and handsome with his longish face, eyes slightly sunken from the stress of bereavement and sleeplessness.

Nduka picked up his white leather fan to exchange a formal salute with Orimili, but the latter halted at the doorway, surveyed the magnificent figure for a few moments, and hailed him by his full titles:

'Ogbuefi Nduka, *ogalanya nwata*!'

'Orimili, *ogalanya*!' Nduka called back.

'Uwadiegwu, *ogalanya ngada*!'

'Eh! Ogbuefi Orimili *atu nnu*!'

Orimili advanced towards Nduka, arm outstretched; slapped the side of Nduka's fan three times with the back of his hand, and once with his palm.

'Hearty congratulations!' he hailed again.

'Thank you, and welcome!'

'It's wonderful to see you fully rigged out in *ozo* attire. I am glad everything went very well for you yesterday. So sorry to have missed it. My, the attire does become you!'

'Oh, really? I'm delighted to hear you say so. Very kind of you to call. You were missed yesterday, of course, but seeing you here now quite makes up for the absence yesterday.' Nduka then called for a kola nut, and when it was brought to him directed that it should be placed before Orimili to say the grace. Orimili gracefully declined the honour. It was the prerogative of the master of the house, he maintained, and he would be honoured to partake of kola blessed by the new Ogbuefi.

'It is very nice of you to say this,' answered Nduka, 'but I mustn't permit you to persuade me that it is all right for me to presume to bless the kola, with you looking on.'

'Still, it falls to you as a natural right.'

'Please do not insist. It is simply beyond my power to do as you suggest. How indeed can you seriously mean that? I'm sure that you will not ask your son Osita to do the kola ritual; what good is it having older men in our midst, if they won't bless kola for us, and speak health and peace on us?'

Orimili was impressed by Nduka's behaviour. He accepted the honour to preside at the ritual. As soon as he picked up the kola, however, he remembered that there was something to make up to the great river god, his protector. Obikeze's prayer earlier that evening had had references to that divine that would not have proceeded from the lips of a worshipper.

He lifted up the nut, and intoned:

> We pray for life and success;
> And we pray for faith in our land,
> And people, and friends.
> We thank the gods who care for us and sustain us
> Orimili, River god and Father,
> Unfailing source of life and fertility for our soil;
> We should be lost, and hopeless.

But for your diverse gifts.
Our Soil, of course,
To us what air is to a bird, and water to a fish;
Mother, far greater than all;
Birthplace of life, which we hold,
And will return at last to you;
Bestower of the sacred rank
The which invests Nduka our friend,
Grant that he in it may thrive.

Orimili felt that he had said enough, and had the nut shared out. He cleared his throat to speak, but Nduka suggested that Orimili should have a drink of wine before he commenced. The man hesitated, believing that a certain sullenness had come through in Nduka's tone of voice. As a matter of fact, the enthusiasm that was written all over him at the start seemed to have dampened, and he wasn't as bright as before. Orimili put it down to the dusk that was quickly gathering outside, and dismissed the edge in his titled friend's voice as the consequence of a sudden recollection. Indeed, had he so quickly forgotten the young man's grievous loss? Well, if he had been carried away by Nduka's splendid attire, it didn't mean that the young man himself had equally been carried away to the extent of forgetting his loss and the new burdens it imposed on him. Orimili took the wine, but he changed his mind concerning the remark with which he was going to open their conversation. Instead of speaking about the induction, he launched out in an exhortation.

'I'm grateful, Ogbuefi Nduka, for your large-heartedness,

which you have kept up even in this season of mourning. I understand the pain which is felt at the death of one's father. It is deep, nevertheless you mustn't forget that you have a duty to bear up like a man. Are you not the one to sustain the courage of your brother and sisters, and your mother too? It is a pity that you are being called upon so early in life to play this role, when some of your age-mates are yet single and free. But it isn't your fault, nor that of anyone; except the haughty shamelessness of Death. That is why the Hoar, unable to find old men of suitable age whose hair to take over and colonize, has lighted upon the heads of the young! You must bear up, for your people are looking up to you for guidance. And, what is more, the title itself which you now hold raises you, despite your youth, to the condition of an elder, and the upholder of the tradition. So there is much to draw strength from, in order not to surrender to grief.'

The speech, however, confused Nduka. There was a filthy story going around, which said that Nduka had sold part of his patrimony in exchange for the title, and people were laughing at him, even though he hadn't sold someone else's patrimony, but his own. Not knowing what had happened, Orimili had been making a eulogy to the Soil and goddess of Okocha during his blessing of the kola, causing his host to suspect that it was meant as a reflection on him. Then Orimili had given his exhortation, which sounded honest enough, and was altogether lacking in ambiguity. His comments about the young man's responsibility in the family could easily have been used to introduce the mocking tone, for which Nduka was on the lookout, still he kept the tone even and well-meaning. Whatever the case, he knew he wasn't alone in having filthy stories going around about him. He had heard about Orimili's bid for the title, and the controversy it had aroused. Let him dare laugh at him, and he would deal him a blow, sharp and stinging: what business had he with patrimonies, having none himself!

He said to his visitor: 'Thanks very much for your fine words. I am doing my best to master the situation. As to leadership, how can one lead, unless the people who are to be led agree to come along?'

He watched Orimili, who was struck by the way Nduka was echoing Obikeze. If he were following the seer's advice, and was therefore circumspect and suspicious, he should have concluded from this coincidence that there was something deeply wrong with the Uwadiegwus. However, he wasn't at all suspicious; and, anyway, here was a game he had entered into with Nduka, not knowing that a game was on and not knowing the rules. It was his turn now to play: he did.

'Yes, it is difficult at the start, but you'll get used to your loss, and I'm sure that sooner rather than later your people will also get used to the fact that you are Edoko's successor. I'd say that they'll be the ones asking you to take them along.'

'Tell me, is it possible to get all the members of a large family to see eye to eye on an issue of importance, especially when outsiders are standing by ready with contrary advice?'

'How can things of that sort be happening so soon?'

'But they are!'

'Oh, that's shameful! I suppose that all your people can do about that is to try to stick together. It won't be long before the outsider notices, to his own confusion, that no one pays him heed.'

Nduka saw how it stood: Orimili knew nothing of the land deal. His suspicion did flare up again when, later in their conversation, Orimili likened the condition of the recently bereaved to that of a young bride, who has to habituate herself to new farmlands, new springs and streams, and new people and conditions, having broken, so to speak, with the land of her birth and upbringing.

Orimili employed many more equivocal images in his responses to Nduka that evening, risking each time the full blast of the bolt which his host had kept in readiness for him. But he remained equivocal enough to keep Nduka hesitant about unleashing it.

He emerged at last from Nduka's magnificent presence into a pleasant moonlight. Just before he regained the footpath on which he had come, he discerned the stooping figure of Obinagu Nwalioba walking down the pathway, with his characteristic long, swinging gait which covered much ground and yet seemed to cost him no effort at all. He was apparently on his way home to Ugwueke. He must have been visiting someone in Edoko's village. Orimili hailed him, and they shouted greetings while he hastened up to meet the man on the pathway. Ah, it was a relief that he was going to have a companion for the long walk to Amanza. It turned out, however, that Nwalioba was to stop over to consult Obikeze's Arobinagu before continuing his journey home. He had been visiting someone in the village.

Nwalioba was glad to see Orimili. Meeting him now

reminded him of the debate at the club over his application, but he wouldn't for all the world mention it to Orimili. How was he going to explain the argument of the other side, even without going into details? No, he wouldn't be dragged into the matter on any account. He must find something to keep them talking, anything that would keep them away from the issue of the debate.

'Oh, you have been visiting Nduka,' he remarked; 'what do you think of him?'

'Nduka is doing his best to cope with a loss which I think he feels very deeply. It appears to me that he is also deeply worried. I think that it should do him good if his more elderly relatives rally together around him, to help him through this difficult period.'

'On the contrary, it appears to me that his relatives are nothing to him. I bet his brother was not with him when you called, was he?'

'Indeed, no!'

'There you are! It was evident during the induction rites that a rift had developed between them. But then, quarrels are common among close relatives in moments of bereavement, since everybody has their own particular ways of doing things. This was what we were all saying among ourselves. But how wrong we were.'

He hung fire.

'A serious quarrel, then?'

'Very serious; you'll be shocked to hear it.'

'Really? With their father having scarcely breathed his last?'

A sneer from Obinagu Nwalioba. 'Their father? The

ancients were wise, I tell you. Have you never heard of Edoko's abomination against his brother, Obikeze?'

'Yes, yes!'

'Then, why are you surprised at what the young people are doing to each other? Isn't it like being surprised to observe that the issue of a mother-snake is string-like?'

'Most extraordinary!'

'Well, this is a new age; and they have introduced a new twist into their old game. Nduka auctioned off a piece of their common land and seems not to have consulted Nzeadi nor any of the family.' Orimili gaped.

'Sold their common land?' he stuttered at last. 'But why?'

'You ask me why?' Nwalioba was sometimes very caustic. One would think from his tone that Nduka Uwadiegwu had offended him particularly. But it was only because the person he would have enjoyed slashing away at was not immediately available. Nduka was the handy victim. 'He wanted to wear his father's red cap; that's why. Did he look to you like one who would be able to pay for a title, or even buy back one for which someone else had already paid without er... doing something altogether stupid?' Ah! thought Nwalioba, hadn't he of his own accord brought in the *ozo* society? and would not Orimili end up asking about the fate of his own bid for the title? Altogether stupid of him, really.

But Orimili did not walk the path which Nwalioba had inadvertently opened up. He spoke rather in a shocked tone: 'Was it so important to him to reclaim the title that he had to trade their common land for it?'

Nwalioba said to his friend, 'Orimili, we have seen

nothing yet in this disordered age; nothing, I tell you. How do you know that by next year we won't be hearing of children auctioning off their parents for money, or for whatever has taken their fancy? Anything is possible now; that's what I think. My one regret in this particular case is that it didn't come to light before the title was actually conferred on the fool. Why should I curse him, though? It is not his fault, nor did he begin it. What is flogging one's patrimony, compared to trading one's own country and people?'

'What are you talking about?' asked Orimili, sharply.

'I mean Onyekwe Ananwemadu. Nduka has only sold his property to a citizen of Okocha. Why should we say that that's an abomination, whereas Ananwemadu has been collecting tribute from the citizens of Okocha in exchange for his warrant chieftaincy? Yet he remains a powerful person in the *ozo* society. Why should poor Nduka not exchange his land for the title?'

'I suppose one could look at Ananwemadu's situation in the light you present it. However...'

'Could any betrayal surpass that? By the way, have you found out why the man's wife was troubling your wife the other day?'

'My wife? When?'

'There, of course,' nodding towards Edoko's place, 'at the memorials yesterday. What do you mean, didn't she tell you?'

'Yesterday? No, I haven't seen her these past two days. Something went wrong in my absence?'

Obinagu Nwalioba stared at his friend: 'Why, you look as if you are coming back from a journey! Emenogha told me that you would be back yesterday: you didn't return then?'

'Oh no; I'm actually on my way home from Okono. Whose wife did you mean, quarrelling with mine?'

'Ananwemadu's, of course. I see that I have upset you by mentioning it. So sorry… I didn't mean to.'

'That's all right. But what was the problem between my wife and Ogbuefi Ananwemadu's?'

'To be frank, I haven't the slightest idea what the problem was; nor did I try to find out. Did you ever know a widower' – Nwalioba was one – 'obtaining an eye-witness account of what goes on among the women? Should he then reduce himself to a gossip by asking around?' He was doing his best to make a joke of the issue, and calm down Orimili; and he actually broke out in a laugh, before winding up: 'I simply forgot about the dispute, or whatever it was.'

Orimili was silent, obliging Nwalioba to resume.

'It isn't something for you to worry about, I should imagine, for it was evident from the way the women behaved that Ananwemadu's wife had been at fault.'

Orimili felt reassured. For Okuata, whose shyness was so well known, was the least likely person to pick a quarrel with anyone, particularly in a public place. This, as far as Orimili could tell, was her first time getting mixed up in a dispute. Ananwemadu's wife must have gone out of her way to bring her out.

Obikeze was preparing his evening meal when they came within sight of his house. The evidence was the smoke which was rising through the thatch of his house. But Nwalioba did not go in immediately to do the consultation, because

Orimili had halted on the pathway in a way that told him that he too had to stop. Orimili wished to know whether there had been a movement towards settling the land dispute with Ikedi.

'I hope I'm not delaying you,' began Orimili, 'but I wish to know how things have got on between you.'

'That dispute has developed in a most extraordinary way,' breathed Nwalioba, heavily. 'In point of fact, that's what I want to consult Obikeze about. The middlemen came to see us today, telling us that we were being given the last chance to accept the boundary they proposed, and that if we didn't put the opportunity to good use, they would move the issue to another stage where it would no longer concern us. That was rather intriguing. So I enquired of them what they meant by saying that they would take the dispute out of our hands; were they talking about their own land or about *mine*? They said that they were talking about *my* land, of course. You want to have seen the arrogance of the men! But why shouldn't they be arrogant? Was it not someone else's land they were trying to dispose of? Of course, both of us said we wouldn't accept such a condition.'

'You mean, you and Ikedi? How strange!'

'Precisely. So, I endeavoured to draw their attention to the fact that the dispute was between me and Ikedi, not between the middlemen and me. Then I saw what they were driving at: to make us fight for the right to our own portions, or whatever was left of it! You see?'

'Quite intriguing,' cried Orimili, 'and a masterly device too.'

'But the price!'

Nwalioba had managed to get Uderika Nwanne, the chief speaker among the middlemen, to explain what they were going to do if Nwalioba and Ikedi failed to come to terms. They would take over the entire property, not just the part under dispute, and they would hand it over to the town to use as a market-place. He also told of the advantage of having such a market-place, since the land in question lay quite close to Guy & Son Trading Company. It would be handy for the townspeople to bring their palm produce and whatnot quite close to the purchaser. Ekwenze Orimili was outraged to hear this. 'What? Use your land for a market? Is that how to go about finding a site for a market-place?'

'Have you seen anything so devious!'

Ekwenze Orimili let droop his shoulder, becoming instantly aware of the weight of the travelling bag which he had been carrying all day. He put it on the ground, but his shoulders did not straighten up. It was as though he supported an invisible load on them. At length, he raised his gaze from the ground, and asked his friend:

'What are you going to do now?'

'The thing is getting confusing, and it is harder and harder to think; it is all the time as if one would explode. That's why I want to talk to Obikeze...' He cast a glance in the direction of the latter's house to be sure that he hadn't gone to bed. However, the smoke was issuing through the thatch as before. So he resumed, 'I want to see whether there are hidden aspects to the case, and then I shall be ready to tell Uderika Nwanne and his friends what I think.'

'Certainly, they deserve to be told what one thinks of that strange plan. Mind you, I'm all for having a market-place near Guy & Son; and if such is to be had, it must be on someone's property. And now that I think of it, it strikes me that the existing market-place, and even Amanza, are both set on someone's…'

'Yes, I have thought of that; and I don't want to give the impression that I won't yield ground if the issue is purely and simply providing land for public use.'

'I see what you mean. You want Uderika Nwanne's crowd to come out clearly with a decision about the actual boundary…'

'And ask afterwards if they want me to donate land for a market,' Nwalioba wound up the argument for Orimili. 'That's exactly what I mean. There should be no problem about that.'

As Orimili was considering what to say to this, another thought occurred to Nwalioba, who now spoke with grim determination: 'You know what, those middlemen are trying to discredit me. They want to be able to say that I refused to settle with Ikedi, and also refused to give up the land to the town. I really should like to know whether Nweke Nwofia has been talking to Uderika Nwanne and his friends; that's one thing I should like to know. For I can't see how else to explain their evil scheme. But wait until I have seen Obikeze. I mean to make things difficult for them. Why shouldn't I? Not only am I going to insist that they state openly the exact position of the boundary, but also I am going to demand that they give me another parcel of land in compensation for my own, if they wish to turn it into a market-place!'

'You will?'

'To show them that I shall not be intimidated. Does it occur to them that I will have to explain to my children why I am giving up their inheritance? No, let Uderika turn his children's inheritance into a market-place. Mine will not be tampered with; not in the present circumstances.'

'Well, see Obikeze, and do let us talk about it later on. There must be a way to solve this problem without going to extremes. I can't believe that it is destined to keep going from bad to worse as it has been doing so far.'

Orimili stooped down wearily, and picked up his grip, but Obinagu Nwalioba did not prepare to leave and go his way. He was lost in thought. Then he took a deep breath, and spoke up, his voice full of labour.

'Ekwenze Orimili,' he said to his friend, who was startled by the uncharacteristic way of naming him, 'we have known each other all our lives, haven't we? Tell me, would you give in to either of the solutions put forward by the middlemen: give up part of your land to a greedy man, or, in the particular circumstances, give up your land to be turned into a market-place? Would you not rather do as our fathers used to do when they were beset by a greedy neighbour? Would you not sharpen your broadsword, and send word to your opponent to sharpen his and meet you at the site? How many such greedy people dared to keep the appointment? Do you think that Ikedi would have been around to press this claim if…'

'God forbid!' cried Orimili. 'What are you talking about?'

'What I am talking about is that I'm afraid I have ruined everything; that I should have taken my stand long ago; and that having failed to do this, I have put myself in a position where someone else tells me: here's what's to be done; instead of me telling them that! You understand?'

'No,' Orimili firmly refused to be swept along by his friend, 'don't understand you.'

'What I mean is that I'm done with retreating. When I finish this consultation, I shall send word to Uderika Nwanne to make up his mind where the boundary is, and state it clearly. Unless this is done, he and his friends are not to come near me or come to the land itself. I shall sharpen my broadsword, my friend, and stand guard on the land. Whoever steps on to my land will not be able to leave it again, unless I am the one who falls!'

'You'll not do anything of the sort,' Orimili quickly told him. He had never said anything more true in his life. For after his consultation with the Arobinagu, Nwalioba had sent and had the middlemen told that he was ready to do battle with them, individually or the whole lot of them together. The news quickly spread, causing much excitement. One of those who had been excited by this turn of events was Ananwemadu, who soon afterwards paid a visit to the manager of Guy & Son, in consequence of which the land set aside for the military people was greatly enlarged. Not long afterwards, much going and coming began to be observed in Nwalioba's property in a way that should have caused the man of action to come out in protest. However, it turned out that owing to the particular circumstances involved, he was constrained not to reach for his sword to put force to this protest.

Orimili parted with Nwalioba in an angry mood. What did the man mean by asking him if he would give in to a covetous neighbour who wanted his land? How did Orimili come into it? Oh, he was tired; had had a most tedious day! Nwalioba couldn't even see that, and was telling him what the old people did when their land was seized. Ah, he should have asked him to say that to Obikeze. He stopped, looked back, but Nwalioba was gone. He sighed, angry with himself for remembering Obikeze too late. He should have stopped Nwalioba with Obikeze's name. Who made him lose all his land and become an outcast? Certainly, it wasn't the children of the day, whom his friend was so glibly condemning. He sighed again, and decided to find something more pleasant to think about. Nothing turned up. He whistled furiously for a while, and then heard Obinagu's voice answer him from within: No, you can't understand…!

He noticed that he could distinguish individual particles of sand on the sandy pathway. What a marvellous moonlight. And how late it was too. His people must have all gone to bed. Shouldn't it have been wiser for him to have gone straight home, and then go out afterwards? Anyway, one made a gain here, a loss there; that was how things were. Osita's sacrifice – that was gain.

By the way, where would be most appropriate to have the sacrifice? He would prefer some out-of-the-way place, and he hoped that the Arobinagu would not specify that it be at Amanza, at the foot of the sacred tree.

Orimili was approaching the intersection which faced directly into Amanza. He knew that at that corner, Amanza suddenly came into view, making one feel as if the square, and the sacred tree prominently stationed at the centre, had dramatically come into being; for one had the sense of having perceived the vestige of a flash of the movement in which the square and its tree had suddenly been brought across one's field of vision, and implanted. This mirage was brought about by the fact that the bushes which grew on either side of the pathway ended abruptly at the corner, where it joined the main road. Orimili knew that. Still, he loved to think of the sudden emergence of the sacred tree into view as an apparition. He watched intently for the apparition.

So intense must have been his vigilance that his mind strayed; or maybe it was the moonlight that beguiled him. However, he missed the critical instant.

Nevertheless, he looked up at the massive tree, whose enormous trunk rose like a great shaft, striving towards the sky. It was a single, towering trunk – no branch – until the very top, where it suddenly spread out like a double-headed anvil; it looked like an enormous hammer, so great that only the earth itself could wield it. It seemed to Orimili that the great shaft had been rising towards the sky as he watched it, growing somewhat narrower as the climb became more difficult, and then despairing at last of ever making it to the high dome of the sky, breaking up and scattering, as it were, into branches and leaves. Oh yes, thought Orimili, ironically, why not strive farther; touch the sky? Go on, touch it!

In its daylight glory, the Ngwu tree was quite awesome. It seemed to dwarf every other thing – tree, house, everything around. Orimili felt that it must be the tallest tree of all, and that no other shrub could attain its height. It was decorated with a band of white cloth which ran halfway round the trunk, just above the level of the head of a full-grown man. Why was the band not made to run right round the trunk? Was it because its priest was saving the cloth? Or because that was the proper way to gird it? Anyway, from the appropriate angle, the white band looked like the white thread around a titled man's ankle. Just below the white band were clusters of feathers which had been stuck to the tree with the blood of the fowls that were sacrificed at its foot. Ekwenze was not sure whether the tree was a god in its own right, or whether it represented the divines of the Soil, or all the ancestors together, or simply the founding father of Okocha. However, sacrifices were offered at its foot in the name of the townspeople, Orimili supposed; and this occurred at intervals of two or three months; usually a small sacrifice involving the priest and a couple of old men. The priest slashed the throat of the cock, rubbed the bloody neck upon the bark of the tree, plucked a handful of soft feathers from the breast, and pasted them on the blood. Orimili's sacrifice for his son should be bigger of course, with his neighbours and Emenogha attending; better at an out-of-the-way place, not at the foot of the Ngwu.

Orimili also knew that he did not care to find out whether the sacred tree was a god in its own right, or the representative of a god. Whatever it was, it was a landmark; a landmark because it indicated the exact spot where the founding father had first set foot on the land; a landmark because it was supposed to be the intersection of the boundaries of the three villages of Okocha – but was not; a landmark because Amanza could not be Amanza without it; it was a landmark, above all, because it had a definite location on the land; it was a feature of the land. Let it try standing on the river – the Mighty River – for Orimili to see how it would get on. Oh no, it could not have been a mark at all, had it sprouted on the river. The Mighty Flood would have laid it low.

If the river had to have a mark, *the* river-mark, Orimili was that mark.

5 | *A Tottering House*

Okuata's distress that day at Edoko's memorial did not in any wise abate after the initial shock which had stunned, and as it were, blinded her. She had felt so isolated and lonely in the midst of the women, but when her neighbours left her alone after bringing her home, her loneliness had seemed to intensify all the more. Long past the hour she was accustomed to see her husband come, he had not appeared. It was dreadful trying to cope all alone with a problem which seemed so large it could bring down a well-built house. Every so often that house heaved, ready to topple over; in the end, it held, as though pulled back again with strong ropes. Still Okuata was terrified that everything might go to pieces before the owner of the house returned. If only there were someone to speak to, perhaps she would be able to hold out until Orimili came home. It wouldn't be any use talking to the children, of course. Suppose she repeated Okwuese's words to Ejike, what could they possibly mean to him?

When the women left her, she had been feeling dazed still. In that condition, she had prepared the evening meal for her children, ate little of it herself, and had gone to bed. She had maintained a vigil most of the night, expecting Orimili to come home any moment. After midnight, she gave up. Her husband would not be coming home that night. The daze which, unknown to her, had sustained her now cleared up. She saw then how hopeless her suffering was; and senseless too. It was sheer torture; and she had broken down completely and cried, convinced that she was the most miserable human being the world had ever seen. It must be said for her that she strove as she knew how to keep her sobs low in order not to disturb the sleeping children.

How was she expected to cope with the shattering blow single-handedly, and not be able to breathe what she had seen to someone? That was why Orimili's failure to return had seemed to her like a stab administered to her when she was down and defenceless, by a grinning fiend, whom she had previously taken for her best friend. This stab touched her to the quick, having come from the very man on whose account she had been knocked down and trampled upon by an enemy full of malice. Thus scandalized, Okuata's almighty rage began to lose its focus. Okwuese Ananwemadu was still discernible as its target, but Orimili was also standing by the side of that fiend. A small rupture had occurred, and a steady stream of concentrated anger had been escaping and gathering at the feet of Orimili, in just the same way as a branch road may draw traffic away from the main one until the main is in danger of going into disuse. Steadily, Orimili's account accumulated, and fumes rose, threatening to blot him out from Okuata's consciousness.

Meanwhile, she suffered on, sometimes with involuntarily loud bursts of crying but mostly in silent tears, oppressed by the very absence of the man whose presence would have had a miraculous effect – lifting from her shoulders the crushing weight of her humiliation, and setting her free. She smouldered with rage and with shame. It wasn't that she felt she had been wantonly exposed; such would have been an abiding danger, if her marrying Orimili had involved for her a descent in social status. Okwuese was the first to suggest that Orimili was beneath notice, and that in marrying, she had gone down to him and ceased to be noticeable. How did Okwuese find the guts to say that? Who was she to presume to speak about another person? Still, she had presumed to speak and had taken Okuata so utterly unawares that she had been paralysed. That was her everlasting shame: she had behaved like one thunderstruck, utterly incapable of reacting to the inexcusable taunt of a fellow woman. Yet it was a moment in which nothing should have answered to the purpose better than striking back immediately; she ought to have done something to Okwuese the effect of which should be similar to what had happened to her – something as instantaneous as it was decisive. What would have answered would have been for her simply to open her mouth, and without the least effort on her own part, except that of exerting an all-powerful will – her own will – drawn Okwuese into this open-and-waiting mouth, and swallowed her, together with her words. She should have obliterated everything. Another solution which should have been equally effective, but which Okuata should not have relished so completely as the first, would have been for the earth goddess herself to open her mouth precisely under Okwuese's feet, draw in the evil woman, and close up again.

But the mother-goddess had not intervened on the side

of the aggrieved woman. Because of the goddess's indifference, Okuata had fallen back on her own imagination, which supplied her with visions of a great many forms of vengeance, none of which seemed to her in the least degree satisfactory. For example, what was the use of tearing up Okwuese's face, or tearing out her eyes and tongue? In what way would they help to cancel out what she had said? Even now, she hadn't found what she wanted. Which meant that if Okwuese were to come round again, and…? Ah! that would be the best thing ever to happen, because in that case, she would beat her until she died. The only reason why she got away alive – unscathed, really – in the first instance was that Okuata had not known what was coming. She had been so unprepared – which was the point she could no longer skirt around. A horribly painful consciousness it was, that she had done nothing to one who had wounded her in her deepest being. How was she going to give an account of herself to Orimili? Wasn't the proper thing to have committed murder on his behalf, and leave him to see about that? How could she say that whatever had come to her mind seemed overtaken even before it was thought of? Shouldn't she have done something, no matter how inadequate? The torment was deep. Okuata was full of self-pity and self-loathing all at the same time. To have surrendered to paralysis in the face of a woman who was not fit to live, or breathe the common air! To have permitted herself to be led away like a foolish lamb – as if she had indeed been the guilty one! To have let the outrage go unanswered; why, she herself ought to have died rather than let it pass! Were she indeed Okuata Orimili, she should have forced the words back into Okwuese's throat until they choked her!

How? In what way? The question returned again and again. She couldn't find the answer to that. All right. What should she do now, or was she to take it that Okwuese could not be answered? That any worthless character could come along any day and repeat the same insult, knowing that she would get away with it? Ah, how terribly shocking even to think this. If only the fiend used the same freshwater stream from which she herself drew water! Then she would go out very early the next morning and waylay her. As soon as she emerged from a corner in the pathway (she knew the precise corner in the pathway to her village stream which should be most appropriate for the encounter), she would present herself to Okwuese, and challenge her. Should she refuse to accept the challenge and put down her water-pot, she would slap her all the same, putting all her power behind that blow. Okwuese's water-pot would topple from her head then (the sound of the explosion of the pot that was full of water echoed in her mind, with an agreeable thud); and before the fiend had recovered from the shock of the explosion, she would find herself wrestled to the ground, with Okuata sitting on top of her, and stuffing her blasted mouth with dust! She should beat into her all the rage which now swelled in her chest, threatening to burst forth – she felt – through her throat. Then she should flay the fiend's face with her fingernails so thoroughly that, if it healed at all, the scars would remain to remind her always that she, Okuata, was not to be trifled with.

But of course Okwuese used the freshwater stream of

Ugwueke; and so the chances that they should meet for the encounter in that most appropriate spot were slim indeed. Was she then beyond the reach of Okuata? And was there no way in which she was to be brought to account for the outrage? The rage soared in Okuata's chest with renewed vigour.

Okuata's people had a metaphor for expressing absolute perversity: they said that the evil-doer was driving smoke underground – a metaphor which has much to recommend it since smoke rises naturally into the air, where it has its sympathies. Okuata was beginning to see herself in the aspect of the evil-doer in the metaphor, not because she had found any wrong-doing of which to accuse herself, besides her failure to blot out Okwuese instantaneously together with her words; her failure to do something, at any rate, if only for the sake of Orimili. What reminded her of the evil-doer of the metaphor was her seeing the rage presently swelling inside her distinctly as smoke; dense smoke, struggling to find its way into the open, and she herself was forcing it back, driving it underground. But she had despaired of carrying on the battle against the insistent uprising of the smoke. There had to be a way to get it off her chest. She had as yet not spoken to anyone about the incident – she would probably talk to her mother about it. She would be sympathetic. As a matter of fact, she was sure that all she could get from her mother would be sympathy, which in itself would not be able to dispel the smoke. The most efficient way to get rid of it would be to beat it all into Okwuese. That was it. And she wept for fear that she might not find the occasion to perform this essential task. How agreeable a task it should be too. She must keep a sharp lookout for an opportunity; the slimmest chance that turned up, she promised herself, would be put to instant use. And while she awaited the opportunity, it was essential, for her own sanity, to speak to Orimili. Apart from the encounter which she had promised herself she should have with Okwuese, the only other way she knew to get rid of much of the smoke was to speak to her husband. Okuata did not worry as to why this should be the case; nor did she wonder where the smoke to be released was to escape into. She must have ruled, without wishing it or thinking of it, that if in speaking to her husband, he welcomed the smoke into his system, it was his own lookout.

Okuata arose in the morning, and went by force of habit towards her water-pot. She usually began her day by making two trips to the stream to collect water for the needs of her family. But she found that she was reluctant to take up the water vessel that morning. What she felt like doing was to go back to bed; and she had a headache too. How was she to bring home the water-pot anyway? She couldn't bring it in her hand, could she? Also she was worried about all the women she was going to meet on the way. No doubt, they all knew what had happened to her – even though only a few of them had in fact been present when the incident happened. Nor was she consoled by the fact that those who had witnessed it had all loudly condemned Okwuese. They all did show her compassion. Difficult to tell, though, whether the compassion was not secretly laced with a malignant joy. She was suddenly weary, standing by her water-pot, being overcome with a renewed sense of her loneliness.

She clenched her teeth tightly together, and picked up

her water-pot. What was she to do? Leave her children without water to drink? If they cried for it, as they certainly would, Orimili would be nowhere to hear them and be moved by their cry. Yet someone was going to have her heart pierced by the cry; well, who else but Okuata? She went to the stream, feeling a shaft of resentment rising from another corner of her breast, struggling with her rage for space, digging into her throat with its sharp point, as if to force an opening there. Then she pulled herself up short, just as she would have pulled Ejike by the ear to drive home an instruction: she couldn't go on that way, otherwise she might be finished off quite easily by the least annoyance she now encountered. Did she want her children to become orphans? Yes, orphans. That was exactly what they would be reduced to, if they looked for her and didn't find her; for did they mean anything really to Orimili, beside Osita? She bent over, holding her water-pot to her head with her right hand, and wiped her tears with the *ear* of her wrapper.

The first woman she met as she branched into the pathway to the stream was Uchendu Oranudu, the aged one's daughter-in-law, and mother of the young teacher, Chiebo. They had barely exchanged morning greetings before Uchendu began to talk about the incident, and to revile Okwuese in the strongest terms. Okwuese was a little, dirty, stinking thing that everybody was doing their best to hide away, and now she had come out of her hiding place of her own accord, a little pig, so daft she did not know she had little to boast about, being no more than the second wife of a common fool, who made his living as the white man's taxi driver!

Well, now, here was something. Okuata felt a certain

warmth, a feeling of gratitude, welling up inside her, greatly reducing the fury of the smoke-storm. How wise she had been to take up her water-pot in spite of everything. What Uchendu was saying deserved to be treasured. She also remembered that Uchendu had been one of the neighbours who had rallied around her that unforgettable moment, and had led her away. It showed how useful good neighbours were. What would it be like to have Okwuese for a neighbour? She wondered that the witch's neighbours had been suffering her, and that no one had challenged her and beaten her to death. She herself wouldn't have been so long-suffering. No question at all in her mind that if she were to be in the same neighbourhood with Okwuese just for one day Okwuese would be dead and buried!

At about midday the leader of the women of the neighbourhood came with two other women and spoke to Okuata. She learned that a meeting had been hastily called immediately she had left yesterday to decide what to do with Okwuese. But, as one might expect, they were unable to talk to any purpose, having been so freshly outraged. So they had decided to take it up at their meeting on the next great market day. However, it was essential that they should have proposals ready to present to the women of Ebonasa on the day of the meeting. For this reason, the leader had called the women of the neighbourhood together that morning, and they had had a long discussion.

It was all cheerful news, of course, the only snag being that Okwuese was, by the admission of the leader herself, quite beyond the reach of the women of Ebonasa. She was an Ugwueke woman, after all. However, they had decided on an enormous fine, which they were going to ask the assembly of Ugwueke women to exact from her, and that until this was done, Ebonasa would not tolerate Okwuese in any gathering anywhere in Okocha, but they would depart en masse as soon as Okwuese turned up. Where the women were stronger was in the home base. They would not tolerate Okwuese in any gathering in Ebonasa; she would be excluded, if need be by force.

Okuata was grateful to her neighbours, and she was lavish in her expression of it. Nevertheless, she was not at all appeased. How much were the sanctions worth, in real terms? And did it not take only determination to outwear even the most stringent of sanctions? Concern was what her neighbours were trying to project, and it was good to know that though private and intensely painful as the blow was, still there were people who knew that it hurt. All, very good; but if it ever came to doing something concrete, which was what she felt needed to be done, nothing could come near her laying hold of the woman. Indeed Okuata continued to nurse the hope that Okwuese should expose herself in some mischief in her presence. She would then seize the opportunity to teach her a lesson. In any case, she was no longer as bitter as she had been during the night. So much had the talk done for her. But as her bitterness diminished, so did her worry increase that Orimili had not yet returned. Might he have had a mishap on the river?

She prepared the midday meal for her children and tried her best to eat some of it, but found the food nearly tasteless and she herself scarcely hungry. Her concern about the welfare of her husband was mounting. The stress she had been through, from which she had not really freed herself, made her highly excitable, and her imagination extremely receptive of the most absurd notions. Orimili had told her he was having trouble with the barge. So it was most natural that she should begin to wonder and terrify herself that the barge may have sunk, and drowned her husband. She tried to get rid of the horrible thought. But the more she tried, the more vivid became the various pictures which her imagination seemed to be stuck with. They showed various stages of the sudden filling of the barge with water, and the boat going down before Orimili and his men knew what had happened. Was the agitation of the previous evening only a preparation for the real horror? Ah yes, how did she bring herself to believe that she had at last begun to *live*; that Orimili happening to her was not merely an interlude in a life which was condemned from the beginning to misery? Oh yes, her self-delusion had come unstuck. In fact, had it not been self-delusion, this interlude? What a fool she had been to have believed that it was real! And, oh! couldn't the dream last longer? Why unravel itself now?

Yesterday's outrage now became a trifle in the face of the catastrophe seemingly unfolding before her. Okuata had never been more sad, more imbued with the sense of utter ruin in all her life. She went to the front yard to take a short walk, and keep an eye on the roadway in order to see the moment when Orimili would emerge into view. All thoughts about visiting her mother to tell her what Okwuese had done deserted her. *What* was Okwuese? That foolish woman's question might well be thrown back at her; now not as an act of revenge, nor even in anger: what was she? Okuata was down, truly down and afraid. The sense of her injured pride was gone; there was no pride to injure now. Her towering rage, which would not be placated without crushing and utterly destroying its object, and which frustrated her because it had been unable to achieve this goal by her merely willing it: that rage was gone. She felt herself now withdrawn into a recess, where she could will nothing and destroy nothing, and where she could be touched by nothing; certainly not by Okwuese, even if she should spit at her. Where she was, only one person could reach her; and that person was Orimili. Evidently, she had overrated Okwuese. Suppose she had insulted her; and suppose the insult was as large and heavy as a falling tree, what would it all mean, if she were to be widowed? Would it matter after that what manner of abuse anyone directed at her; what with her having received the ultimate blow from the fates? Would her very life still mean anything? Her death even; except as a most welcome end to all her troubles? Alas, she knew – and with what force the certainty rose from one corner of her mind, and impressed itself upon her consciousness in an unchallengeable way – that once the gods had dealt her that blow, they would know that she was finished with; and they would kick her contemptuously aside and pass on, omitting to extend to her the final act of mercy which, in that case, would be to take her life!

After her eldest, Ejike, had returned to the school for the evening catechism, she began to stray more and more into the front yard. She found herself so frequently in that yard that she decided to find something to keep her busy there in order not to have to keep going and coming. If only the avenue had not been recently weeded! That should have been ideal for keeping herself busy in that frontage. What else could she take on? She finally lighted on the kola tree; it would be well to build a low fence around it for collecting sweepings every morning as a source of manure. Strange, she had never thought of that. Well, just as well. Okuata was busy at this employment until Ejike returned from the catechism lesson, and reported that he had seen his father on the way to the school, and he was going to Amanna to see Edoko's people. This piece of intelligence struck Okuata as very much like what was told in folklore about the headless ghost of a murdered man haunting the place in which he had been killed. She got no end of goose pimples from it. However, she completed her task, and went into the kitchen to prepare the evening meal.

Ekwenze finally came home. It was quite late when he entered. His young children heard him from the kitchen where they were eating their supper. They abandoned their meal temporarily to greet him. The welcome ritual was well practised. As they said their good evening sir, they made a dash for his grip, which he let one of them capture. Then they all left him and went after the one who had the grip. At this point, he called a truce, retrieved the bag from the winner and took from it a loaf of bread, which they seized and ran away with to the kitchen, amid great commotion. There their mother divided it among them. Orimili suffered the ritual to run its course, then he fell heavily into his sling chair, calling after the children running away to the kitchen:

'Do tell your mother to bring me my supper, for I'm famished.' They didn't hear him, of course, but Okuata did.

She brought in the supper looking extremely moody, and she wouldn't look into Ekwenze's face even when she greeted him, and enquired whether he had been delayed on account of the problem he said he was having with the barge.

'Yes,' replied Ekwenze, wearily. 'The leak was getting worse and worse. Still, I didn't think for a moment that it would take a great deal of time to repair. Well, it is done, now; and here I am. Were you thinking I had wrecked the boat somewhere?'

'No, I knew it was the repairs, but I was surprised that it took two whole days. It must have been very bad?'

'Pretty bad, but I'm sure I won't have to worry about that hold for a good while. It cost a lot of money too.'

'What is that to your being able to come and go? I'd say that the money has been put to very good use.'

'You look somewhat distressed; is anything the matter?'

'No, there is nothing the matter,' answered Okuata, without trying to sound convincing. The time didn't seem right yet to bring out the little speech she had prepared for her husband, and she was actually having second thoughts about it. It didn't seem to be right at all to say anything hard to Ekwenze.

Ekwenze rephrased his question: 'Did someone annoy you in my absence?'

'No, no one annoyed me in your absence.'

Ekwenze's temper rose sharply, but he checked it, and ate in silence. Why was Okuata refusing to tell him about her quarrel with Ananwemadu's wife? Maybe she was waiting for him to finish his meal – which meant that the thing was deep; deeper than he had feared.

'Did the children go to school today?' Let her have all the time she wanted.

'Yes, they did go to school, of course. You better eat your supper. I'll be back.'

Ekwenze finished his meal, but it was Ejike who came to remove the dishes. He waited. Okuata did not return. He gave her more time. Finally, he sent for her. But she took her time, first putting the children to bed, and coming out at long last to say:

'Yes, did you want me?'

'What is the matter with you?' asked Ekwenze, cutting out all the preliminaries, and doing nothing to deaden the glint of his temper showing clearly at the question's edges.

'Nothing, except that I wish to go home to my mother.'

Ekwenze Orimili reeled, profoundly shocked. Then he looked hard into her face, as if to check if the peculiar turn he had heard in her answer matched with her demeanour – a perfectly natural reaction in a boatman, who knew a great many shades in the sky, and the value of each. Was he heading for a storm? No doubt of it, the sky was overcast; face swollen, as if with recent weeping; which was where the analogy broke down, as he knew that the sky had a particular lightness about it after a downpour. Ekwenze backed down instantly, and adopted a very mild approach. He would treat the matter very lightly; so lightly that the idea of going home to one's mother would appear even to the speaker as too ordinary to be worth mentioning.

'Is my mother-in-law unwell?'

'Did I say she was sick?'

'Are you sure?'

'There is nothing wrong with my mother!'

'Ah, if you say so, then I'm relieved. But you sound so vehement that one would have thought that there was something really wrong; I mean, back home at your mother's place. I'm relieved that it is otherwise. Of course, you should go and see your mother any time you need to. I'm sure that this is not your first time of paying her a visit; and yet there is nothing special about the present visit to seem to make it necessary to ask permission.' Orimili made a noisy gesture of rising from his seat. 'Well you have permission to go; no problem about that.' And he settled back again, his eyes on Okuata. 'Was that all you wanted to say to me?'

'Yes, that's all; and I mean to go back to her!'

'Oh, were you talking about going this night? I didn't realize that. Don't you think it is quite late now to go calling at people's homes? I should have thought so myself, unless, er…' narrowing his eyes at her, 'are you sure that my mother-in-law is all right?'

'Oh, leave my mother out of this! I've told you she's well, why do you keep asking me?'

'Oh, very well. In that case, why not go and see her tomorrow morning? I'm sure you'll be able to come back in time, and get food ready for the children.'

'Thanks indeed for your concern for the children. I'm sure, however, that I didn't say that I intended to return.'

Ekwenze knew of course that this was what she meant

to bring out from the very beginning. Nevertheless, he was enraged by the retort:

'You-' he stammered, and then fell silent. All right, he said to himself. What was the use getting worked up? Much better to hold his countenance and remain self-possessed. Ekwenze Orimili even permitted a smile, or the appearance of one, to play on his face.

'What do you mean, you won't come back?'

'Just that; no more.'

Ekwenze said, 'Strange!' and fixed her with a hard gaze. To be frank, he knew how to stop this nonsense; of course he knew. Only accuse Okuata of wanting to go away because she had found some other fellow, younger and handsomer than Orimili. Get her defending herself, and swearing her loyalty; then just walk out and go and rest his old bones from the fatigue of these two days. Next morning, then, tell her he was surprised that she took him seriously last night; of course he had only been joking; and sorry, anyway. That would take care of this foolish hide-and-seek they were playing. Another thing it would take care of was that quarrel with Ananwemadu's wife: he would never know what happened. Play a little longer:

'All right. Let's say you won't come back. Who is going to look after our children for me? I can't very well split myself in two: be at work upon the river, and be here at the same time, minding them, can I?'

'Most extraordinary! *Our* children? This is the first time I've heard you speak in that way, but...'

'Okuata! Just what do you mean by that?'

'Let's face it; since when have you cared for my children?

You can't have been favoured with a revelation at Okono, to make you say *our* children? Or was it the great river god himself that told you? I don't know what you are talking about, for I shall take my children with me!'

Ekwenze Orimili was now quite sure that his wife was determined to drive him mad. He swallowed a lump, and glared at Okuata.

'Okuata,' he said, trying once more to assert command over himself, 'this joke has gone on for too long. Let's put it aside. Tell me what went wrong while I was away.'

'What went wrong was simply me seeing that my children are nothing to you, and that as far as you are concerned, Osita is your only child. Why should I stay on, knowing that I am only a visitor? That's why I decided to give up the joke, and go home, I and my children!'

Orimili took his turn to enquire as to the way in which his wife had attained this revelation. Had she had an apparition from the goddess of the fireplace or from that of the freshwater stream? Were this the farming season, he would have enquired also about the goddess of cocoyam and of the cassava.

The wife then answered that the initial impulse had indeed come from a goddess, though one less well known than the ones her husband mentioned. That goddess was Okwuese Ananwemadu. After that initial impulse, it was quite easy for her to deduce the rest for herself.

The anger which Orimili had been trying to hold down had in fact been building up all the time. As if ruptured by Okuata's mentioning of Okwuese's name, it now came bubbling with great force to the surface, making it difficult for him to speak coherently. The words came in jerks, while his throat contracted and expanded in succession, as though the fumes of rage were forcing their way through the torrent of words, hampering the torrent and being in their turn impeded. What he was trying to say, Okuata discovered by slow stages, was that he couldn't tolerate his wife having a row with anyone, for any cause; didn't she know that such things rebounded adversely on a family? Just look at what they had been doing all evening, trying to communicate, but beating about the bush all the time; that was the kind of thing one expected, when one's wife had grown so brazen as to be having public rows!

Okuata struggled, manfully, to weather Orimili's storm, and then coolly tell him that if he knew what Okwuese had done, he would wonder why she didn't kill her! But just as she was beginnning to feel that she was succeeding, her eyes began to fill with tears, and her lips to tremble. Before she knew it, she had broken down. Orimili stopped and waited, but Okuata's sorrow appeared to be enormous. She cried for a great while before she mastered herself sufficiently to stammer out her own story about what had passed between herself and Okwuese at Edoko's place.

When she had finished, Ekwenze Orimili said to himself that one thing he wasn't going to do was to take the least notice of Okwuese. Why should he quarrel with a woman, and bring himself down to her level? Never! Why should anyone stop her from saying whatever she wanted to say? Certainly, not Orimili Nwofia. If she thought that in saying something outrageous, she would discompose Orimili, she had never been more mistaken in her life.

He said to Okuata:

'Aha, I have it! What you were telling me was that you had found out from Okwuese that Orimili was nobody; and for that reason, you would go back to your mother, and have nothing to do with a nobody?'

He had the impulse to add: 'Go back, then, to her, and let's be done with it!' But he restrained himself. It wasn't right to say such things in such a grim atmosphere, for they could do profound harm to one trying to overmaster a deep sorrow. Orimili got up from his seat, and walked to his bedroom, muttering under his breath as he went: 'No one knows where Orimili comes from; and so what?'

Ekwenze put out the light which had been left for him in his room, and lay down in his bed. 'Do they know where they themselves come from?' he muttered into the darkness. His mind was blank. Nothing could be farther from his mind than sleep. So he made no effort to compose himself to sleep.

Then he told himself that it was quite as well he didn't tell his wife that she could go home and be done with it; at the very least, that would have shown that he was angry. Angry? he vehemently denied; who with? Okwuese Ananwemadu? Who was she, anyway? The thing he should have said to her in fact was, in an off-hand manner, 'Was that what made you so moody?' He should even have smiled ironically, as he said that, and added, 'I'm quite surprised at you!' Orimili was so pleased with the way he seemed so unperturbed that he would have wished Okuata, that minute, to have a glimpse into his soul, and see for herself how peaceful it was! What was the use of wasting words, telling her not to worry, and knowing that she would take it as a mere front, rather than as an expression of the true state of his mind? So, let her see the soul for herself; after that, she won't need to be told to make nothing of the incident!

Ekwenze Orimili congratulated himself for his manliness, and did not wonder why he hadn't fallen asleep, nor why he didn't feel at all like sleeping. Wasn't he the one who had been so tired?

Orimili's body had been drawing energy from unknown sources, as if consciously preparing for a long night. At the moment, however, his mind was not ready to begin the session which his body had so quickly made preparations for; which was quite understandable, since it had been confronted with a challenge that it intuited to be altogether unanswerable. What it was faced with was that which could not be thought; that before which the mind could do nothing but fall back.

Ekwenze Orimili was faced with a certain actuality, the roots of which were in the creative act. For his people spoke of this act as being brought to completion, when the Creator had branded the individual with a secret mark, selecting the spot above all others, where it would hurt the individual most, should the branding come to light. He was then released into the world, without knowing himself to be branded. The unanswerable personal attack was like wantonly confronting a person with his own secret mark, like leading a person down a corridor which was that person's mind, and bringing him to a point where he would see for himself what the guide already knew: that he was naught! It was like pulling away the sheet in which one's self-confidence was wrapped to reveal a void. The uncovering of such a deep secret necessarily gave Orimili's people sleepless nights, which explains why this manner of a personal attack was referred to as *insomnia*.

Ekwenze Orimili had been confronted with the secret and humiliating brand of his creator. True enough, he had long enjoyed the privilege of knowing about his brand, but it was not a crushing knowledge, as long as one could go on as if it were unknown. Now the privilege was gone, shattered by the coming of insomnia. Appropriately, Orimili remained wakeful throughout the night, his mind steadfastly declining to come to grips with what had happened. At first, his consciousness seemed to be blank; and the ideas which floated through it seemed to be all opaque, and not to call for identification and exploration.

Later that night, Orimili began to be aware of specific ideas, one of the first of which to impress itself with any force upon his consciousness being the fell stun that Edoko Uwadiegwu had received from the evil spirits, which had pursued him for a good while and had finally overtaken him. These same spirits seemed to have turned to Ekwenza Orimili, brandishing the infernal club. Ekwenze was amazed to find that he was in the mood to answer, 'Here I am!' He pondered this reply. To answer thus, he reasoned, was to say that he was ready for death; how was he to be sure that the fiends wouldn't take him to be in earnest? Yes, come to think of it, wasn't he in earnest, really? Of course, the fiends were malicious in diverse ways; and did not their high malice contain a very strong streak of sadism? How else was one to explain their trick of striking down their victims in the very bloom of their career? He could see them making merry at such an achievement. Consider what had been happening in his family. Allowing that Ekesi was a well-known case, what about his grandfather, who died in battle? What about Obiako his father? A man who had worked very hard all his life; then, just before he could retire to enjoy the fruits of his labours, the fiends took interest in him, and did him in! Was it for nothing that they were referred to as they who destroyed life when it was most full and most joyful? On the other hand, they wouldn't touch a desperate fellow, who offered them himself as a willing victim! Perhaps the best way to deal with them was to be utterly indifferent. Orimili, therefore, let the spirits know that he didn't see any difference between life and death. If one was fighting for one's life, did it really make sense as one was only trying to keep it safe for death? So the fiends were welcome, any time. That was beating them at their own game!

Nevertheless, there was something to be said for remaining alive. Osita should still need him, shouldn't he? For Osita then. Why should such a promising young man be left utterly parentless? Also – he gave further ground – the other children needed him; and Okuata too. What did she mean by saying that he didn't care for his younger children, though? Of course he cared for them. She herself should be willing to admit that if he passed away right now, it would affect Osita more, in that he would not have the advantage of seeing his remains in state, before they were put away; but the younger children would!

For some reason, which Orimili did not trouble himself to examine, he ruminated on these morbid thoughts in a matter-of-fact way. It did not even occur to him as odd that he should have these thoughts; rather it seemed natural enough to have them. He went all the way with them; weighing every side of the question, seriously, as though to see very clearly what his gains and losses would be, before finally making up his mind to live or die. It was as though there was not the least question in his mind whether he would put an end to his life, if his conclusions warranted it; and if the invisible participants to his internal conference showed any reluctance to strike him down when he gave them the word.

But he had reached no conclusion on the matter before his mind drifted, at last, to the cause of his wakefulness. The injury hovered, as though suspended in his consciousness, for some moments. Then he faced it, manfully. It was true, what Okwuese had said; penetratingly true! But did it mean that whatever was true had to be uttered? Weren't there some which were better left unspoken? He tried to dredge up another example of such an unspeakable truth. He failed. Did it mean then that he alone of all human beings was in the outer rim of things, where one had to try not to be seen; whereas the rest of the people of Okocha danced around within a circle of light, free, and unable to be embarrassed?

Orimili felt in an excruciating way the pressure of the overwhelming fact which he carried with him wherever he went, from which he was attempting hopelessly to protect himself. It was as if he had only freshly put his shoulder to this fact; feeling its weight for the first time. He ground his teeth from the sheer weight.

All right, granted that he could not shift the burden and cause it to slip from his shoulders and crash to the ground; yet why should Okwuese take it upon herself to point it out, and remind everybody that he had the hunch upon his back? Was it on her back, that hunch? So what had she to do with it? Perhaps there ought to be something to do about that presumption. However, his mind did not rise to the occasion. Rather, on being called upon to suggest what might be done to Okwuese, it seemed to smile on him with grave sympathy, and then draw back to a more quiet corner. Why? Was this something to do with fatigue, this refusal to come up with ideas? He shook his body, felt every muscle respond like a spring, and wondered why his mind seemed to have been beaten so early this night of nights when he must keep a vigil. As if in consequence of thus shaking up his body, and as if in answer to his problem, the idea of the *ozo* title pushed its way through, like a fish pushing up smoothly from the deep waters, and presented itself to his consciousness. No! Before that! – he heard himself speak out loud; and then, kept still for some moments, fearing that his unintentionally loud command to his mind to find something else had awakened someone. How embarrassing it would be if his wife had overheard him. At the same time, Ekwenze Orimili sagged on his bed, terribly depressed that he couldn't work himself into a fury; the sort that should make him go out there and then to Ananwemadu's place, and have it out with somebody there!

It was most shameful of him; quite unusual too, that he hadn't quickly decided on what he must do. He decided to visualize the scene of his wife's humiliation; perhaps that should be of help. But the only help which came to him was the reassurance that had he been there in person that fateful evening, he should simply have drawn his broadsword, or borrowed one from Ogbuefi Emenogha – more likely the latter, since he himself rarely carried his broadsword even during ceremonial occasions; and in any case, the instrument hadn't been whetted for years – he should then have walked across to where the women were, picked out Okwuese, and brought the edge of the sword down on her head. All this would have taken place without him causing the least stir among the crowd. He, for his own part, would have walked back, after the act had been done, and calmly resumed his place among the elders to continue watching the dances which would have been performing.

The key quality of this reflection which made it pleasing to Orimili was its serenity. It suited him perfectly that nothing be disturbed in the execution of this vengeance. Even the representation of the scene in his mind was totally without drama. It was just as if a voice with no passion whatever, and no authority, was casually narrating it to him. This man's serenity had never been put to the test through physical suffering. In fact he seemed to have everything going for him, and was the envy of his neighbours and fellow townspeople who frequently told him in jest that life was partial towards him, smiling on him whether or not he did anything to deserve this. Few of the townsmen had any idea of the burden of Orimili's self-consciousness. Not even his bosom friend Obiefuna Emenogha had an idea. It would have been a burden and a terror altogether private and secret, had not Okuata been drawn into it. But she had been spared the dread her husband had felt all along for a dark and terrible hand lying in wait for him, to arrest him, plunge into his bowels, and pull out everything in one determined and fatal movement. That horrid hand had now appeared, and Okuata had seen the flash of it, being so near; and this was what had knocked her flat.

In point of fact, Okwuese's thrust, flawlessly homed in, was but a manner of putting a question Orimili was already familiar with. It was a question he had mustered up the courage to face about a year previously, and had gone to the *ozo* society to sort out for him. Wasn't it after all the judgement of that ruling class against a man he thought to be innocent; a judgement given despite his own testimony, that had led him to sue for membership in the society? What Ekwenze Orimili had gone to seek with the heads in Okocha that wear the eagle-quill was a clarification of their estimation of him, which he thought to be hidden in that judgement. When he had seen the full significance of Okwuese Ananwemadu's 'What is Orimili?', he had known that he was ready to take the answer of the *ozo* people, whatever it was.

Orimili neither slept that night, nor managed to work up his fury. But he was thinking more and more of the patriarchs of his line: his father, and the grandfather who died in battle long before he was born. Later his thoughts dwelt on his ancestor four generations back; and the more he thought of him, the more he was displeased with the man. For, as far as he was concerned, that ancestor, Muodi, was the absolute beginning of his line, being the oldest name in it. However, Muodi should not have had that distinction, if he had remained in his homeland. Why, for goodness sake should a man leave his homeland and never go back? Merely to be the head of a line? And why, of all places, should he choose to settle in Okocha? A legacy of suffering, of never knowing the meaning of home, to bequeath to one's successors. If only his grandfather had survived that accursed battle! It seemed to him that whatever was known of the family background must have died with the ill-fated warrior, since he had learned nothing from his own father on that subject. If only something had been left him by means of which to find his way back to his homeland, then all would have been plain-sailing. He would have taken his wife and children with him, and Osita, and gone back to his own people. He could see them going ecstatic with joy the moment he told them who he was, and who Osita was, and who the children with him were. How they should all clap their hands, play the great drums, and fire cannons of welcome! Could he blame the people of Okocha for treating him like a leper? What security could there be for a man, whether alive or dead, as long as he was cut off from his ancestral homeland – and never to know it?

Instantly, Ekwenze experienced a tremor, which travelled in a wave down his entire body. He was terrified. What if he were to die and going down to the land of the ancestors, find no welcome among the ancestors of Okocha? if they asked him what he sought there; and which of the lines of the sons of Okocha he thought he belonged to? Could anyone blame him then if he took hold of a halter, and did himself in – a second time? Or were there no halters to be had in the land of the ancestors? Now that the thought had occurred to him, he began to wonder about the welfare of his own ancestors. The shock which he had experienced earlier returned now with redoubled force as he thought of the four patriarchs of his line hanging about at the outskirts of the land of the ancestors of Okocha. He saw them wandering in an open country, which was very much like the grassland between Okocha and Amofia. He held the image; tried to scrutinize their faces – to see how they felt, being where they were. He knew which of them was Nwofia, his grandfather, who had died, fighting for Okocha. He was heavily built, just like Orimili himself. Strange! He tried to make out his face, to be sure; but the man seemed to bend his face to the ground, intently. He couldn't make it out. He wondered now how many generations it would take to build up a proper community of ancestors for his line. No, he let go of the vision – the dead could not be so heartless!

Almost at the same instant, Ekwenze heard his wife stir. He lay very still, his heart beating loudly. The water-pot scratched against something. It seemed to Ekwenze that this was the most encouraging scratch he had heard in all his life. It gave him the sense that relief might be had in this horrid affair: Okuata would stay, it seemed.

He remained in his bed. When he heard his wife return from the stream the first time, he felt the desire well up suddenly that he should go to her, and say… oh, how was it going to be? How put it in one utterance, which would be absolutely concise, and persuasive? It would be rather unremarkable to go simply and say: 'You won't go back to your mother, will you?' The moment passed, without his coming up with the absolutely convincing word.

He broke his vigil finally, when he heard the kitchen come alive; and he had finished preparing himself for the day when Okuata brought him his breakfast. He lifted up his eyes to her morning salutation; looked into hers, held them for a moment, and then looked down again upon the food before him. But just as Okuata was breathing out, in one forceful act of getting rid of the breath which had stuck to her throat when his bloodshot eyes had held her own, she heard him say:

'Do you wish to bring me down utterly, and complete Okwuese's infernal work for her?'

'God forbid! What do you mean anyway?'

'What I mean is, stay with me!'

The meeting with Emenogha could not be put off. Never before had Orimili felt like not meeting his great friend. He would have been glad to be left completely alone to wallow in his depression. It didn't even occur to him that he should try to pull himself out of the condition, rather there was something good and honest about not wanting to make an act of will in any direction whatever. It was also congenial just to sit around and think how terribly easy it was to undo a man; well, maybe not every man. So the thing was how dreadfully easy it had been for a simple woman to undo Orimili! It did occur to Orimili that if he would be honest to himself, perhaps he should be best to let himself go: to cry and make a lament for his hard fate. But it retained the distance of a supposition. Every receptacle in his being was filled to overflowing with lethargy; every emotive function was permeated. The only thing that stood aside, untouched by this disease was the certainty he felt that he should see nobody, and be seen by nobody. He could not bear the very thought of being seen; now that he had been exposed, his greatest need seemed to be to open a hole in the ground, and hide away like a rat.

The experience of the previous night had developed by day into a feeling of a great empty space in himself at the edge of which he trembled, and in danger of tumbling inwards and crumbling up, at the slightest push. It was just like bending over a basin of water to look at the sky-dome beneath, and suddenly feeling dizzy. Yet another way in which Orimili felt his tragedy was as though the ground had opened under his feet, but had withheld from him the relief of being sucked in and covered over.

He met his friend, in spite of everything. Emenogha had heard what Okwuese had done, but he must give it wide berth during their conversation. He felt it, he imagined, as keenly as Orimili himself must feel it; and it embarrassed him. As a matter of fact, he let a thin shell of self-delusion persist in his mind that Orimili had not heard it, or that if Okuata had mentioned it, being the sensible woman she was, she must have done it in such a way that Orimili should somehow remain unaware of the deep malice of it. So he did not dare even to show the least sympathy to his friend; how agreeable it should have been if the meeting were taking place in the night – in the dark – so that he would not be caught out avoiding his friend's eyes. What helped him was his keeping before his consciousness the reason for his coming. Were it simply to tell about the debate at the meeting of the *ozo*, he would have put it off for a day or two until he could assure himself that he should be able to look into the man's eyes and allow him to look into his, without batting an eyelid. He had pressed himself into coming because of Okwuese; but he wasn't going to talk about her. Quite the contrary, he was going to carry on as if he didn't know of her existence. What he was going to talk about was the debate. *Ozo* affairs were going to be reduced to a mere subterfuge. In speaking about them, he would be aiming to make Orimili feel his solidarity with him against Okwuese; letting him feel his burning hostility towards her. It is hard to imagine how Emenogha would have managed all this in the dark. At any rate, that preferred setting was not to be had. So he abridged the preliminaries and went straightaway into a detailed report on the first debate of Orimili's application for the title, stressing that the prospects did not in any way appear to be bad. He said that Oranudu might have been more helpful to him; but he suspected that the old man would rather stay aloof and not influence the decision. That, he made haste to point out, was far better than if he had raised the least objection. In the second place, the one stridently hostile point of view had been that of Ugonabo, allowing that Nweke Nwofia seemed to be somewhat interested in what Ugonabo was saying. However, towards the end, Nweke seemed to be coming round to the majority viewpoint. Ogbuefi Emonogha was determined that he should not have the occasion of outlining for Orimili what precisely the argument of the opposition was. So he entered into a long discourse on the plan of action which he and Nwalioba and Udozo were trying to put together. If that plan worked, he was quite sure that Orimili would be a titled man within a year. The plan consisted mainly in canvassing the title-holders who had been silent during the last meeting, because he was sure that the more people who spoke in favour, the more ridiculous the opposition would appear. Moreover, the case was to be brought up for discussion as often as the club met, until the opposition was worn out.

Orimili had listened in silence while his friend was speaking. He permitted a further interval to elapse before he rejoined with a comment which Emenogha found quite disappointing:

'I think you have done a fine job. I am gratified, and I thank you sincerely. The title; certainly it should be a nice thing to have. But I have been thinking, why not put by the money for Ejike – I mean my little fellow?' Orimili hung fire, going over in his mind what he had said, and wondering whether it was a suitable answer to Emenogha's speech. For the life of him, he couldn't recall anything specific from what his friend had been saying, even though he had listened very attentively – which is scarcely surprising after his awful night. At any rate, he was saying to himself, concerning the idea of saving up money for Ejike: yes, why not? For this was a brand new notion; and it seemed to have come to him entirely of its own accord, all formulated and wrapped up. Oh, it wasn't fair what Okuata had said, about his not caring for her children. See how naturally the plan for Ejike had tumbled out, unbidden, showing that the thing had been at the back of his mind all the time – in his *mind*, he meant to say, not at its back.

After a moment of silence, Obiefuna Emenogha asked,

'Do you mean him to have the kind of education which Osita has had?'

'Yes, yes; I think that something of the sort should be done for him, and the others too; so that when I'm gone they should be able to say to themselves so-and-so was what my father did for me! He would have done a great deal more, if he had lived!'

'Shouldn't that be something!' Emenogha answered, and paused, before pointing out that Ejike was of course very young, and it should be a long time before it was going to be necessary to start saving for him. 'Do you know,' he concluded, 'that I wish to do the same for my son; I mean, to have him do as my son-in-law has done?'

'Really?' Orimili asked with sudden animation. 'Do you really mean that, Emenogha?'

'Yes, it is one reason why I want our two families to stick so together. So you know that I'm not opposed to your wanting to do something fine for your little ones. Still, the title is a sensible investment in many ways; you must agree with me.'

'Of course, it is a valuable thing to have.'

'So the plan remains unchanged?'

'It remains exactly as it was.'

Obiefuna Emenogha beamed. Getting up from his seat, he walked across to where Orimili sat, and shook him by the hand, saying,

'Ogbuefi Ekwenze Orimili, you are a manly man!'

'Thank you,' replied Orimili. 'Any, by the way, I'm going to have some festive sacrifices offered for Osita. The time and place are not yet fixed, but do keep it in mind, will you?'

'Of course; just let me know when. What…'

'You will bring your family, mind you.'

'All right. Is it something to do with the match?'

'No. Not directly, at least,' amended Orimili. 'I have learned that Osita is a river spirit. So there ought to have been a reincarnation ritual for him long ago…'

'The sacrifices are to supply…?'

'Ah, I won't waste a moment when he returns: I shall take him through the reincarnation ritual straightaway.'

The conversation with Emenogha did much to lift up Orimili's spirits. This surprising outcome was because Orimili had perceived that his friend was determined to stand by him in both his high and low moments. It made him somewhat self-conscious, but it also helped to lighten the shade of isolation which he had felt to be closing round him. He was pleasantly affected by what Emenogha had said he wanted to do for his son. Oh, it was nice to hear him say that! He had begun a new trend in Okocha; had, in plain language, become the measure of success for the townsmen! Wasn't that something? He took the issue of this achievement several points higher: A time might come when people would be saying to one another, let's ask Orimili about this; he should be able to tell us what to do! Okwuese might think she had wiped off his social identity, and brought to naught his hopes of becoming one of the leading figures in Okocha. What did he want to be a leader for, if not to give the cue and have everybody looking up to him? Now, wasn't that what he had got? He had made his mark in Okocha: Okwuese or no Okwuese. Of course, Orimili didn't see as part of this achievement the split that was beginning to appear in the high government of Okocha. He was inclined to see this budding split as signs of jealousy and resistance to himself. However, he quickly realized that if Ugonabo and his other opponents wished to keep him from the club out of jealousy, then there was no chance that he would ever get in. They would oppose him to the last. He heaved a breath, and sagged as a fresh wave of depression assailed him. He would never be made an *ozo* since every member had almost an equal say in the matter. Any old fellow could say he didn't approve of Orimili; and that would be that – unless he afterwards said he had changed his mind in favour of him. So in spite of being a measure of success, he would continue to encounter rejection everywhere in the town; oh yes – he stoutly maintained against a voice which challenged him from within – Okocha's sons didn't want him. What was Ugonabo's objection, after all? Emenogha was only being delicate not to mention it. He knew what it was all about; he had known all along that that would be the sticking point but had deluded himself – against the facts of an older case – that the *ozo* were high-minded men, who would examine the issue on its own merits, and not go digging under his feet. What had happened now? Okwuese Ananwemadu had said it loud and clear, shouting it into his ear, to make sure that he heard. Did she do it entirely on her own? Of course not. One of the sayings about the great river which the man had also appropriated was its being utterly unamenable to human influence. How come that a single person – a woman, at that – had so discomposed Orimili and shattered his very will to defend himself? It soothed his crushed ego better to think that the feat had been the work of the whole town; or at least, that there had been a conspiracy against him. The people of Okocha had got together and whispered to Okwuese Ananwemadu to go and do it; yes, go! And they had sat back to see how she got on. Of course, Emenogha wasn't in the team that had been sent to her, nor had he joined in planning it. One knew that without taking the trouble to investigate. Nor was Nwalioba, nor Obikeze Uwadiegwu. And Orimili would reward them by inviting them all to the festive sacrifice for Osita: all his friends in fact, Udozo, Udeagu, Okandi Echebido, Oranudu. Ah! Make it a gathering of friends. He put his hand to his cheek, and stared at it. A new sodality?

So, shouldn't he hold the feast at Amanza? The danger was that at Amanza it was likely to have the appearance of a public event, and spoilers, such as Ananwemadu, might turn up uninvited. In that case, he strongly urged himself, make it defiantly private! Tell the fellow, quite simply, that he was not wanted there.

Orimili did not deceive himself that he would do this for any cause. Defiance was not going to serve his purpose at the present. So long as his application hung in the balance, and had the least chance of slipping through, he could not afford to defy even his adversaries. He might indeed exploit the festal occasion to buy him support at the club. Orimili's bitterness surged at this thought, rising very nearly to the brim, where it would have suffocated him altogether. What, he asked himself, should be the purpose of trying to buy the support of a people who despised him merely because he happened not to be one of those whose ancestry could be traced until it disappeared into the soil itself? The idea of a line of descent disappearing into the soil seemed to him to be an apt way of putting it. For, how else could one explain the arrogance of the people, unless their origins were sunk into the soil in as physical a way as the roots of a plant are sunk in it? Whereas his own roots had lost themselves in the river down which his ancestors were said to have come. To plant one's roots in the river was to have them obliterated; didn't he remember from what he had told the sacred tree only yesterday? Clearly, it wasn't sufficient that one's ancestors were buried in the land; that didn't mean that one's roots were buried in the land – so much he had learned from the sons of Okocha. Being rooted in the soil had to be something more physical and vital.

The question had not really been dealt with, and so it re-presented itself to his consciousness: should he use the sacrifices as a means of buying support, or should he make them a defiant act? Now, here was a dilemma. Orimili decided to leave it to Obikeze's Arobinagu to determine the circumstances of the sacrifices. Why should he bother about that, when the Arobinagu could decide it quite easily, by simply looking it up in the sheet which lay before him always, as Obikeze had said, in which the past and the future were displayed? He smiled now with grim irony to notice that Obikeze's Arobinagu was not alone in having the knowledge of the past and future. Perhaps it excelled only in matters relating to the future. For had Okwuese Ananwemadu not shown how good she was in matters relating to the past? Did she not delve into his own past, and bring up from it a fact which he desired so much to keep buried where it was? Had she not tortured him with her find, like a fiend?

That instant, Orimili's past unfurled before him like the great sheet kept by Obikeze's Arobinagu. But only one part of the sheet was shown him. Orimili thought that he could see, out of the corner of his eye, the other half of the sheet, folding up and held down in place by a pair of hands: a woman's hands, no doubt those of Okwuese Ananwemadu. Furthermore, what appeared clearly in what was being shown him were things he had forgotten, and never wanted to recall.

Out of this mass of facts, an incident which had occurred over forty years before beamed at him with particular intensity. Ekwenze Orimili beheld himself, arms flailing in mid air; the white of his eyes protruding unnaturally, the black having disappeared behind his skull; Orimili saw himself submerged in water right up to the lower jaw. And this was taking place in the great river itself. The image enlarged itself, becoming pellucid, as though it had been polished to a sheen by the same hand on the sheet, the hand of Okwuese Ananwemadu. As the image grew larger and more brilliant, so did it seem to erase from Orimili's consciousness everything that had contributed to making the man. Were Orimili required to set down in writing what he remembered of his past, it seemed that this image meant him to set down the narrative of a little boy in frantic despair – no more! Something else which Orimili found distressing about this image was that whereas he knew that his association with the great river began on the night of his reincarnation ritual, he was now being told that he was on the verge of drowning in the great river, even before the ritual took place. Ekwenze said to the vision, 'No.' But it was no use. The vision was unconvinced; and no more could he thrust the sheet away from his consciousness.

Ekwenze Nwofia and his playmates, Obiefuna Emenogha, Obinagu Nwalioba, Okandi Echebido, the youngest of the group, and Udozo Anaeso, had been having a swim in the river. Obinagu Nwalioba was the oldest boy in the group, but Ekwenze was by far the ablest swimmer. He swam faster and could dive and remain submerged longer than any of the others. On the day of the incident which now overshadowed and crowded out everything that had been represented to him from the past, he had swum as usual; outpaced his friends, and dared much farther out into the deeper parts of the water than he had ever done before. Ekwenze had sailed back triumphantly and rejoined his friends, who had hastened back to the shallows as soon as they encountered the cooler waters and faster currents of the deeper parts of the river. They had played at the shallows, splashing water into one another's eyes, a favourite sport, which they performed sitting on their heels in the water, and driving their palms across the surface of the water, fingers pressed together, and angled to discharge water on the faces of the others. One had to splash in all directions at the same time, to protect one's eyes, by driving against the gusts of water coming towards their faces, and to score hits against the others. One's eyes got bloody-red and irritating the more often one was hit in the face. It also made breathing difficult. The first to concede defeat that day was Obiefuna, breaking out from the circle and striking out towards the deep waters. The others quickly abandoned the sport and went after him, each one trying to go farther than he had done before. When they returned from this stint, they went ashore. However, they found that they were not ready to go home yet. Ekwenze was the first to step back into the water, once they had all agreed to have another go at it. However, he stepped on clay, losing his footing at the edge of the shallows. He panicked, and crashed into the water. The laughter of his friends who were yet on the shore echoed in merriment. Within moments, however, Ekwenze was out of the shallows, swept along by a current which had come from nowhere into the deeper parts of the water, and he was struggling frantically to regain his foothold.

In an instant, he had hit the bottom, and was propelled by the impact back into the air. In breaking the surface, he had pushed up a great white column of water, which broke into hundreds of fragments shining brightly in the sun, and he was clawing at the water and the air in a frenzy, the black of his eyes buried behind the eyeballs – the very image which the hand of Okwuese Ananwemadu had forced on his consciousness. It was at this very moment that some of his friends, perceiving that something was amiss, ceased their laughter and dashed into the water to save him. To save him! People were always saving Ekwenze Orimili Nwofia! Why was he always needing to be saved? What a tragic fate to be perpetually in danger, and to find oneself for ever being plucked out of ruin at the last moment! Who else had a similar fate? Obviously, no one; for he himself had never had the good fortune of saving anyone. But they were always saving him. Right at that moment, Ekesi, and Obikeze's Arobinagu – and the man himself, Obikeze – were fighting to save his boy; in short, to save him, because in spite of Okuata's shocking reminder that he had other children besides Osita, who didn't know that if any harm were to happen to Osita, Orimili himself would cease to be? Such would be the last accident from which no one could save him – in point of fact, no accident at all, but the final treachery of his invisible enemies, and the people of Okocha as well, that is, minus those who did not consent that he should be tortured. So it was he himself that Ekesi, Obikeze and the Arobinagu were trying to save. Then again, Emenogha, Udozo and Nwalioba were also engaged in saving his cause; in saving him at the sodality!

Orimili was more lonely and depressed than ever. Not being able, apparently, to do anything for himself, but rather having things done for him was a great source of misery indeed. The one person who had depended on him, and whom he ought to have saved, if need be with his own life, was Ekesi. But didn't he, Ekwenze Orimili, let her slip through his fingers and die? He wouldn't go all the way with a thought which had secreted itself into his consciousness, suggesting that he in fact had helped to cause Ekesi's death. He thrust the thought from him.

The thought he couldn't get rid of was the one which mocked him for being rescued by his youthful friends from the clutches of the great river god. Was not the very ground of his faith that he was in community with the river god? The image of the little Ekwenze in a moment of extremity forced itself so powerfully on his consciousness that it was as if it meant to say to him, 'How now, fellow? Is that you, the shadow of the river god himself?' The demonic taunt cut Orimili to the marrow.

Slowly, however, it dawned on Orimili that there was, probably, more than one way of looking at the incident. It was some kind of a rescue, all right, but at the same time, wasn't it the river god's way of reclaiming to himself what was his? It wouldn't have been wanton destruction. The argument was pleasing to him, and he greeted it with a grunt. After this, however, he still confronted himself: where was he now? Was he in the river god's inner circle, or did he belong to Okocha, whose sons – it was not to be denied – had rescued him?

Thoroughly baffled, Orimili tried to analyse the issue point by point. The river god had been exceptionally good to him; that was beyond question. Even the townspeople themselves, who were unconcerned one way or the other, confessed it, seeing how the god had prospered his business. But for practical purposes, Orimili must see himself as tied to the people of Okocha. Quite simply, his situation was an in-between state, living between the great river and Okocha. Quickly, this in-between state assumed a dramatic form in his consciousness. As a result of a conspiracy of the fates, he had been placed in the centre of a great tug-of-war: the river god, with Ekwenze's elemental comrades, tugging at one of his arms, and Okocha and his sons at the other! Ekwenze Orimili's unconscious wish had been to hold together in his very person the two essences that had meant so much to his people: the spirits of the land and the great flood; Okocha and Orimili. The god, Orimili, seemed happy enough to have the man for his servant. With Okocha, it wasn't so in the least. But Orimili had agreed with Emenogha to struggle some more, little suspecting that he was being led, as it were, to a height where he was to find himself staring futility in the face.

In the first movement of his life's struggle, however, at the stage where he was fighting literally for his life, the difference had been made by his friends who had been with him. Seeing that he was actually drowning, they had fanned out towards his flanks, only for him to go under again before they reached him. Nwalioba told them to move further back, in case he drifted downstream. In the same instant, Ekwenze surfaced again, quite near Obinagu Nwalioba, who had the presence of mind to give him a shove. This shove was enough to flatten Ekwenze upon the river, breaking the pattern of his death dance, and enabling him to use his limbs to effect. He struck out and kept himself afloat, while the others rallied round him, steering him towards the shore. He collapsed, then, when he stumbled to the shore. Seeing Ekwenze collapse, Okandi Echebido – who up till that moment had not understood that what his older friends were engaged in was not a special entertainment for himself – thought that he had died. His own merriment died abruptly, and he ran off towards the town. He did not stop running until he reached Obiako Nwofia's house. In spite of his wildly beating heart, and great difficulty in catching his breath, he did manage to get out the story that Obiako's only son had died at the water's edge.

Obiako gazed at the youngster, but did not comprehend immediately what he was saying. Then he gave one agonized cry, which he cut out abruptly, as it flashed through his mind that the informant was a mere child, who should not be trusted to know what he was saying. Nevertheless, he left immediately for the river, maintaining a steady trot, until he met Obinagu and the others bringing home his son. Okandi Echebido, of course, followed the old man, who had completely lost awareness of the youngster, and did not even know that he met anyone on the way to the river. Many a townsman who saw him trotting towards the river, with the expression of utter disaster written all over him, tried shouting an enquiry into his path; none of which could stop him, for he heard nothing. So Okandi picked up the enquiries and told them all they wanted to know. The result was that hardly had Obiako met the party leading his dazed son home than he was joined by a great number of townspeople, making a great commotion as a sign of concern.

They did not take the exhausted boy home to rest, but stopped to interrogate the rescuers about the circumstances of the accident. Then they all went to the edge of the river to see the spot where the drama had happened. It was agreed by all present that there was something mysterious about the incident. How was it that a champion swimmer, such as Ekwenze was, should be swept away at the shallows, where there was scarcely any current to begin with?

Ekwenze had been recovering, meanwhile. Having recovered his senses sufficiently to take in the situation, and to understand that he himself was the spectacle at the centre of the townspeople's excitement, he had grown so self-conscious that he had tried to sneak away. In consequence of this, the townspeople thought that there was something sinister about the episode, suggesting that Ekwenze himself might have the key to the mystery.

Not long afterwards, Obiako consulted a seer, and it was found out that the boy had had a spectacular escape. For he had been on his way to answer the call of his allies, the entourage of the river god, and that unless the ties with these invisible allies were immediately broken, Obiako could very well count himself childless, for the elementals had sworn that there was going to be no escape when next they came calling.

6 | *The Debate*

Orimili's Song
Mighty River, Life-source of all
The fish teeming beneath your waves;
Bronzed flood, life-blood of Orimili's Boat,
To you Ekwenze brings his thanks.
    You too sustain Okocha;
Same way as Orimili's life is owed to you.
Long ago, the seer saw and affirmed
That he's Okocha's guardian's offspring;
So have you ever been his sire.
    Mighty River, Orimili *atu nnu*,
Bearer of the enormous fish;
The greatest of the lot that swim your waves;
The same Orimili's ship;
    So Mighty Flood, be for ever
The source of all his fortune.

Orimili Nwofia had been having his busiest season of the entire year. The harvest season itself, which to him was the accustomed high tide of freight and money-making, was as busy as usual. There had been a full load of merchandise each market-day to ferry to Okono. As it was also the period when Guy & Son had the most abundant supply of cash crops, Orimili had freight for several runs a week to Okono. But this was all heavy work, which kept him toiling all day, and for much of the night too. By contrast, he had been doing an average of five trips a week during the past month – one more than the average at the peak season. He wouldn't have been able to squeeze in that extra run were it not for the fact that the work this time was much less fraught with toil and stress. It consisted largely in ferrying to Okocha the supplies which were destined to be used in the construction and furnishing of the facilities ordered for the colonial defence force. The officers arrived as soon as the buildings were ready, and commenced recruiting volunteers for service abroad. It turned out that fetching up the materials for the construction was only a phase; the major phase of Orimili's work during the period. The second phase began not long after the officers arrived.

Orimili was especially glad about this turn in his fortune because it occurred at the beginning of the rainy season, a time when his work seemed to be least fruitful. The farmers would be preoccupied with tending their farms, leaving him with precious few passengers to ferry to Okono on the market-day. And those who made the journey had less still by way of merchandise to take to the market. But Orimili would not think of breaking his schedule, fearing that such a change would cost him more in the long run, as well as force him to stay longer on land than he imagined was good for his health. He persevered, not daring to complain aloud even on a day he found that Guy & Son had only two sacks of palm kernel in their warehouse. He took them, and went his way to Okono. This was the early planting season and Orimili was doing exceptionally well. That must be a reward for his perseverance; also, his namesake and protector was quite obviously wide awake. What was more, he had had the premonition, as it were, to repair his barge, and have everything in readiness for this boom. It showed that the old saying was true, namely, that if a man's guardian spirit took up his position beside his ward, even the cleverest and most assiduous enemy would not be able to find a way to get at the man.

So it was that after the peak period, Ekwenze Orimili had gained a new contract. The new recruits were committed to him to ferry to Okono, from where they continued their journey to the colonial capital. To Orimili, the undertaking was most agreeable, for the men took care of themselves. So his day with the volunteers was short, involving little or no work on his own part. All he did was navigate the boat to Okono, and back again to Okocha. The pay was excellent too. It all went to show Orimili that handling cargo was actually mere drudgery – something that one had to put up with, if not pretend to enjoy doing, only because one got paid for it. Were it possible to earn one's living by merely sailing up and down the river once a day, Orimili would have been the man for the job; for, from Okocha to Okono, and back again, there wasn't a boatman who had done as many days on the water, and who was less disposed to thoughts of retirement, ever, from the job. No, Ekwenze Orimili would die well before it was time to retire – or rather, just before. Orimili was contented with the chance which his day with the volunteers afforded him to earn his money without drudgery, his only discomfort being the shortness of the day itself. Okuata had insisted that it did him good to have those half days, but he doubted this, complaining that he did not know what to do with himself during the long evenings. Apart from this minor inconvenience, Orimili was disposed to admit that he fared a good deal better now than he ever did at that season of the year.

So preoccupied was he during the busy period that he forgot to have a letter sent to Osita. The young man did not give him time to recall this omission and redress it, before sending him yet another letter. And Orimili was fairly ecstatic with joy on receiving it, knowing that it was Osita's – who else ever wrote to him, except Osita? Of course, he had promised in the earlier letter to write again very soon; and he had done exactly that, giving his father yet another proof that he was indeed faithful to his word. Oh, his word was good, and a dutiful son he was too! With this came the pang that the father had been remiss, and had not answered the last letter. It was a pity not to have done that, especially because of the wonderful news he had been meaning to surprise and delight him with. Ah, to have failed to enter the competition, when he had been so certain of winning! Well then, Osita had entered alone; and his good news was probably in the letter he now held; he would still tell his, of course, but it would not be as nice as it would have been, if the letters had crossed. The best he could do now was to promise himself to write very soon.

Thinking now of the marriage he was arranging for Osita, Orimili quickly fell into a self-congratulatory mood. Had it taken a whole year to arrange, it should still have been worth every moment that had been spent working towards it. That it turned out to be the achievement of one and a half days made it all the more intoxicating to contemplate. Orimili visualized the ceremony of exchange of consent: his 'daughter', as he increasingly thought of her, perched on one knee, wine-cup in one hand, out of which she takes a sip, and presents the cup to Osita, amid the applause of the onlookers. His son would understand then that although he had not been prompt in answering his letters, he had been taking every chance which came his way, and turning it to the young man's advantage.

Orimili left the barge as soon as it had been moored along the Guy & Son quay, and hurried into the office to speak to Onyeme. Onyeme looked up from his desk and greeted Orimili, adding that it was as if the older man knew what was going on in his mind; how he had urgent business to see to at Okono the next day, and how he had been meaning to go straight from the office at the end of the day to Orimili's house to ask for a ride.

'Certainly,' answered Orimili. Then as a jest suggested itself to him, he adopted an aspect of irony, and asked, 'Have you found yourself a mistress over there in Okono? That must be, else it'd be hard to understand your enthusiasm!'

Onyeme guffawed. 'I wish you were right,' he finally countered. 'In that case, you wouldn't have seen me at all, for I would have gone off straightaway, on foot too, to Okono. Do you think I would wait around here merely for the advantage of having a ride? Well, not if I had a mistress, instead of work, waiting for me at Okono! No, I'm not a lucky man. What I have to do at Okono is infinitely less interesting; important, all the same. Have you got news of interest to us?'

'Oh no; not the sort that would warm your heart, and make you set off overland to Okono. No, it is a letter from Osita; you will be able to come over and read it to me, will you?'

'Yes, certainly. I could call for a few minutes this evening, if that will suit you.' Onyeme was a good deal more forthcoming today. One wouldn't have suspected that he secretly resented attending Orimili at his place to read him Osita's letters. He never knew why the man insisted on his coming to the house to perform the charity, as if he was doing him a favour asking him to come to his house. However, he was the first to ask a favour today, so he should reciprocate.

'Aha! You can come this evening! Splendid. Do bring your pen along, so you may copy out my reply at the same time. For I haven't written to my son for over four months now; in fact, I didn't reply to his last letter, which I got a month ago. Remember the letter I asked you to come and read for me? You never came; why, Onyeme?'

'Come? Oh! I forgot about it; I'm sorry.'

'Oh, never mind. Someone else read it to me. I'll see you in the evening then?'

'Emh... You know, as there is going to be a reply to be copied out at the same time, why not let's do the whole thing together the day after tomorrow? Remember, I'm coming with you to Okono.'

'Yes, of course. But we aren't going this evening; so why can't you come?'

'You mean this evening? I have a great many things to do

this evening to prepare for the trip tomorrow. You know, since there is going to be a reply as well.'

'Well, then, why not tomorrow evening? We should be able to return to Okocha late in the afternoon, unless, of course, you mean to spend the night at Okono.'

Onyeme agreed that he hadn't thought of the opportunity which could be availed of the following evening: 'In that case,' he wound up, 'tomorrow evening then.'

Orimili had won a bargain. He beamed with satisfaction as he left the office. What he should do now was to think of the various things which he must say to Osita. The news concerning Adoba was the most pleasant to dwell on. However, he mustn't forget to warn him to stay away from that war they were fighting in Europe. There was a saying about a little boy trying to avenge his father's death; if he wasn't careful, he may end up suffering a fate similar to his father's. Ever since the grandfather died in a battle, Ekwenze's people had known that their race was unlucky in things related to warfare – as a matter of fact, they were cautious even as regards sports, especially the violent ones. That was why Obiako had steadfastly refused that his son should so much as wrestle with his age-mates. His instruction to Ekwenze had been very simple: If anyone boasted that he could beat you in a wrestling match, say, oh yes; I always knew that! Ekwenze was never to get into an argument with anyone. As to Osita, he was just as marked as the others before him. There was the football match long ago, for an instance. Didn't everybody's child go home at the end of the day, treading the ground firmly with both feet? Osita alone came home limping! He must keep mentioning to Osita to keep away from the war, until he was sure that there was no longer any danger of his getting involved. This time, he would go so far as telling him that if his city was threatened in any way, he must take ship and return immediately to Okocha. For a one-eyed man was by that fact indebted to blindness, and was liable to be seized at any time. On the other hand, someone who had a palm nut roasting in the fire – a single nut – would not suffer it to burn in the fire, nor somehow to get lost! It flashed through his mind that Okuata had disapproved of such metaphors which seemed to suggest that he thought of no other besides Osita. No, he didn't mean that, of course; and he didn't owe blindness anything. All the same, he'd better be careful how he spoke in her presence. How was one to speak to show that even though one had several eyes, and several nuts roasting in the fire, still one particular nut was… well, not more valuable, but… See, now, Okuata – he mentally reproached her – you see how it gets one in a jam minding what you say!

Orimili commenced to hum a tune to himself:

Okocha can boast of towering figures:
Emenogha, friend of Orimili is such;
And so are Nwalioba and Udozo; men,
Who speak the heart and mind of Okocha.
    As to Orimili, Mighty Flood
Is his domain, the giver of
His blessings; chief of which
Is Osita, Orimili's son, and
Pride of all Okocha.
    For which, Orimili

(That's the Mighty River itself,
And the favoured young man's father, both)
Is the name which most beseems Our Pride!

Orimili abandoned the tone of song as he wound up his exhortation, calling upon all that the people of Okocha held sacred: the soil, the great river, the ancestors, and all the gods to bring him back his son, in the fullness of time, safe and sound.

Ogbuefi Obiefuna Emenogha called out to Ogbuefi Udeagu, when he approached the latter's house.

'Eh!' answered Udeagu from within. As his house lay facing the pathway, and the front yard opened directly on to the pathway, without an avenue, one could fairly hold a conversation with Udeagu from the pathway.

'Shall I wait for you, or will you rather come along when you are ready?' Emenogha called back.

'Oh no; just a moment. Let me put on something, and I shall be ready. You can't be in such a hurry since you didn't call the meeting.'

Obiefuna paced the pathway until Udeagu joined him, and he was thinking how to suggest ideas to Udeagu concerning the title debate, which he was going to bring up again at the meeting today. To his dismay, Udeagu had said nothing during the last session; not even Ugonabo's vicious attack on Orimili had proved sufficient to bring him to help in the defence.

Udeagu joined him soon afterwards, and they fell into

pace. 'Have you any idea,' asked Udeagu, 'why the meeting has been called?'

'No,' answered Obiefuna, 'but whatever it is, I'm determined to bring up Orimili's application. As a matter of fact, I am going to this meeting especially for this purpose; and that is all I care about at the moment.'

'I suppose that it should be brought up again,' agreed Udeagu. 'Have you seen our in-law, Orimili, lately?'

'Oh yes; only a few days ago.'

'I wonder, did he give you any ideas how to deal with the objection raised by Ugonabo?'

'Oh, we didn't discuss that part as I can't see that there is anything he can do to help us to win the case.'

'I see what you mean,' answered Udeagu, 'that it is through his friends he must help himself. I have been thinking as well that we have a particular reason to try to push the case as far as it can go, for it should be a nice thing if our in-laws are not only rich, but also titled.'

'Ah, that should be nice indeed,' said Emenogha, irritably, 'only that it isn't Osita's title we are concerned with at the moment.'

'Of course. But if his father has the title, is it not as good as he himself having it?'

'You're quite right, but I was thinking of a particular aspect of the case, which is what our friends at the sodality seem not to grasp. Orimili deserves to be conferred with the title; that's the point. He is a reliable, and well-meaning fellow. He is rich and well-travelled. Do not our people say that the traveller has a larger fount of wisdom than the sedentary hoary-haired man? The club, I think, has much to gain from his experience. His son is an asset too, and he is set to rise to great things. The way things are going, we may yet all gather around him for shelter; you see what I mean? Think of the palm-wine sellers on a holiday at Amanza; without the Ngwu tree, could their wine remain fresh for one half of the evening? If we can foresee the time when we may have to gather together to take shelter under Osita's wings, I think it will be tragically short-sighted of us not to do what we can now to clear the way, in order not to have anything to be ashamed of, when the day comes. It is said that an individual who has too many enemies to contend with, should conciliate some, if need be take a keg of palm wine along, in order to be sure that he is not turned down! Don't you think that we should be inviting Orimili to come and join us, instead of his asking us? When children fight over their food, who sues for peace? Is it not the one who has seized the *foofoo*? Certainly, not the one who has the soup. So?'

'I think that the problem is to get this argument across to the others. I'm sure that even the opponents will withdraw their objections, if you speak to them in this way.'

The point, of course, was that in order that the argument should carry, it should come from someone else, not Emenogha, or any of the well-known friends of Orimili. Obiefuna Emenogha said to Udeagu: 'Yes, I'd say they'll withdraw their objections all the sooner, if the argument were to be presented by one who has so far seemed to be neutral; you, for instance. Wouldn't you agree?'

'Yes, yes; but don't you think that Orimili should have been asked to help us with ideas as to how to clear up the question raised by Ugonabo; not that it matters to me, but in order that it will not look as though we are not sufficiently circumspect – you know, as if we are asking the club to make a gamble.'

Emenogha's enthusiasm went limp when he heard Udeagu's argument. '*Gamble* sounds rather... umh... umh... unfair; I mean strong,' he lamely returned, after an interval. 'Also I think it is unfair of Ugonabo to insist on an obscure question, mindlessly obstructing a good cause. That question is really uncalled for. We have no law that I know of, which says that anyone whose remote ancestors have come from elsewhere cannot be admitted to the society. All that we have is that our tradition, or in fact, living memory, does not furnish us with an instance of one in circumstances similar to Orimili's receiving the title. My idea is that the fact that we don't have such an example does not in any way prove that it cannot be done. Why should we let Ugonabo hold us back from doing what we know to be right?'

'As far as I can see,' answered Udeagu, 'we won't be able to push the case even one step forward, unless we find a way to get around the problem. Whether or not it was called for, when Ugonabo first mentioned it, the fact we must now face is that it has been brought publicly to the notice of members; and something must be done about it, before we can make progress.'

'You mean that you will not come out in support, unless it is disposed of?' Emenogha was pressing Udeagu a little hard, and he knew it.

'Of course, I think that our in-law should be allowed to take the title. In point of fact, I'm of the view that no one should be debarred from getting what is his due on the basis of what is *not* remembered from the past. For that is what Orimili's handicap boils down to. It is not remembered whether any of his people have ever held the title, and it cannot be remembered where his people originally came from. How do we know that his people were not originally from Okocha; that the coming of his great-grandfather or someone like that was not a *return?*'

'Ah! That his people may have set out from here, and then returned?'

'I see nothing improbable about that!'

'That sounds really good. Why don't you bring it up during the debate today?' Emenogha seemed to be clutching at everything in sight, in the hope that it might be put in service.

'Can it stand on its own as an argument that will win a case? I should like to be able to feel that it can, but I can't. For it only sidesteps Ugonabo's objection, whereas we want to be able to overcome it.'

The main business which dominated the meeting of the titled men that day was not the debate on Orimili's application, which Emenogha and his friends had tried to prepare themselves for. The problem was the takeover of a parcel of land near the river for the use of the officers of the colonial defence regiment, who had been stationed at Okocha during the past month. As soon as the officers had taken in their first recruits, they had begun to do a great deal of clearing of grounds, fencing in a huge area of land, which included the plots of several townsmen, some of whom were Obinagu Nwalioba and Ogbuefi Ikedi.

Nweke Nwofia was the first to speak, outlining all the

reasons why the goings-on at the riverside were not welcome. He complained about the white men, who since their coming had been doing all sorts of outrageous things, ranging from taxing the people and trying to impose on them what they called a 'chief' – in fact, a tax-collector – to gulping up their land, 'the burial place of our ancestors'. There was no way of knowing how far they meant to go, but there was no doubt at all that they meant to go far indeed. He asked the peers to stop a while and think, and they would find that every so often the white man had introduced something new; and it was always a demand, an encroachment, a new form of oppression.

'Not long ago,' he continued, 'several plots of land were taken over in order to construct a military barracks. In answer, our people said that if the soldiers were human beings, and meant to settle in the place for a while, they couldn't very well settle on the air or on the river. They had to settle on the land – on someone's land. Have they not now begun to expand and to take over more land?

'However, taking over land is a small matter because they are not going to eat the land, or somehow run away with it. The issue which, to me, is like the sudden announcement of a murder case, which then reduces the one of theft previously under discussion to a minor incident, is the enlisting of the children of Okocha to fight in a war the causes of which they could not account for. No doubt some of the recruits are unprofitable young loafers; and one should not have bothered at all if the thing were limited to that sort of people. One could in fact say: good riddance! Unfortunately, one can't say that for some of the people being enlisted are responsible young men.'

Ogbuefi Nweke Nwofia ended by asking his titled friends to look into the matter, and answer him whether Okocha should continue to retreat as it had been doing since the white man came, or whether it should rather come out now, and say that enough was enough.

Pleased with his harangue, he sat down to observe its impact on his fellows. The latter remained silent for a while; and Nweke thought their silence to be a good sign.

One of those who had been very thoughtful during this interval was Ogbuefi Ananwemadu. He had an assurance of sorts that the recruits weren't intended to be actively involved in the fighting. But he had his usual dilemma as to mentioning what he had heard from official sources. In this case, it was not only that he would implicate himself, showing that he had been consulted when the decision was being made, but also he was unsure of the manager of Guy & Son. How was he to know that the volunteers were not to be involved in the fighting? He couldn't imagine what else might be the purpose they were being enlisted for. He was still ruminating on these matters when Obinagu Nwalioba saluted the meeting, and made the following observations:

'I think that Ogbuefi Nweke Nwofia has done very well to call our attention to a case which we have all been looking upon with dismay. As you know, I am personally concerned, not from the point of view of the recruitments, but because I have lost some land. I have had to think deeply about what's going on, and I'm afraid I can't see that much can be done about it. It is just like a harpoon launched at someone's belly, which causes an option of difficulties to the bystander: he cannot pull out the lethal thing without hastening the victim's death; nor can he easily overlook the natural impulse to try to get it out. Yet the victim will die, if the weapon remains in his belly.

'Frankly, I can't see what is to be done. Still, many of you are a good deal more imaginative than I can ever hope to be. So, maybe there are some who can see a way out?'

'Isn't it strange,' Ugonabo took up the argument straight-away, 'that ever since we have known the white man, we have been moving from one crisis to another. No sooner do we get used to one– none is ever solved – than another quickly darkens the horizon.

'It is quite true, what Ogbuefi Nwalioba has said. The white man is a harpoon in the belly of Okocha. Still, I think we should try to do something about the present problem. Let us send and let every householder know that they are not to permit their children or dependants to sign up. I'm sure that the soldiers will quickly leave, if they no longer have custom.'

Ogbuefi Nweke was enjoying the discussion immensely. It wasn't leading anywhere, of course; nor was it intended to. What mattered was that at his behest the full assembly of title-holders was talking seriously about something. He was the one showing leadership.

Emenogha now took the floor. 'I believe that the two last speakers have said all that there is to say about the recruitment of volunteers in our town. There is little to be done now, it seems to me, except that everybody should try to restrain their children from enlisting. I suspect, though, that many a young man will not agree to be restrained, in as much as by enlisting they have a chance to travel abroad like Orimili's son!'

There was some laughter when Emenogha said this because what had been going around in the town was that one could now go abroad on the cheap – merely by signing up. It was thought that many had enlisted simply for that. Emenogha went on then to thank Ogbuefi Nweke for acting promptly to get the leaders together to discuss the matter, urging him to remain watchful, and call them together again if there were further developments. Having put the present question to rest, he introduced one of his own:

'And talking about Orimili's son a moment ago, it reminds me that we talked much about the father during the last meeting, trying to reach a unanimous agreement that he should be conferred with the title for which he has applied.

'Now, this application is something we can deal with, and swiftly too; quite unlike the one we have just finished discussing. To get the debate going, and since I know, and we all do know that it is in our best interest to have Orimili as a member of this club, I move that we give him the full honours of membership in our society; and further, that this motion be adopted without further delay!'

Ogbuefi Nweke was alarmed that the meeting he had so carefully planned was about to be taken over by Emenogha. Therefore, he interposed, before the others began to pass remarks on the motion:

'Just one moment, Ogbuefi Emenogha.' Then he thanked his titled friends for the way in which they had taken up the issue he had put before them, professing himself to be greatly encouraged by their attitude, and promising to remain watchful as Emenogha had enjoined upon him. He was also sure that enough had been said on the case to enable them to move on to another item. However, just before moving on to that other item, he wished to put a question or two to Ogbuefi Ananwemadu concerning the plots of land that had recently been taken over.

'The question, Ogbuefi Ananwemadu, is whether the district officer mentioned to you that the land will be returned to its owners when the soldiers finish their work and go away.'

Ananwemadu moved towards the bait, his voice tight; nothing of the rounded resonance his friends were used to. He hated being on the spot, and it was as if all the life and energy had passed from him to Ogbuefi Nweke. The energy would later come flooding back, not merely to his voice but to his great muscles. How his reply was only, 'I believe that it should be returned; I see no reason why it shouldn't.'

'Do you mean that it wasn't specifically mentioned?'

'No, there was no mention of it.'

Ogbuefi Nweke was pleased with his resourcefulness. He had had no information that Ananwemadu had been consulted over the takeover of the land. However, he had got the warrant chief to make the admission himself. This was a wonderful opportunity to give the man a sound drubbing, and perhaps silence him for good. The time was auspicious too, for Ananwemadu's wife had publicly insulted Orimili's wife. If he handled the incident cleverly, he was sure that Orimili's friends would desert Ananwemadu, and his isolation would be complete. As a matter of fact, he had carefully weighed another method of approach to the showdown he had planned for this meeting. That alternative method would have been a two-pronged attack, aimed at Ananwemadu on the one hand and Orimili on the other. Orimili would have come under attack for the contract he entered into with Guy & Son, which had made the construction of the facility possible. But his bitterest words would have been reserved for condemning the man for ferrying the volunteers to Okono, as though he were ferrying sheep, or even palm-kernel sacks. The problem he saw here was that even though he could have shown Orimili to be utterly callous in ferrying other people's sons to an ambiguous fate, while secreting his own son away to a place where he would be safe, someone was likely to answer in defence that Orimili was only doing an honest job, and that the administration would have found a way to bring up their construction equipment to Okocha, and transport their recruits as well, if Orimili had turned them down. The plan he finally decided on was quite simple: use Orimili to knock down Ananwemadu, pick up a few good friends, and put off further the discussion of Orimili's application.

He now put the plan to work, speaking in a deliberate and lucid manner, his brow wrinkled a little as he concentrated in the pursuit of his deadly assault on Ananwemadu. 'One problem which I have pondered ever since the officers arrived was why of all places they chose to set up their barracks here in Okocha. Ndomili is farther down the river, and nearer to Okono; yet they didn't care to stop there, but lighted on Okocha. Further, they did not set up the facilities at Amofia, where the district officer lives. Instead the volunteers from Amofia travel to Okocha for examination and selection. All this made it clear to me that Okocha was chosen because of an advantage which is not offered by Ndomili or Amofia. That advantage is free land. I should say that the warrant chiefs in those places know precisely how much ground to allow the administration.

'Ogbuefi Ananwemadu has confirmed here before you the conclusion which I reached on my own accord, that land has something to do with the selection of Okocha for the facility, and that he was consulted before the decision was made. For some strange reason, however, he neglected to obtain a guarantee that our land will be returned to us, when the soldiers go away. I want to know whether the warrant chief has presumed to sign away our land without consulting us. Yet the land is ours, and it is we who must decide what it might be used for, and who might have access to it.'

At this point, Ananwemadu attempted to interrupt Nweke's speech with a point of order, but Nweke brushed him aside, saying that there would be time enough to explain.

'One only needs to look at the thing closely to see that Ananwemadu and his people are intent upon bringing this town to ruin, or maybe to take it over for themselves, for ends known only to themselves. Those of you who were not present at Edoko's memorial – who were spared the outrage of witnessing the fact for themselves – will have heard of the way Ananwemadu's wife publicly insulted the wife of Orimili, for no just cause. I am yet to hear that Ananwemadu has shown any concern over what happened; has he even disciplined his wife? One cannot suspect that there is more to it than meets the eye.

'I leave it to you to decide whether Ananwemadu is welcome to play havoc with this town, or whether he is going to be required to follow the rules of conduct by means of which our town had been going from strength to strength, until quite recent times. For my part, I suggest we exclude him from further participation in this society, until we determine what is to be done with him.'

Nweke ceased. At the same instant, Ananwemadu sprang to his feet, and was in the act of hurling a challenge at Nweke when Udeagu ordered him to desist and to sit down. Perhaps it was something in the tone of the command that made Ananwemadu cast a glance in the direction from which the order had come. He saw that Ogbuefi Udeagu was on his feet and was trembling with rage. Ananwemadu returned to his seat.

Udeagu then roared out a handful of barely coherent utterances, charging Nweke with attempting to split the town, and with irresponsibility, so much as to interest himself in the meaningless squabbles of women. How, he demanded, could a sensible man suggest that a fellow householder had instructed his wife to insult the wife of another man?

Udeagu concluded by saying that he was going away, and would attend no further meetings of the society, until he was assured that such irresponsible behaviour as Nweke had showed that day should be severely punished in the future. He walked out, followed by Oranudu.

The meeting had come to an end most unceremoniously.

7 | *A Bend in the Road*

Ekwenze Orimili, lounging in his sling chair at home, a little more than a stone's throw away from the club meeting place at Amanza, would not have believed that as he sat waiting for Onyeme he was being accorded a brilliant defence before the titled men by no less a figure than Ogbuefi Nweke Nwofia, who was widely believed to be the most eloquent speaker in the fellowship of title-holders. What more could Orimili have asked, if his case was being taken up by the one man who, it had been feared, would use his considerable gift of oratory and great influence among the leading people in Okocha to block Orimili's admission into the sodality?

However, the strange role which Nweke was playing did not help the applicant's case in any way. He was no nearer his goal now than when he first began his quest for it; in fact, he had never been farther from it. There was little doubt that such key objectors as Ugonabo would have been a great deal more persuadable if Nweke were to have declared his support publicly for Orimili. But then, Ogbuefi Nweke had not done this. He had endeavoured to let the impression flicker on in the minds of many a peer who was favourably disposed towards the applicant that he had only stopped short of making the public declaration.

He didn't mind at all if they took it that all in all he still held the door ajar, and might yet open it wider and step out to join them. The great new obstacle was the sudden closure of the forum itself in which the merits and demerits of the case were to have been argued. And this was as effective a block as if Ogbuefi Nweke had openly told his titled friends that they must choose between him and Orimili. It was even more effective for the very reason that the argument could not now be carried on; thus was nipped in the bud the chance of forcing the opponents to admit that they were objecting to the man, not in the interest of the traditions of Okocha, but in their own. Nor could Obiefuna Emenogha put to work the trick of which he had told his friend, how he was going to bore the opponents to death by bringing up the case as often as the sodality met – a brilliant approach that would have unfailingly caused the staunchest of the defenders of the opposite view to fall silent. Suppose for the sake of argument, that the forum still functioned, that Emenogha's strategy had worked, and had caused the opponents to fall silent, would they have come joyfully to join in Orimili's initiation rites? One could hardly suppose from the way they nursed their hostilities that their silence would necessarily have meant consent. It might in fact signify that the division in the fellowship had been further deepened and complicated.

As it turned out, Emenogha never followed up his idea beyond outlining it to his friend. The opportunity never came. Still silence did reign; and this was what Ogbuefi Nweke had achieved by showing so great a concern for the injured feelings of Orimili as to take up his cause, turning it into a weapon for finishing off his enemy of longstanding, Ananwemadu. He put the man's case to silence; and in that one blow silenced Orimili's defender and opponent alike. That stroke was altogether precise and inimitable. It was a marvel the way it brought to pass the very effect intended by the titled man, which was to cause Orimili's application to be sidestepped. But what made it more remarkable still was that it went a good deal further, and caused to become manifest a certain potency which one would not have suspected to inhere in Orimili's name. Thus was opened yet another side to this man, Orimili.

Though Orimili was wont to read deep meanings into events, names were the last place he would have thought of finding hidden meanings. The great magic he saw in them was that every single name he knew had the power to call up a distinctive picture in his mind, and that each had a mood or a range of moods going with it. There were such favourite names as Osita, Ekesi, even Emenogha. There were others he wouldn't care to call to mind upon awaking of a morning. Okwuese Ananwemadu was such a one; and therewith, Ananwemadu himself.

Were he himself to have been asked what sorts of mood he thought he evoked in other people's minds, he would have answered readily that they would have been in the main happy ones, as he was outgoing, understanding and good-natured. No doubt there were some, since Okwuese, who would think of him with feelings of triumph. But what was the meaning of their triumph since he wasn't crossing swords with anyone, and never had, not even for what Ananwemadu's people had done to him? Cross swords?

Well, not he, who would readily grapple with the earth itself, if by so doing he would avoid doing so with one of his fellows, even in mere sport. In the present case, however, his fellow townsmen had not merely refused to be drawn towards him. His very name had caused them to break apart and scatter, where previously they had been able to work together in mutual understanding.

No; Orimili did not know that his name had magic beyond calling up an image and moods. To be sure, he would have been delighted and thankful to his gods, if he were to perceive that it had a power for good. But he would have gone with all possible haste to make enquiries with Obikeze's Arobinagu, were he to have had the least inkling that one could use it in a way that it would cause harm to a fellow townsman, to say nothing of its causing so complete a breakdown in fellowship among the leaders of Okocha as it had done in Ogbuefi Nweke's usage. Were the Arobinagu to have explained, in answer to his anxious enquiry, that being the great river god's double gave him a certain dimension, whereby he himself became immense, he would have thought that he wasn't being told something he didn't already know. Wasn't it after all the very ground of his self-awareness? The man had stumbled upon that berth long ago in his unconscious search for his roots; he had docked, and had held it unshakeably ever since. It was safe and cosy too, and there was no occasion for him to justify himself. Well then, had not the seer, Obikeze, once hinted to him that his godfather was not only bountiful but also devious? Most likely, Obikeze would not have been surprised at the present mischief, even if his client did not see the connection. But the seer himself would have admitted that it was a considerable leap from being the agent of mischief in the midst of the leaders of Okocha to being the reincarnation of the ancient ancestor, who had founded and given his name to that town. Yet that was something that came afterwards to be said about Orimili! What could such a title have meant to Orimili, notwithstanding that there were traits he held in common with the Ancient One? For instance, their both being wanderers, and their having a common desire to settle and give their offspring an inheritance. But having a desire was one thing; settling and giving one's name to a place was quite another. His view of his life's struggles would have been that he had desired in vain; and moreover, had left behind him a trail of destruction: witness the demolition of the fellowship of elders and title-holders, which was quite as if in revenge for having been unsuccessful in getting himself made an *ozo*. Who in his shoes, if he had failed in so small a matter, would not have been suspicious of the far greater title of progenitor? His quest for the *ozo* had been like trying to give the old tradition a certain twist; trying in fact to lay down a new law, and not being believed. It was bad enough not to be believed by one's fellow elders and peers – which was what had happened to Orimili at the sodality; but what was far more important now was the attitude of the youth towards him. It had been a goal of his to arrange their lives for them, being determined apparently to stop the flight of the enthusiast by having him conjoined to the old and static. Just as in the case of the elders, he was soon to find out what the young people thought of his industriousness; and then, he would have cause to be much more greatly surprised still.

No one knows what good it would have done him – or anybody, for that matter – if he had succeeded as the reshaper of tradition; but there was much harm, if not in rejecting him, at least in the manner of doing this. For, in invoking his name at the club, Ogbuefi Nweke did bring about the bursting open of the worm-eaten under-belly of the *ozo* sodality, cleaving asunder the leadership of Okocha. Ogbuefi Nweke Nwofia understood what had happened as one would understand a physical fact. But there was a deeper significance, considering the very place itself where the incident had happened. It was Amanza, after all, where the town came together, not only for their evening refreshments on the weekly holidays, nor only at ceremonial occasions, but also physically as the place where the boundaries of the villages met, with the tree commemorating the Ancient One at its centre. If Nweke had been aware of that particular aspect of the question, he didn't at all show it, nor let it perturb him. What bothered him was the misfiring of a plan he had carefully laid out, and further, what that boded for him in the club. He was surprised that in invoking Orimili's name he had produced the sort of effect one might expect from gunpowder ineptly handled. This was the first time Nweke's strategy at the sodality had worked so against him. It was such a profound turn for this man that he had to give himself time to analyse fully the damage to his own prospects for a hegemony in the *ozo* society. The prospects had been very good indeed, and he had been moving from success to success, used his growing influence to great effect, carving out a bloc in the fellowship of which he had been the undisputed leader. Now, all of a sudden, the whole thing had blown up in his face; and with it, his credibility as a leader. How could he afterwards present himself in that guise, when he had been so inept as to cause by his own direct action such a deep confusion in his very band? No man with such high pretensions was ever known to have been at the same time so clumsy as to plunge himself into so deep a hole. However, to have gone down a deep hole was reprieve enough for that peer, who might be expected to climb out again when everything was felt to be safe on top, and he had the means of getting himself out. It wasn't at all so for the man, Orimili. Happily for Ogbuefi Nweke, it wasn't the particular gunpowder he had ignited that had burned Orimili. There had been a coincidence – a rare coincidence indeed for a man who had been sailing along a current different from that followed by the rest of the townsmen. What had happened was that an unsuspected source of trouble had burst forth upon Orimili just at the same time that his name was being invoked at the *ozo* house to the end of wreaking havoc there.

Nweke's mischance also had an aspect whereby it became a mixed bag, instead of an outrightly bleak one. For, what had he ever desired in the sodality, other than the right to call the shots? And was that not what Ogbuefi Udeagu had handed over to him? Nweke Nwofia knew now that the leaders would not reconvene unless he himself undertook to call them together. Still, he wasn't rejoicing that he had got what he wanted. If he were to send out the call, the first business must be to clear up the mess he had made; a thing that would certainly involve humbling himself before them, and submitting to their wrath. What sort of shots would he be calling after being kicked around by the elders to their hearts' content?

Following Okuata Orimili's discovery that sanctions in Okocha took only determination to be outworn, Ogbuefi Nweke decided to do nothing until tempers cooled. As a result, for many a month, the people of Okocha farmed their fields, and had their harvests, while their self-appointed aldermen met once in a long while in their own villages for very low-level business. At their meetings in Amanza, which came much later, it was clear from the start that the men had far longer memories than Okuata's fellows would have had. Confusion reigned there, even when the issue was merely the dividing of gifts from the families of their deceased members.

Ogbuefi Nweke Nwofia found a golden opportunity a few years afterwards to reassert his authority. The time was remarkably well chosen, and the issue sufficiently in the public eye as to seem unlikely to arouse a controversy. News had begun to reach them in Okocha about their son, Osita Nwofia, who was proving himself a significant figure in national politics. This was the issue that Ogbuefi Nweke had seized upon and quickly got the sodality to agree to hold a reception for the young man, give him a feathered crimson cap for his head, which was balding rather early, and a pair of *ozo* threads for his ankles. That was the first time in Okocha that someone was given the *ozo* title as a symbolic act, without his having to pay a fee and go through a scrutiny by the elders. Nor did they have any second thoughts as to the propriety of what they were doing. Like all the nationalist leaders of the time, there was a noise and a glitter that went with the clever young man from Okocha. But the people of Okocha did not suspect that there was another besides their very own Osita Orimili. The phenomenon was overmuch for them; for never before had such a noise and such a glitter been attached to any of their citizens. The more reason then why they delighted in their bright young man. For a while, it must be said, they did hold their breath, fearing that the magic might fail and the bubble vanish. But the noise only seemed to gather force, and the young man to shine out more brightly still. Then did the people of Okocha let themselves go, basking in his light and letting themselves be deafened by the noise.

The decision to hand over to this young man the crimson cap and anklets was swiftly reached; and it was even suggested that this would bring honour to their town. There wasn't the least hint how that was to come about; but there was no hair-splitting over it. What mattered was that their young man had a light which they could see and in which to delight – they cared little even to try to see by that light.

Osita Orimili would not have hated to think of the accolade as a fee as from a client who wished to be taken along on one's band wagon. Were he by any means sarcastic, he might have called it a bribe to let them be in his mob as his henchmen. He was rather a hard-nosed politician. That was why he called it *his* achievement. A 'hard-nosed politician' might in fact be rather much to say about this bright young man – and a great many of his peers among the nationalist leaders as well; to say nothing of their successors. What should be more to the point is that the young man and a great many of his friends were campaigners first and foremost. Whether or not they were also the moulders of national consciousness and fighters on behalf of their nation has been hard to substantiate. That claim was on the ground that they had fought for and won independence for their country, but the speciousness of the notion has been manifest from the first few years of nationhood. The campaign for independence has continued to rage regardless, now under one slogan, now under another.

Orimili had reconciled himself to his lot to the point that he gladly called the event what Osita had called it; and he was too overly taken with it to wonder at its significance; namely, that it was as if his son had appeared unexpectedly at the town's gate, having taken a long detour; and while the elders were still stunned, had seized the inheritance of the sons of Okocha, which Orimili before him had sought and desired with all his soul but had been denied. He didn't wonder at it because of the unspeakable relief it had brought to his tortured mind, that justice was, after all, deep down in the order of things. Still, the man who had known what it was, through a well-intended act, to bring chaos to the placid face of a deep underwater sky; had seen his whole world turned upside down, and himself nearly dashed to pieces at the same time – almost in consequence of his having put his fist through the dome in which he had felt himself encased; this man now had the prudence to keep to himself that renewed confidence in the justice underlying things.

Orimili Nwofia had been present at the reception,

though not at the meeting in which the decision had been reached to honour his son since he was not a title-holder. Like many another townsman, he had been fascinated by the noise and glitter being stirred up and irradiated by the gang of which Osita was a part. Therefore, it was entirely without irony that at the reception he had spoken of the great pride he took in the young man, and had gone further to say that he would not spoil things by claiming for himself anything beyond a reflected glory. He was entirely happy the way things were, for it went to show what he had discovered long before, that the Moon had finished with the older generation, and had the young especially in mind in dispensing its light. Strangely enough, Osita's achievement affected Orimili with the sense that he was truly passing out; and he had been a good long while at this passage.

The passage had begun years before, on the exact day when Ogbuefi Nweke Nwofia had clashed openly with Ogbuefi Ananwemadu, the warrant chief, at the meeting of the *ozo* sodality. This had initially made it difficult for Orimili's friends to carry on the fight on his behalf at the club. Further complications arose because the main circumstances had been disimproving markedly, owing to the completion of the new road along which one went overland to Okono. It was as if his entire world was suddenly collapsing all around him just as he was on the point of taking the high ground that had so dominated his vision. For the rest of his life, he remembered the precise moment when that passage began – when, as he himself later put it to Emenogha, he ceased to be Orimili. That mode of statement, which was entirely symbolic, came naturally to

Orimili, who prided himself with knowing when precisely he became Orimili.

As Nweke was making his speech at the club, Orimili had been waiting for Onyeme to come and read him Osita's letter, and was wishing that Ejike knew enough to take care of things of the sort for him. Soon he saw Onyeme entering the front yard. He waited in his chair until the young man had shaken hands, and seated himself. Orimili then went to the cupboard which he kept in his room, and returned with a bottle of gin. He enjoyed treating Onyeme to a shot of the spirit, comparing this to the legendary drop in the seer's eye, by means of which he could see the spirits as if they were flesh and blood. Orimili gave Onyeme a shot of gin now, that he might see very clearly and decipher most intelligently Osita's letter. He took one himself – perhaps to improve his hearing. Then he put away the bottle and gave ear to Onyeme's translation of the letter.

Osita, Onyeme read, sent his greetings to his stepmother, and to his half-brothers and-sisters. He hoped that his father recalled from his earlier letter that he had promised to share some good news with him. The news was good indeed, although he didn't know how his father would take it. Therefore, before going any further, he wanted to assure him that he was studying as hard as ever, if not harder, in fact. His father was not to imagine that his studies were suffering on account of the joy that had come his way. Quite the contrary, he was doing a deal better on account of it, and he was sure to complete his studies on schedule and return to Okocha the following year.

Orimili interrupted Onyeme, and gave thanks for the

most important communication he had got so far, which was that Osita would return to Okocha the following year. Excellent, he concluded, and asked the young man to continue reading.

The good news, Osita continued, was that he was now engaged to marry; and that the marriage would take place within a month!

Orimili was alarmed to hear this. He commanded Onyeme to go over the section again. The alarm turned into a complete stun when Onyeme (might Adoba Emenogha be his after all?) went over the section again.

Ekwenze Orimili was still; very still.

'He says,' continued Onyeme, throwing a glance at his host, 'that he is a little sad that he will be all alone at the wedding, as his father would not be attending. However, he will do the whole thing over again when he brings his wife home, hopefully by next year's harvest.'

He looked up again, irritated that Orimili was not attending.

'You heard what he said? That he will come home with his wife at harvest time next year?'

Orimili made not the slightest move. He only sat, eyes glazed, and looking straight before him.

Onyeme was now exasperated. 'What does he mean,' he scolded under his breath, 'asking me here to read him his letter, and then refusing to listen?'

He folded the letter angrily, quite sorry that he couldn't do what was several times more agreeable: crush the letter in his fist and throw it at the man as he departed. As he sought to slip the folded paper back into the envelope, he was suddenly frightened because of what appeared like derangement in the man's eyes. He cared not to be sprung upon by a mad man and knocked senseless; all for being so charitable. With his hands a little shaky, he found he couldn't get the folded letter back into the envelope. That made him more panicky still. So he scrambled to his feet, dropping the letter and envelope on the seat he was vacating, and then backed out the front door, watching the man all the time. His feet felt extraordinarily light as he hurried across the yard towards the road. Only after gaining the road did he heave a breath, and say to himself that it wasn't his fault after all that the young man was getting married without obtaining his father's leave. Also, it served him right, trying to stuff his mouth with both hands in one go. One hand at a time, Onyeme ruled; and this was all he desired for himself: that he should not be stopped from putting one lone hand into his own mouth!

Orimili remained where he was for a long time. When he finally got up, he staggered as if he was drunk. This surprised him, and he fairly fell back into the chair. He told himself not to struggle, and to be calm, lest he do himself harm. Quickly, he relapsed into his former state in which he saw nothing and heard nothing, and everything was at a standstill. By and by, he began to pick out objects, which showed him he was still alive, and looking into the front yard. There was the road, the fence, the kola-nut tree… He observed that the tree seemed to have doubled itself. Quite strange! He didn't check to see if the fence also doubled itself, or if the doorposts also doubled. He tried to hold the slightly shifty double image in his gaze, and found the exercise tricky; quite fascinating. Orimili noticed that the unsteadiness of the double image seemed to follow a pattern of movement. There were two trunks which seemed to move apart, rather gently, until they came to what must be the farthest extent they could go apart, then they began moving back inwards, as though they were going to merge into a single trunk. As they seemed to merge, Orimili saw the outer edges of the trunks again moving apart. He didn't know whether they actually crossed, or only stopped and reversed their movement on reaching a certain point known to both trunks. He found himself focusing closely on the pair as they resumed moving apart, determined to see if they did separate completely. He must see the moment when they went totally apart; it mustn't elude him again. Not only must he watch carefully, but also he must strive to hold them apart when they did separate. Perhaps the fence might be seen through the gap between them. Maintaining this careful watch so assiduously, he had given himself a headache. No, it wasn't a headache at all. It was a wire implanted in his skull from behind. He felt it forcing its way, in a zig-zag movement, towards the top of his head. It seemed then to stop at that point, unable to go any further; at the same time, something commenced tugging at the wire from behind him. It must have knotted itself into the crown of his head because it failed to slide back when it was pulled from behind.

Orimili made several attempts, by force of reflex, to get hold of the wire hanging out from the back of his head, by means of which he was being tormented. He failed, of course. But his greatest need seemed to be to hold the sides of his head in order to prevent them falling apart when the wire was pulled.

He staggered to his feet, still holding the sides of his head.

Osita!

What's got into your head? – if he thought the young man to be the fiend pulling at that wire hanging out behind his head.

Osita!

Ekwenze Orimili's knees were giving way, and he fell back heavily into his chair.

Talk of a lineage… Never had a man given so much for a cause, only to have it all shoved back in his teeth. What youth, his entire lifetime before him, would forget his need of his ancestors to the point of raising his fist so outrageously against them as Orimili's son had done? How can things go well for… Orimili deprecated this last thought and gave attention to his headache.

Something had to be done about that headache, or Orimili would simply split down the middle. He shut his eyes, to calm himself. This act did not bring him a welcome darkness; instead he perceived before his eyes a grey horizon, with thin patterns of darkness hovering in the greyness. But the patterns seemed to be quite alive. By degrees, they settled into the silhouette of the double kola-nut tree. The two trunks were now distinct. All movement ceased.

Now, was this supposed to be madness?

Ekesi, where was she now, to see the treachery of the lone palm nut against the roaster!

By nightfall, Orimili had become much calmer; so calm

that he had begun to wonder what really had happened to him; was it real – it didn't seem to have left a mark on his body – or was it only a vision-experience? He also wondered how long it had lasted: had it all happened in a twinkling of an eye, or had it lasted several moments? And what did it all mean? There were also moments when he doubted whether Onyeme had in fact been in his house that evening, and whether he had in fact read him Osita's letter. However, he had retrieved the letter from the chair in which Onyeme had dropped it, and he knew that it had been read, because it had been pulled out of the envelope. He himself never opened letters, judging that it would be like a vulture hobnobbing with a barber: to what end? So, if the letter was actually lying apart from the envelope, instead of inside it, and sealed, it meant that it had in fact been read. Ah, would that he knew how to get to where Osita was; and he would go and tell him to give up the woman he said he was going to wed, or be responsible for his death, because he wasn't going to live to see him do as he proposed. Unable to transport himself by a miracle to where Osita was, he pleaded earnestly with him to give her up, in the name of everything he held sacred. How was she to be accounted for? Where was his young man of policy, *his* Osita? For if ever a man had put faith in his son to take after him, Orimili was that man; and Osita was that son! Ekwenze Orimili thought that the very circumstances of their existence made it absolutely necessary that his son should carry on in his own footsteps. For everything he had ever done in his entire life, down to the marriage he had been arranging for Osita, had been motivated by policy. Had not the objective always been to root his family deeper in Okocha? And now this; sweeping away in one reckless act his life's work! Every sensible person acted in such a way as to open a way, or to leave one open towards a goal. Where did Osita think he was going from here?

Orimili was even quick in urging alternatives on the absent young man: at least, let him delay the marriage with that other woman he didn't know, until he completed his arrangements with Emenogha's people. Such a delay, he argued, would save Adoba from the indignity of becoming a second wife, after having been promised, so to speak, to be the one and only!

Ekwenze Orimili could not get rid of the double-image he feared to be pushing him towards the edge. He never did get rid of it; for it haunted him during the rest of his life, following him as though it were a personal fiend. And it seemed to take a ghastly delight in the man, to approve of him even, for being secret with these terrors; never breathing a word. He endured them dutifully, wordlessly, as if out of respect for the good opinion of that fiend. In any event, he could hardly think of putting them into words. Not even Okuata would have understood. Most likely, she would have supposed him mad. And wouldn't such a supposition have been quite sufficient to bring him over the edge? To his friend, Emenogha, he could say only that he no longer felt like *Orimili*, letting the other conjecture that he was referring to his premature retirement from business.

However, the fiend gave Orimili not one moment to recover from the shock of the afternoon, but followed it up; no doubt, with a purpose, so that Orimili would never again look proudly ahead of him, marking out goals for himself, and seeking ways of achieving them. The fiend wanted Orimili never to forget him.

Thus did the double-image appear in his dream that night; complete with the movement in and out. Orimili watched it. Then the upper part of the tree disappeared from his field of vision. In its place, there appeared something that was like the silhouette of a human head. Maybe it was the upper part of the tree that had transformed itself into the figure of a head. He was sorry to have missed the moment of transformation. Orimili could never have enough of moments of transition, yet he seemed to see so few of them.

Orimili watched that head with concentration. Had it a face? Or was its back turned towards him? Presently, the features of a face seemed to appear on the head. He became instantly aware of three names: his father's, Osita's, and his grandfather's. How Orimili wished it were the face of his grandfather! That should have been a rare opportunity to see what the old man was like. It seemed at that moment to be a great disadvantage not to know what the face of one's grandparent looked like. Were Osita to ask him now what his grandfather had looked like, what answer could Orimili give him?

About the Author

REV. FR. AMECHI AKWANYA is a writer and professor born in 1952 in Anambra state, Nigeria.

Akwanya gained a BA in philosophy and theology at Bigard Memorial Seminary before moving to Maynooth College at the National University of Ireland where he studied English and geography. He returned to Nigeria in 1989, having achieved his PhD in English.

Akwanya is the founder of the *Africa and World Literature: University of Nigeria Journal of Literary Studies* and was editor of *Okike: An African Journal of New Writing*, founded by Chinua Achebe. Akwanya's debut novel, *Orimili*, was shortlisted for the Commonwealth Best First Book Award in 1992.